MADISON HORTON

KINGDOM
OF THE
STARS

First edition: May 2024

Cover design by MiblArt

Map by FantasyMapShop

ISBN 979-8-9871968-3-0 (Paperback)

ISBN 979-8-9871968-4-7 (Hardback)

ISBN 979-8-9871968-5-4 (Ebook)

www.madisonhortonauthor.com

For Cheryl and Aaron

May you have a love for the ages.

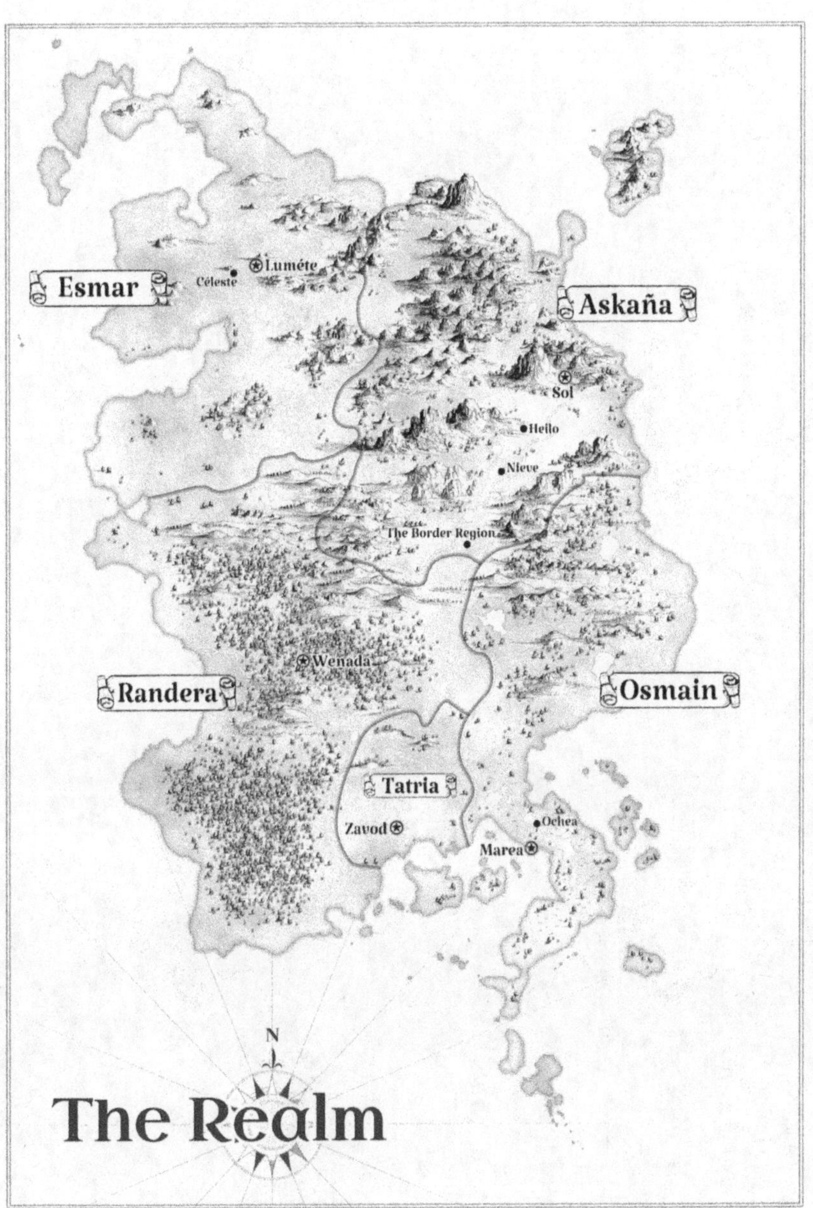

Esmar
Askaña
Céleste
Luméte
Sol
Heilo
Nieve
The Border Region
Wenada
Randera
Osmain
Tatria
Zavod
Ochea
Marea
N
The Realm

"Please wish Prince Charlie the happiest of birthdays. I can't wait to see how he's grown since I've seen him last. I hope everything is well in Esmar."

Daniel DiAngelo to his friend Marius Roche, day 75 of spring

PROLOGUE

Year 728
Day 88 of Spring

*M*arius couldn't hear anything over the sound of his heart beating. He ran as fast as his legs would carry him to his parents' bedchamber. Servants raced after him, shouting instructions to stay calm that fell on deaf ears. By the time he reached his destination, Marius was struggling to catch his breath. He fought his shaking hands and forced himself to open the door.

The sight as the hinges creaked open was worse than he could have imagined. His parents lay side by side, their faces pale and foreheads glistening with beads of sweat. Blood seeped from the several puncture wounds on their torsos, staining the pristine white bed sheets a deep crimson. Doctors were everywhere, working desperately to staunch the bleeding. Marius choked back a sob as he watched their chests slowly rise and fall, each breath more labored than the last.

After a moment, Marius forced himself to tear his eyes away from the grotesque sight before him.

Servants surrounded him in a flash and it felt like the room was spinning as they spoke over one another, their explanations melding into incoherent babble as he struggled to ground himself.

"It happened in the village square."

"The arrows were poisoned. They each had to have been hit at least two or three times."

"If they don't die from their injuries, they will surely die from the poison."

"We don't know yet what the arrows were poisoned with. The doctors have been mixing all sorts of different antidotes—"

"We haven't apprehended a suspect yet, but we believe it to be connected to the other murders."

"We are just lucky that Prince Charlie escaped unharmed."

That caught Marius's attention. The world came back into focus. Charlie.

Marius looked around the room. There, in the corner, stood the young prince. He shook violently, eyes wide with shock. The blood of the roi and reine stained his clothes, only hints of what must have been an extremely traumatic situation for a boy of his age to endure. Today was supposed to have been a happy day for him, and now this.

"Charlie!" Marius exclaimed, running to his younger brother's side. "It's going to be okay."

Charlie didn't respond, tears rolling down his cheeks. Marius's soul ached for him. He was so young, but already Marius could see the innocence of childhood leaving his eyes. It was enough to break his heart, but he bit back any trace of emotion. He had to stay strong for his brother.

Marius heard a cough from the bed, bringing him back to his parents. He ran to his mother's side as one of the healers applied pressure to her wounds. But there was so much blood. Too much blood. The doctor mixing another possible antidote for the poison in her system stopped grinding up herbs and helped those working at the royal bedside, but it was no use.

"Maman!" Marius cried, but she didn't respond. He looked for her eyes, to catch the gaze of the woman who had held him when he was a small child, who had taught him so much as he'd grown, but there was no light left in them. She was dangling by a thread.

Her chest rose and fell, but a trickle of blood escaped her lips and Marius could see how hard she fought for air. She struggled to take one last breath but didn't quite succeed. Her body stilled.

"No!" Marius screamed. The servants tore him away from his mother's body, muttering their condolences and trying to calm him, but Marius once again turned his attention to his brother. "Get Charlie out of here!" he demanded.

"But Your Highness—"

"He's only seven. No, shit! He's *eight*! He doesn't need to see this!"

"We thought he might like to say goodbye."

"It's his birthday, goddammit! Get him out of here!"

Marius could hardly breathe. He held his head in his hands and tried in vain to steady himself as his world crumbled around him. Charlie wailed as he was taken out of the room. Marius wished he could be there to console his brother, but this was for the best.

"Marius," his father croaked weakly.

Marius was at his father's bedside in an instant. He clutched the roi's hand as his father's wound continued to bleed and his breaths came shorter and shorter. The doctors still buzzed around, hoping to save their roi.

"I'm here, Papa," Marius said, tears welling up in his eyes.

"You are"—he coughed weakly—"my pride and joy."

"You're going to be fine," Marius said, shaking his head in disbelief. "You're going to get better. You have to. You can't leave me!"

"You are all they have," his father said, his words coming out almost as a whisper.

"Don't say that. I can't— I'm not ready!"

"You will make a fine Roi." His eyes closed, his hair matted to his forehead in a coat of blood and sweat. It churned Marius's stomach to look at the shell of his once-commanding father, but he forced himself to keep his eyes fixed for as long as he could in the time they had left.

"Not yet," Marius whispered. "Please."

"Make me proud, son."

His father did not speak again.

When the roi's hand finally went slack, Marius stepped back, speechless. The room was silent as the doctors slowly packed their bags and left, morticians replacing the healers who had just surrounded the royal bed.

Marius's head pounded. His hands shook at his sides. Everything seemed to be flipped on its side—wrong. Marius tried desperately to right himself as his balance disappeared. Everything had happened so quickly. The day was supposed to have been a celebration. It should have been about Charlie. It should have been about anything but *this*.

Marius lost track of time as he fell to a knee by his parents' bedside. He could have been there for minutes, hours—days, even. He wouldn't have known the difference. Eventually, an aging woman stepped into the room. As close to the royal family as a servant could get, she acted as both head of staff and an advisor to the roi. Despite the tragedy that had befallen her home, Amélie appeared as composed as ever, quill and paper at the ready to take notes and cross items off her perpetual to-do list.

"What would you like us to do about the funeral arrangements, Your Majesty?" she asked, her voice soft, almost pitying.

"I don't know," Marius muttered, shuddering at the sound of his new title. *Your Majesty.*

"Should we do a public or private ceremony?"

Marius turned to face her. "I said I don't know, Amélie!"

"Your Majesty—"

"Don't call me that!" Marius snapped, turning back to look at the lifeless corpse of his father. His father was roi. Not Marius. Marius couldn't be roi. He was barely eighteen. He was supposed to have more time.

"You are roi now," Amélie said gently. "You must make these difficult decisions. I know their deaths must be a shock to you, but we have to keep moving forward. Your people need you."

"Am I not allowed one day to grieve?" Marius cried out.

Amélie was silent. The answer was clear. The roi didn't have the time to mourn. His new title came with weight. Responsibility. He had to make his father proud.

"I don't care what you do for the ceremony," Marius finally conceded. "Just give them the respect they deserve."

"Will there be anything else, Your Majesty?"

Marius nodded. "Find out who did this. Track them down. Across the whole realm if you have to."

"Rest assured, the guard is on it. We will bring this criminal to justice," Amélie said.

"Good," Marius said, hardening his jaw and picking himself up off the floor. "Because it looks like I have work to do."

"My good friend, the duc des Étoiles, has agreed to marry your mother. He is a powerful man, and his resources will no doubt sate your desire for revenge. You are no longer my responsibility. Please don't contact me again."

Nicolas Marqueza to his illegitimate daughter, Sibella Bellerose, year 730

1

Year 738
Day 3 of Autumn

The entrance to the study swung open. The servant pushing the heavy, ornate door was pale-faced and nervous, and Sibella was sure she didn't look much better herself. Raphael Lavigne, the duc des Étoiles, looked up from his desk. His generally unpleasant demeanor turned downright chilly when he spotted Sibella, a scowl forming across his hardened features.

She didn't dare enter the room, standing instead in the doorframe as her stepfather glared at her with all his might. She held her hands steady by her sides and made sure her face was as placid as possible. There could be no sign of weakness when confronting Raphael, or he would feast upon it like a bird of prey on a sparrow.

11

"There is to be no wedding, I assume?" Raphael asked.

"No," Sibella replied curtly.

Silence. She briefly imagined that Raphael might get up from his desk and pummel her right there, but he just stared at her, deep in thought.

"You have a lot of nerve showing up here," Raphael said finally.

"I live here," Sibella said. Her voice threatened to waver, but she just held her chin higher and faked a confidence she didn't possess.

"You live in Osmain now. Or did you forget the arrangement?"

Sibella scoffed. "You of all people should know that I wouldn't simply walk away from an opportunity like that."

"Then tell me," Raphael said condescendingly, "what happened?"

Sibella considered her options, trying to figure out what answer would anger Raphael the least. There were many reasons why her engagement with Principe Daniel of Osmain had fallen apart. Her original plan had been simple: she would present herself as an eligible bride to the principe, offer him political advantages through her connections to a powerful man in Esmar, seduce Daniel if necessary to secure the match, then ascend to the throne of Osmain.

The deal would have been fruitful for both of them. Daniel would have gained a wife with ties to a wealthy kingdom, and Sibella would finally have more money than she would ever need to keep herself and her mother comfortable. She had suggested the arrangement to her stepfather, seeing promise in the young principe, and for once, Raphael had agreed. He'd set up secret plans with Imperatore Antonio, Daniel's father, for Sibella to court Daniel.

It should have been easy to persuade Daniel to marry her. Instead, Sibella had found herself facing off for the crown of Osmain against her cousin, Princesa Luciana. Luciana and Daniel had forged a true connection, and no amount of scheming on Sibella's part could make up for it. Every attempt to appeal to Daniel had only driven him further away. Luckily, she'd made an ally of him in the end. The same couldn't be said of Luciana, with whom she shared a mutual loathing.

"The principe is already engaged to someone else," Sibella said flatly.

Raphael raised an eyebrow. "Why didn't you win him first?"

"I tried," Sibella said. "But she already had her claws in him."

"So?"

"So, he chose her over me."

"And why would that be?" Raphael asked with a fake sweetness that sent shivers down her spine.

"I'm not sure I follow," Sibella said.

"Why did he choose this other girl over you?"

The honest answer was that Daniel had claimed to

be in love with Luciana. Sibella wasn't sure whether she believed in love, but she knew for certain that Raphael didn't. He would never accept "love" as the answer to his question. No, he'd almost certainly only asked her why she'd been sent back to Esmar because he wanted her to humiliate herself, to humble herself in front of him. She shook her head and said, "I don't know."

"Because, Sibella," Raphael said, standing, "you're a failure."

As he rose to his full height, Sibella fought the urge to run. She planted her feet and forced herself to wipe any emotion off her face. She'd been called every name in the book in her lifetime. Mistake. Whore. Bitch. They had all stung the first time, but over the years, Sibella had developed a skin thick enough that most insults didn't bother her anymore.

"I give you the opportunity of a lifetime and you squander it!" Raphael said, growing red in the face. "I think you're getting spoiled. After everything I've done for you, you're still just the ungrateful little bastard child you were when I married your mother."

Sibella took a deep breath. She wouldn't—no—she *couldn't* react.

"You're lucky I'm not throwing you out on the street for this," Raphael continued. Despite the underlying threat of becoming homeless the next time she failed him, Sibella breathed a small sigh of relief. She still had a place to stay. For now.

"Let me be very clear," Raphael said, coming closer.

"Your father is dead, meaning that my promise to him to take care of you has ended. You are a grown woman, and I no longer have an obligation to keep you under my roof. But because I am a charitable man, I will allow you to earn your keep here."

Sibella opened her mouth before she could stop herself. "Earn?"

"Your mother was the Askanese royal seamstress some years ago, correct?"

"Yes," Sibella said, unsure of where the conversation was going.

"So, you must have learned some valuable skills with a needle and thread, yes?"

"Yes."

"Some skill" was an understatement. If Raphael had ever paid any attention to Sibella, he would have known that she spent most of her days crafting her own garments, since she'd never had enough money to buy a new wardrobe from a modiste.

"Then it's settled," Raphael said, turning to sit back down at his desk.

"Wait," Sibella said. "What's settled?"

"Isn't it obvious? You're going to earn your place here by working as a seamstress."

"But how—"

"Again with the stupid questions, Sibella? Now that I think about it, you might be too incompetent to be of any use to me," Raphael said, waving her off.

"No, please!" Sibella said, and wished she could take

the plea back as soon as the words left her mouth. She'd shown weakness, let it slip that she was afraid of being sent packing. But to her surprise, Raphael didn't capitalize on her mistake. He just sighed.

"I will see to it that you have a small shop in town. Any profits generated will, of course, come back to me to pay for your accommodations," Raphael said.

Sibella bit her lip. This situation was far from ideal. She was now essentially a slave to Raphael. As far as the kingdom of Esmar was concerned—at least as far as Sibella knew—no one knew that she existed, much less that she'd gone off to Osmain to try and snare their principe. Raphael didn't talk about Sibella in public, which made her rejection slightly less embarrassing. But it also meant that she had no allies, no means to leave even if she wanted to, and now she would have no time to earn money behind his back. But Sibella nodded solemnly. He'd already gotten enough reaction out of her today.

They stared at each other in silence for a moment before he said, "What are you still standing there for? Get out of my study."

Sibella nodded again and hurried away, picking up the packed bag she'd left in the hallway along the way. She hadn't seen her mother or stepbrothers since arriving home from Osmain, but she didn't care. She wanted nothing more than to be alone for a moment.

Sibella reached the grand staircase and glanced at the large portrait of Raphael's first wife, Madame Juliette, who seemed to watch Sibella as she climbed the three floors from his study up to the loft where she slept. She threw the door open. The room was stuffier than she'd remembered, but besides a fine layer of dust over everything, the space was exactly as it had been when she'd left it. She looked up at her ceiling, smiling at the view.

As an unwanted guest in Raphael's home, Sibella had been given lodgings in what used to be the observatory. The domed ceiling of her bedroom was made entirely out of glass. While the light of the sun kept her from sleeping in, she loved her view of the sky. When she lay down in her tiny bed at night, she could see the stars twinkling above her.

Sibella loved the stars. She'd spent hours as a child studying astronomy. Her shelves were filled with books on star charting, constellations, and space. There were even a few on reading the stars. Esmar was well known in the realm for its star readers, people capable of telling fortunes based on the stars' positions in the sky. She smiled as she glanced at the dusty books on her shelf, happy to be back in her room despite herself.

The golden glow from the setting sun cast shadows across her bedroom, drawing her eyes to the sewing machine sitting on her desk in the corner. She would have to move it to her shop in town soon. The thought of working for Raphael forever made Sibella's good mood disappear, and she slung her small bag onto her bed in frustration.

She'd tried so hard to overcome the circumstances of

her birth, and it had all been for nothing. She thought of every letter she'd written to her father while she was growing up. While starving on the streets of Céleste, a small province outside the capital city of Esmar, she had saved every coin she had to buy stationery for her letters. She had hoped for years that he might recognize her, perhaps even love her as his own. Year after year she wrote to him, and year after year there had been no response.

She'd been tempted more than once to stop trying to reach out, but she couldn't bring herself to do it. Not until her eighteenth birthday, when she'd finally had enough. Even if her father, Rey Nicolas of Askaña, wouldn't recognize her as the heir to his throne, the least he could do would be to provide for his only child. While Sibella didn't regret blackmailing her own father into helping her and her mother, she did hate the situation that writing that final letter had left her and her mother in.

Raphael and Nicolas had been old friends, and when Raphael's first wife, Juliette, suddenly disappeared, Nicolas had quietly married Sibella's mother off to Raphael in an attempt to kill two birds with one stone. Raphael would have a wife to keep up his perfect image, and Nicolas would finally be rid of Sibella's demands. Her cheeks flushed in anger at the thought of her father, but she forced herself to unclench the fists that had formed at her sides. Her father was dead now, killed by his own subjects, and that would have to serve as justice.

She took a deep breath to try to clear her head, and opened her bag. There wasn't much inside. Sibella dug to the bottom where a small purple purse sat. She lifted it gingerly and poured the money it held onto her palm, satisfied by the weight of the gold coins in her hand.

As she'd left Osmain, Daniel had agreed to sponsor Sibella for one social season in Esmar. The season usually started on the first day of autumn and would last until the first day of winter, which marked both the new year and the end of the social season. Given that the season had already begun while she'd been traveling home, she now had less than ninety days to find herself a husband if she was to ever have any hope of escaping Raphael's control.

There was a knock at her door. Sibella scrambled to hide her coin purse. She was just barely able to close it and throw it back into her bag before her bedroom door swung wide open. Her older stepbrothers, Leo and Simon, stood in the door frame.

Leo was four years older than Sibella. He was tall and thin with tan skin and blonde hair almost as light as hers. There was always a look of intensity to him, his features sharp and intimidating. He was the type of man who might have been handsome if he wasn't an absolute monster on the inside. She wasn't afraid of him like she was Raphael, but he could be a thorn in her side if he wanted.

As for Simon, who stood behind his brother, he was the closest thing Sibella had to a friend. He always appeared happy and approachable. Even his resting face seemed to hold a perpetual smile lifting his lips. Between that and his bright eyes, he appeared more youthful than other men his age. How Leo and Simon could be as close as they were was beyond Sibella. Their differences were more than skin deep.

Sibella and Leo stared at each other for a moment. She waited for him to state his business, but Leo just looked at her with a stupid grin on his face. She pursed her lips.

"What do you want?" she asked.

"Nothing," he said, shrugging.

"Fine." Sibella rolled her eyes. "Simon, what are you doing here?"

He shrugged. "Following Leo. I don't know."

"So, you walked up three flights of stairs and barged into my room for no reason?" Sibella said.

"I knocked!" Leo insisted.

"Yes, thank you," Sibella said. That was at least an improvement from Leo's usual behavior. Simon's presence must have pushed him to use basic manners.

He stared at her for another moment, but when Sibella didn't say anything else, Leo finally cracked. "Papa says you're not invited to dinner."

"What?" Sibella said.

"He's disappointed in you. Just thought you ought to know," Leo said.

Sibella sighed. She should have seen that coming. It wasn't the first time Raphael had done something like this when she'd "disappointed" him. She knew better than to ask her brothers if it was a joke. It would only make her seem weak.

"Anything else?" Sibella asked.

"Oh yes, actually," Leo said. "The Comte de Cieux is throwing a masquerade ball in two days. I need you to design and make a costume for me."

"In two days?" Sibella asked, raising an eyebrow.

"Yes. Will that be a problem?"

Sibella eyed him suspiciously. He had to know that two days was an impossible amount of time in which to get a project like that done.

"Why haven't you seen a tailor for your suit yet, if the ball is in two days?" she asked.

"I'm a busy man, Sibella. Besides, Papa said he wants us to start using you to have our garments made. I'm sure your work can't compare to that of actual professionals, but orders are orders. Right?"

Sibella crossed her arms and fought the desire to spit in Leo's smug little face. But she swallowed her pride and sighed. "What would you like your suit to look like?"

"Something that will get me lots of attention from the ladies at the ball. I don't like to leave a party alone," Leo said.

Sibella rolled her eyes. Leo never failed to be classless. "Give me a theme, color, fabric, anything."

Leo thought for a moment, then finally he said, "I like silk."

"I can do that. A storm cloud theme maybe? Something silver and striking."

Leo looked at Sibella for a moment, then burst out laughing, so much so that he doubled over. Anger rose in her chest. This was what she got for actually trying to help. If Leo was now her most loyal customer, her life was going to be a living hell.

"A *cloud*?" Leo said between deep laughs. "That's the stupidest thing I've ever heard."

"Then what do you want from me?" Sibella asked, her patience wearing thin.

"Just make me something trendy. Not too flashy. Maybe blue? And I want to look devastatingly handsome," Leo said.

"I can do that."

"No, I mean, I want to have a girl on each arm all night. I want them to fight over who gets to be the first to take her corset off for me."

"I'll do my best," Sibella said, flashing him her fakest smile and trying not to grimace at his remark.

"You'd better come through for me, or I'll make sure Papa knows how much you let me down," Leo said. Then he turned on his heel and left the room.

Sibella rolled her eyes again and focused her attention on Simon. "I assume you want a costume, too?"

Simon shook his head, much to Sibella's relief. "I got my costume a few days ago. Monsieur André and I are going to wear matching outfits."

Simon had begun courting the heir to a massive fortune while Sibella was in Osmain. It was unusual for couples to form attachments outside of the social season, but Sibella had been overjoyed for her brother when she'd received her first letter from Simon recounting how he had met Monsieur André. While she worried how she would fare without her only friend should their courtship blossom into a marriage, she knew it was more important to support Simon in his happiness.

"That's wonderful!" Sibella said. "I take it your courtship is going well, then?"

Simon blushed. "I have a good feeling about him, Sibella."

Sibella beamed. "I'm glad to hear it."

"I wish you could come to the masquerade ball so you could meet him," Simon said sadly.

Raphael had made it clear to Sibella long ago that she was not and would never be allowed to attend any societal functions. So she'd never met Monsieur André—or any other noblemen for that matter—and she didn't know how she was going to be able to find a husband this season, even with Daniel's money to help her. She would be too busy sewing her idiot brother new clothing to even try to think of a scheme.

Slowly, Sibella's mind started swirling with ideas for Leo's costume. A silken suit. Blue fabric, maybe with white trim. A matching mask. Leo would be unrecognizable as the annoying stepbrother who only chased the latest fashion trends and never dared to try anything new.

Sibella paused. *Unrecognizable.* If Leo could go to a party and hide his identity, what was stopping Sibella from attending in the same way?

It would be a lot of work. Nearly impossible, in fact. But she had Daniel's money. She would need to gather supplies, but Sibella knew—this masquerade ball would be her best chance to escape.

2

Day 4 of Autumn

"You have ten minutes, Your Majesty," Amélie said. She held her pocket watch so tightly Marius thought it might break into pieces. "If you're going to make it to the concert on time, you will have to be ready to leave before the end of the hour."

Marius sighed and set down the contract he'd been drafting. He took off his reading glasses and tried in vain to massage his pounding headache. It had been a busy summer, and autumn was shaping up to be just as awful.

The trade contract with Tatria that had been established before Marius had taken the throne ten years ago was set to expire at the end of the season, and he'd been working overtime drafting and revising the terms of the new agreement, hoping to have a solid place to start negotiations once the Tatrians arrived. The trade contract had undoubtedly saved thousands of Esmarish lives since its inception, as Tatria's rare plants were the basis for excellent medicines to treat common illnesses. Marius was glad that Esmar was rich with precious metals in turn. The mines in his kingdom were full of silver and gold, which made excellent bargaining chips in trade negotiations.

In addition to the end of Esmar's old deal with Tatria, the realm had seen a massive political shake-up over the summer. Askaña, a fairly large nation, had endured a revolution and a total change of power. While Askaña wasn't the most influential country in the realm by any means, the new Askanese rey had already made an enemy of the Osmainians.

Luciana Marqueza, the sole surviving member of the Askanese royal family, had become a prime target of the new leader—Rey Hugo and his court—following her escape to Osmain. But just as suddenly, he had dropped the matter. Marius didn't know the terms of the agreement that had since been settled between Askaña and Osmain. He only knew that one moment, the realm had been gearing up for war—Marius himself preparing to receive Askanese refugees—and the next, there had been peace. Tension, of course, but peace. Principe Daniel and Luciana were set to be married any day now, and Marius planned to host them for their honeymoon.

He and Daniel were similar enough in age, both the

heirs to their respective thrones, and they had been close as children. Marius had even learned Osmainian to keep up their correspondence. But when his father died and Marius was thrust upon the throne, he'd grown apart from his friend. He was hopeful that this visit might turn the tides and renew their friendship.

Still, no matter how much he wished things were simple, Marius knew he'd have to reach out to Rey Hugo of Askaña soon to make an attempt at goodwill. Hosting Daniel and Luciana without making peace with Askaña first would make it look like he'd chosen a side in their problems, and the last thing Marius needed were foreign tensions of his own. Keeping his own country from disaster was difficult enough.

"Your Majesty?" Amélie prodded.

"What is it?" Marius ground out.

"You really should get going," she said, standing impatiently by the door.

Marius sighed and stood up, pushing in his desk chair. He would have to come back to the contract later. No matter how hard he worked, something always seemed to pop up. Being the Roi of Esmar was a great responsibility, one that he was proud of, but deep down, Marius longed for a simpler life. He missed the days before his father had died, when all he had to do was be himself. The carefree side of Marius had died with his parents, and all that was left was a man who only paused work to attend shallow social functions.

The next few hours transpired in a blur. Marius was

so consumed by his own thoughts that he was dressed for the concert, pushed into a carriage, and seated in a private box before he brought the world back into focus. Musicians tuned up their instruments as the curtain behind him parted and a young woman entered his box.

Marius turned his head to look at her as the guard on duty announced her presence. "Your Majesty, may I present Mademoiselle Noyer, the eldest daughter of Baron de Cométe!"

Marius tried to smile as she came into view. The girl was certainly pleasing to look at, with her spotless olive skin and slick black hair. Marius tried not to get his hopes up. This wasn't the first time he'd been set up with an eligible lady hoping for marriage.

Despite his situation, Marius refused to marry a woman with whom he didn't think he would be compatible. The pressure from his advisors had been quite annoying over the past few years, as it seemed like they were all nervous that he might somehow die before producing an heir. But Marius had remained steadfast. He knew he wasn't likely to love his future bride. For a man like him, holding out for love just wasn't an option. But he didn't want to be miserable, either. As long as he got along well with his wife, Marius supposed he would be happy enough.

Mademoiselle Noyer curtsied before him, flashing a dazzling smile. "It is an honor to be here, Your Majesty."

Marius gestured to the empty chair next to him. "Go ahead and sit. The show should be starting soon."

"Of course," Mademoiselle Noyer said, taking her seat. She sat so lightly on the cushion that Marius wasn't entirely convinced she was putting her weight on the chair. But her posture was perfect, and she was elegant in her navy-blue evening gown.

"Thank you for joining me tonight," Marius said.

"Thank you for the invitation," Mademoiselle Noyer replied. "I am most impressed with your private box. Everything is so beautiful up here."

"Thank you," he said. The truth was, he only used the box once a season or so. It wasn't even decorated to his tastes, the carpet and chairs still untouched from when his father had decorated it decades ago. He knew he was only fooling himself, but he liked to imagine he would have the time to redecorate it sometime soon. Marius had always been too consumed by his work to think about something as inconsequential as his box at the concert hall. He desperately needed to do something for himself soon, or he was worried he might explode.

"So, tell me about yourself," Marius said.

"Of course!" Mademoiselle Noyer replied. "What do you want to know?"

"How about your name, to start?" Marius laughed. He'd expected her to go into a full recitation of her history. Most women he'd met in this sort of context didn't need explicit permission to talk about themselves.

"Of course! My name is Félicité," she said.

"It's wonderful to meet you, Félicité," said he responded.

"And you as well," Félicité replied. "And may I say, you are even more handsome than people say you are."

Marius fought back the heat rising in his cheeks. This was clearly a soulless attempt at flattery meant to soften him to her, but it was still nice to be complimented.

"Thank you," Marius said. "So, about you. Where did you grow up?"

Félicité cocked her head. "Um, in Cométe?"

Marius shook his head. Her home had been announced upon her entry. How had he forgotten already?

"My apologies," he said.

"It's quite alright. I'm sure you meet people from all over the realm."

"Yes," Marius said, still slightly embarrassed.

"And I'm sure you've seen much of the realm yourself," she continued.

He drew in a breath. He had seen some parts of the realm, that much was true. He'd visited Osmain multiple times as a child, and he'd passed through Randera on his way to and from those visits. But other than that, he'd never traveled. While part of him wished he could see the rest of the realm, he knew he'd already seen all that he needed to.

"I know my country very well," Marius said. "I've been to every province óf Esmar, and I pride myself on that."

"But you could travel all over the realm, yes?" Félicité asked.

"Of course. But I'd have to bring my work with me. This job doesn't exactly pause when I want to take a vacation."

"Oh," Félicité said with a twinge of disappointment in her voice. Marius made a mental note—this one was into travel. Not a deal-breaker, but certainly a hobby for someone with significantly less commitment to the kingdom than himself.

"That's alright," Félicité said. "I'm sure the château here is spectacular."

"It is," Marius said. "It's the crown jewel of Luméte."

Félicité smiled. "You'll have to give me a tour, then. I have an affinity for shiny things, and I've heard tales of the château's silver decor."

"Those tales are true. Many of our accent pieces are made of pure silver."

Félicité sighed. "Think of how much money is wrapped up in that place, with all those precious metals."

Marius narrowed his eyes at her words. The silver was certainly an interesting feature of the château, but it was no secret that it was there. Esmar was known for their silver. It could hardly be a surprise to her that the château contained samples of the nation's most profitable export.

"And all of the rooms that there must be," Félicité

continued. "I'm sure the ballroom is huge. Do you throw parties often?"

Marius smiled awkwardly. "Not exactly. I usually throw at least one per year, but I don't do the planning. I trust my advisor to handle everything."

"That's incredible," Félicité gushed. "So, you just sit back and enjoy your riches while your servants do all the work? What a life! My family has a small staff, and we are often very involved in everything that takes place at our estate."

Marius fought back a laugh. He didn't want to offend the girl, but her rosy-eyed view of his life wasn't at all true.

"It's not that simple," he replied. "I still have many responsibilities. Being roi isn't easy. The woman who becomes my reine will have to understand that."

Félicité nodded dismissively. "I do understand. Becoming reine is nothing to scoff at. The woman you choose will be responsible for being the social face of Esmar. She will set fashion trends! What could be more important than that?"

Marius opened his mouth to reply, but he couldn't find the right words. He was grateful when the orchestra finally struck their first notes and silenced the crowd.

Perhaps he would have to be more direct in the future with the women who attempted to court him. He needed a bride who would support him in his work and lend a helping hand when he needed it. Someone who would serve as an advisor. And from his conversation with Félicité so far, it was clear that she was only interested in the material gains that being reine offered. She hadn't asked Marius a single question about himself.

He sighed. This was not his reine. Amélie wouldn't be happy with another rejection, but he didn't care. Love had never been easy for Marius. Even before he'd become roi, he had never been one to fall head over heels for anyone. He'd seen through every façade.

He'd met girls who wanted authority and power, girls who wanted money, and girls who wanted fame. But he'd yet to meet a woman who wanted *him*, even as a friend. And even though Marius knew that true love was a near impossibility in his situation, a small part of him still wished to find his perfect bride.

The concert passed by slowly. Marius found himself thinking of all the things he needed to do when he returned home—all of the worries he had to face. As soon as the last song ended, he left his box without even a goodbye to Mademoiselle Noyer. Amélie met him back at the château with a broad smile on her face, but it fell instantly when she noticed his sour mood.

"Not again," she said. "What was wrong with this one?"

Marius shrugged. "She was only interested in my money. I'm not looking for someone who will just sit around begging for treats like a show dog. I want a partner."

Amélie pursed her lips and said, "You're going to run

out of eligible young ladies sooner or later, Your Majesty. You'll have to pick a bride soon. I just hope you haven't offended everyone by the time you make your selection."

"Who knows?" Marius said. "Maybe Charlie will marry and produce an heir, and then I won't have to rush."

"Maybe I'll do what?" a voice said from behind him.

"Your Highness." Amélie curtsied quickly before the prince. "I should leave you two alone to talk, yes?"

As she departed, Marius turned around to see his brother stumble further into the château. He wore the plain clothes of a peasant, no crown in sight, and stains dotted the rough fabric of his tan shirt, which looked like it could have belonged to a farmer. His hair was unkempt, his long brown locks tangled. Charlie tried to lean casually against the wall but ended up losing his balance and grabbing the corner for support instead.

Marius crossed his arms. "I thought I told you to stop going out this late," he said.

"Thanks, Papa," Charlie said sarcastically. His voice was surprisingly clear for someone so obviously drunk, his words barely slurred.

"This isn't proper behavior for a prince," Marius continued, unfazed.

"Oh, you'd know about being proper, wouldn't you?" Charlie spat. "Perfect Marius, saving the kingdom one day at a time. Give me a fucking break."

Marius took a deep breath. He had to keep his

composure. There was no point in trying to reason with Charlie when he was drunk, except that just happened to be most of the time these days. Marius had tried many times to stop his brother's partying ways, to no avail. Charlie would disappear for hours—sometimes even days—at a time, leaving Marius and the servants worried sick. But he always came home eventually. At this point, Charlie's occasional check-ins were about all Marius could ask for.

Anything could happen to a wealthy man in a bad area of town. Marius tried not to judge Charlie for spending his time at taverns and brothels. Just because Marius had never been drawn to that lifestyle didn't mean that other men weren't. But he was concerned for Charlie's safety, and his reputation. Gossip about the prince coming home drunk every night was also sure to affect his prospects. Marius almost laughed to himself at that reminder. There was no way Charlie would marry before him. He would be surprised if Charlie married at all.

"Let's just get you to bed, Charlie," Marius said. "We can talk about this more in the morning when you're feeling better."

"I'm not tired," Charlie said.

"Yes, you are. Now come on." Marius tried to gently lead his brother to his bedroom. Charlie tried to escape, but Marius pulled him tightly toward him and forced him to keep walking.

"I don't need your help," Charlie insisted.

"Yes, you do."

"Would you please just leave me alone?"

"No."

Charlie flailed his arms, trying to escape his brother's powerful grip, but in his intoxicated state, it was no use.

"Let me go!" Charlie shouted at the top of his lungs.

Marius just sighed and kept walking. The first few times Charlie had come home drunk like this, the servants had been at Marius's side, ready to help. But the more common it became, the less the servants rushed to his aid. Marius didn't really want them there anyway. He would rather there be no rumors circulating about Charlie, at least not any stemming from his staff. Marius took the responsibility upon himself to take care of his brother. As much as Charlie frustrated him, he was all Marius had left.

"Stop fighting me," Marius commanded. "The less you squirm, the quicker I'll leave you alone."

To his relief, that seemed to work a little. Hopefully, the walk to Charlie's room could now take place in relative peace. But Charlie had other ideas. He said, "Why don't you just leave me alone? I can take care of myself."

"Sure, you can."

"There you go with that condescending bullshit again. What, you think you're better than me?" Charlie spat.

Marius sighed. "No. But I do think you're making some poor choices."

"I'm an adult. I can do whatever the fuck I want," Charlie said.

"Barely," Marius replied. "You only just turned eighteen."

Charlie scoffed. "Some of us like to have a little fun, Marius. Not all of us are total sticks in the mud like you."

Marius ground his teeth. Charlie's attitude was wearing him down fast. "When I was your age, I was running all of Esmar. Unlike you, I didn't have the luxury of getting wasted at all hours of the night and squandering my allowance on prostitutes."

"Forgive me, oh holy Marius, he who can do no wrong!" Charlie said, spitting on the ground as they made their way through the gilded corridors of the château.

"That's not what I—"

"Yes, it is. You think you're so much better than me, so much better than *everyone*. But in reality, you're just as big of a failure as I am."

Marius's grip on Charlie's arm faltered, and his brother used that as an opportunity to break free. The two stood face to face. Marius didn't say anything. He didn't want to hear any of Charlie's opinions about how he chose to govern Esmar. He'd been doing the best he could since day one. But that didn't stop Charlie from running his mouth.

"Look at you. You're twenty-eight. Unmarried because no one likes you. Letting your kingdom and the line of succession slip away. You're a house of cards, Marius. You work all day and worry all night." Charlie stepped closer, enough that Marius could smell the aroma of booze on his breath. "Eventually you're going to come crumbling down. And when you do, I'll be right there, reminding you that you're a screw-up, too."

With that, Charlie shouldered past him and stumbled down the hallway. He was headed in the direction of his bedroom, so Marius didn't fight him. He just bit his tongue and watched his brother until he rounded a corner and was out of sight.

Marius shook his head. As much as he hated to admit it, Charlie was right. Marius was a mess, and unless something changed, it wouldn't be long until he cracked under the pressure.

"You are cordially invited to a masquerade ball at the estate of the comte de Cieux to officially kick off the Esmarish social season. Please bring a mask and wear a themed costume if you'd like."

Arthur Martin, Comte de Cieux, to Marius Roche, day 1 of autumn

Day 5 of Autumn

"*O*uch!" Leo complained, squirming as Sibella pushed her needle through the fabric of his suit.

"Hold still," Sibella commanded.

"How can I hold still if you're poking me?" Leo whined.

Sibella closed her eyes and took a deep breath. She was almost done with his stupid suit. She just had to finish the last few alterations, and then she would be free.

She had been working non-stop on Leo's suit for the ball, and she'd completed it just hours before he was to waltz onto the comte de Cieux's estate. It was hardly even a costume. She'd made it as simple a design as she could get away with, just a silk suit and a matching mask.

But despite its simple appearance, Sibella could tell that Leo liked it. He'd tried to scowl as she entered and helped him into the ensemble, but his eyes twinkled with excitement. It filled her with an odd sense of satisfaction to see that she could make even Leo happy. He was probably going to use that joy to seduce and deflower some innocent woman at the party, but Sibella chose not to think about that aspect.

She tied off and clipped her thread, then stood grandly. "Okay, you're ready for the ball."

Leo nodded approvingly. "It's sleek. Fashionable. Look at you, Sibella. A woman who can take orders."

She cringed and tried her best not to sneer at him. He was always making disgusting remarks about women and seemed to revel in Sibella's discomfort, a smug smile at the ready to throw in her face after making her horribly uncomfortable.

"I'm glad you like the suit. Enjoy the ball tonight," Sibella said, turning to leave.

As she left Leo's room, she heard him yell, "Oh, I will!"

Sibella practically flew up the stairs to her own bedroom, where a half-finished gown lay waiting for her. She quickly pinned the skirt fabric into place and prepared to stitch it all together. She had to work quickly if she was going to finish her dress in time for the ball. For once, she was glad her room was in the highest loft in the estate. No one would hear the whirring of the sewing machine as she toiled away.

She added eyelets to help her lace up the top, and slid boning into place to add structure to the bodice. For the skirt, she added a sparkling trim to complete the look. Just as the sun began to set, Sibella finished the last seam on the gown. She stood with a flourish and hastily tried it on. She had been making her own dresses for as long as she could remember, and it was no surprise that it fit perfectly.

Sibella examined herself in the mirror. She'd taken her storm cloud idea and poured every inspiration into this one gown. An iridescent silver fabric sat beneath a layer of sequined silver tulle, which flared out past her knees. The bodice pushed up her cleavage and would ensure every gentleman at the party looked her way. The design of the sleeves left her pale shoulders bare. She slipped on her finest shoes to go with it, a pair of shiny boots that matched the color of the dress.

Next, her hair. She'd bought a wig for herself, as the last thing she needed was for Raphael or Leo to recognize her at the ball. The long, flowing silvery wig accentuated the color of the gown and would help hide her identity. She pinned up her own golden locks and put the wig on, letting the waves of someone else's hair flow down her back. The wig was of high quality thanks to Principe Daniel's funding, and to the untrained eye one could almost mistake the wig for her real hair.

Sibella grabbed the mask that went with her

ensemble and fastened it around her head. She'd added blue rhinestones to the mask, the only pop of color on the outfit, to draw attention to her face. The blue was a perfect match to her eyes. Lastly, she slipped on her gray elbow-length gloves.

She took one last glance in the mirror. This was it.

Sibella took a deep breath and smiled at her reflection, then tore herself away. She grabbed her longest cloak, covered all of her hard work, and opened her window, climbing down the makeshift ladder of lattice that led to the ground below. She was vaguely aware of the danger posed by climbing down five floors in a ballgown, but she'd made the trip enough times over the years that she didn't falter, even for a moment.

Finally, her feet touched the ground. She smoothed her dress and cloak, pulling up the hood to conceal her identity, then quietly crept through the shadows to the edge of the Étoiles estate. Then, looking over her shoulder to make sure she wasn't being followed, she quickly opened the gate and slipped out without a sound.

Sibella had snuck out before but never to a social event, never mind one to which family would also be attending. Her heart was pounding in her chest so hard she thought it might jump right out. She forced herself to take a deep breath and keep walking. As she rounded a corner onto the streets of Luméte, she glanced around in search of her carriage. She had paid for her transportation to the ball using Daniel's money as well. The château wasn't too far of a walk from the Étoiles estate, but Sibella wanted to fit in with the other guests.

She made her way down the cobblestone streets to the corner where she'd arranged for the driver to pick her up. As she waited, Sibella glanced around. This was to be her street corner soon. The small shop at the end of the block was to be hers in a matter of days. The fading light made the empty store look almost foreboding.

She should have been excited to have a business to her name, but all Sibella could feel was resentment. All her hard work would amount to nothing once Raphael got ahold of her profits.

Her thoughts were interrupted as a small blue carriage turned onto the street. It was slightly run down and shabby, clearly the type of carriage that someone would rent, not own. The silver trim was covered in a layer of grime from the dusty streets outside of the city, and the coachman's coat had a few threadbare patches from overuse. But it would have to do.

The carriage slowed to a stop and the coachman raised his eyebrow at her. Sibella had not revealed her identity in her letters to arrange the service, and the coachman had no idea who he was to pick up. He only knew the time and location at which he was to meet her.

"Are you my passenger?" he asked.

Sibella nodded. "I believe I am. Please take me to the masquerade ball at the estate of the comte de Cieux."

He eyed Sibella's old cloak suspiciously. "Do you have an invitation to this ball?"

Defensively, Sibella put her hands on her hips. "What exactly are you implying about me, monsieur?"

The coachman shook his head. "Nothing, mademoiselle. Hop in."

Sibella let out a satisfied "humph" and opened the door to the carriage. The step up was steeper than she thought it would be, and she struggled to climb in without assistance. As she gathered her skirts and shut the door, she cursed herself silently for spending so much of her money on materials for her dress and not on a better carriage. It would be humiliating to have to scramble out of the cab without aid.

The coachman started the drive to the comte's estate without another word. The rest of the ride was spent in silence, the carriage jostling as the horse trotted down the bumpy cobblestone streets. The sun dipped below the horizon as she neared the ball, stars beginning to peek out of the darkness, illuminating Esmar in their glow.

Finally, the comte's estate grew closer. Sibella could see a few stragglers making their way into the ball, but it seemed like most of the guests had already arrived. She sighed in relief. The fewer people who saw her embarrassing herself by climbing out of the hired carriage, the better.

The horses drew to a halt in front of the grand staircase leading into the estate. Sibella shed her cloak, ready to make her grand entrance. She opened the door and nearly fell out of the carriage, but caught herself just in time and gently lowered herself to the ground.

"Thank you, monsieur," Sibella said, nodding to her driver. "I will signal you when I'm ready to depart."

The coachman left without even an acknowledgement of what she'd said. Sibella worried he might be gone upon her return, along with her heavy cloak, but there was nothing to do about it now. There were more important matters to attend to. She needed to find a husband tonight. The money Daniel had given her had been enough to sponsor her for the season, giving her funds with which to buy clothes and some necessary services, but had been nowhere near enough to allow for her and her mother to escape Raphael's clutches on their own. Marriage to someone of means was her only hope.

Sibella turned to the ornate silver doors that marked the entrance to the ballroom. She ascended the staircase slowly, trying not to lose her breath. The last thing she needed was to make her grand entrance huffing and puffing. When she reached the top of the stairs, the servants standing by pushed the doors open for her. She was glad they hadn't asked her to present an invitation, or her entire plan would have failed before it had truly begun.

She entered and stood on a balcony overlooking the party. The room was bigger and grander than she could ever have imagined. Sibella had attended balls before. Most recently, she'd been Principe Daniel's guest to a gathering in Osmain. But where that event had been in honor of the military and was far more boisterous, this was decadent.

The room was decorated with beautiful crystal chandeliers hanging from the ceiling. Light from the candles inside reflected spots around the ballroom. Music was being played somewhere, and couples swirled around the floor. The masks made it impossible to recognize anyone, and though she looked, Sibella couldn't see the suit she'd made for Leo on any of the men in attendance.

As the song ended, Sibella stepped forward and set one gloved hand on the railing. Despite the lack of an announcer to give her name to the crowd, she could feel heads turning toward her. She wasn't sure whether to smile with satisfaction or be nervous at the attention, but she took a deep breath and made her way to the staircase that led to the dance floor.

As she descended, the eyes of the guests followed her every step. Sibella was glad she'd elected to wear a gown short enough that she didn't have to worry about tripping on her hem with everyone staring.

By the time she reached the floor, a crowd of gentlemen stood waiting for her. She smiled humbly at them, hoping to make a good first impression. She had never been formally introduced to society, and even though no one would know who she was, she considered this her debut. It was a lot of pressure for one night, but she was certain she could handle it.

"Mademoiselle, may I have your first dance?" one gentleman asked.

"You look ravishing this evening," another commented.

"I don't believe I've made your acquaintance," a third chimed in.

Sibella smiled politely, but she hardly had time to begin a reply to one man before another cut in. She had never been the center of attention like this, and not knowing where to start or what to do, she let them fawn over her until a loud voice cleared her path.

"I believe I would like to lead the lady in her first dance."

The men that had formed a crowd around her parted, and she caught sight of a gentleman in an unconventional blue and white ensemble. His coat was long, almost flowing down to the floor, and it had a hood on it that hid his hair. His mask almost looked like it had been carved from marble but carried the same white and blue colors as his jacket.

He didn't look at all like the other men at the party, most of whom had chosen the same plain style of suit and matching mask that she had made for Leo. This man was unique. Sibella couldn't help but be drawn to him, and with each step she took toward his outstretched hand, her heart beat faster.

She looked into his eyes, a deep blue color that reminded her of the shores of Osmain, and took his hand. He smiled at her, but Sibella was so transfixed by his eyes that she couldn't think straight enough to smile back.

"May I have this dance?" he asked, kissing her hand gingerly, lingering for just a moment to look up at her. Her lips parted slightly, and her knees felt weak under the gaze of this dashing stranger.

"You may," Sibella said, nodding. The musicians struck a chord, and a new song began to play. It was a slower melody, the kind in which there would be very little time apart from her dance partner. He gently pulled her into the proper position and led her around the floor.

Dancing with this man was as easy and as natural as breathing. His hand on her waist was firm but gentle, and the way he looked at Sibella as they moved was intense but kind. He'd clearly been properly trained in ballroom dancing, neither of them missing a step. The song ended all too soon. Sibella had been so caught up in the moment that the time had flown by in the blink of an eye.

She curtsied politely before him and began to pull away, but he said, "Would you like to dance again?"

"Again?" Sibella asked. She glanced around the room. Surely she should dance with more than one man. Then again, dancing with the same partner two dances in a row would only make her more desirable to the other men in attendance, and she had all night. She nodded, and her partner brought her back to a dancing position as the band began to play once more. The song was slightly faster this time, less intimate, but the steps were simpler, which made conversation easier.

As he led Sibella around the dance floor, the man said, "I don't believe I've seen you at court before."

"You haven't," Sibella said truthfully. "I've never had a social season before."

He smiled. "For someone who doesn't have much experience, you certainly know how to make an entrance."

Sibella beamed. "Thank you! I'm just glad I was able to find a dance partner."

"I don't think you'll have any trouble with that this evening." The man laughed.

"But it will be so hard to choose which gentlemen to dance with," Sibella teased, the masked faces of the men who had swarmed her earlier flashing in her mind.

"There are worse problems to have," he said, spinning her around and then pulling her back into his arms.

She shrugged. "That's true, I suppose. But I'd much rather focus my attentions on a few gentlemen at a time. That way, I might get to know the eligible bachelors in society and find a respectable gentleman to marry."

Her mystery dance partner smiled. "And what, might I ask, are you looking for in a husband?"

Sibella thought for a moment. What *was* she looking for? She knew that she could only afford to hope for three things: money, a title, and escape from Raphael. Low-born women, if they managed to marry into the nobility, could hardly be picky about the kind of man they married, and Sibella was no different. No good could come from getting her hopes up. Seeing her cousin so in love with Principe Daniel had made her wish for the briefest of moments that she could have a romance with her eventual spouse. But it was all so far-fetched that she couldn't allow herself to follow that train of thought. Until now.

"I'm not sure," Sibella admitted. "All I know is that my dream husband would be someone I couldn't stand to be away from, someone who made me feel less alone. What about you?"

The man smiled, a dazzling sight that made her heart flutter. She couldn't even see his whole face, yet his grin was so charming that Sibella fought to pay attention to the steps of the dance.

He said, "I'd like someone who wants to support me. I've met plenty of women who only wanted my money, but they didn't fool me. I know that out there is someone I can be happy with, and I won't settle down until I find her."

Sibella smiled and nodded, but she felt oddly exposed at the same time, as if he were going to sense the financial reasons why she'd come to the ball. Not for love, but for business. His candor about the women he'd met awakened a sinking feeling of guilt in her gut. This man was genuine, and he wanted a love-match. As inexplicably drawn to him as Sibella was, she would have to leave him after this dance to try a different partner.

There were plenty of men at the ball for her to dance with who simply wanted a wife and weren't hoping to fall in love.

The song ended with a final sweep and Sibella stood up straighter, ready to make her formal departure. She looked around the room at the rest of the guests. There were still plenty of eyes on her. It would be easy to find another gentleman to dance with.

Before she could step away, the mysterious man's hand was on her arm. "Come with me."

"I'm not sure, I should probably—"

"I'd like to continue speaking with you, but somewhere quieter than here," he said.

Sibella cocked her head to the side, trying to decide what to do, but the mystery man didn't wait for an answer. He took her hand, and together they practically ran from the dance floor. Sibella laughed, delighted at the surprising departure from protocol as he led her away from the noise of the ballroom and onto a private terrace overlooking a reflecting pool that glittered in the moonlight.

"Here we are," the man said, gesturing grandly, as if to show off the space. "I imagine you'll learn more about me here than on a crowded dance floor."

"Did I really impress you that much? You want me all for yourself?" Sibella joked.

"If you wish to return to the party and dance with other partners, I won't stop you," her companion said.

"But there's something magnetic about you. I'm not sure what it is, but I can tell you feel it, too."

Sibella didn't know what to say. She didn't even know who this man was, and unless she wanted to reveal herself as well, she didn't dare ask about his identity. Yet he was right: she *had* been drawn to him instantly. So what if he wanted to marry for love? Wasn't Sibella capable of love? If she didn't enjoy his company, she could always run back to the ball and choose another eligible bachelor to court. But if she did like him… well, didn't she owe it to herself to at least try to win the mystery gentleman's favor?

Her eyes fell to his suit, and before she could even think, an unrelated question came tumbling out of her mouth. "What is your costume supposed to be?"

"That's what you want to know about me?" he asked, a laugh ready on his lips.

Sibella sighed. So much for impressing him with her dazzling conversation. "I guess it does sound silly."

"No, it's fine. I'll tell you," he assured her. "I'm the rain."

"I thought so," Sibella said, smiling with satisfaction. The fabric's blue stripes were like the streaks of water that would run down a windowpane during a thunderstorm. "I went for a bit of a rain cloud theme with my costume myself."

"I can see that," he said. "It seems like our meeting tonight was meant to be."

"It is very strange that our costumes work together,"

Sibella agreed. This man was coming on strong, and Sibella wasn't sure whether to run to him or away from him.

"Exactly," he said, flashing his perfect smile. "That is one astonishing coincidence."

"There's no such thing as a coincidence," Sibella said, leaning against the balcony railing.

"You don't think so?" he said. She shook her head in response.

"Fate, perhaps?" he asked.

"I'm not sure," Sibella said. She didn't want to admit it, but she was beginning to think she'd been drawn to the ball tonight in order to meet this mystery man. The other guests suddenly didn't seem to matter as much as the one in front of her.

Sibella didn't believe in luck. She believed that life was a series of uphill battles and disappointments, and this meeting—this man—wasn't likely to change her mind. Her brain told her the truth. This flirtation wasn't likely to result in any offer of marriage. But her heart protested, unwilling to let her walk away. No one had ever drawn Sibella in so immediately.

He said, "Whether it's chance, or destiny, or whatever else—"

Hard work. Resourcefulness. Ambition. Sibella knew *she* was the only reason she'd gotten as far as she had, and she would be the reason she would reach her potential.

He placed his hand on top of hers. "I'm glad you're here."

His hand was warm and sturdy, leaving sparks where he touched her.

He laughed. "Your hand is cold."

Sibella jerked her hand away. "My apologies."

"No," he said, "let me warm it for you."

She raised an eyebrow and placed her hand in his open palm. He pulled her closer, the heat from his body bringing warmth to her cheeks. Sibella turned her head to hide the blush.

"Tell me about yourself," he said. "Do you ride horses?"

Sibella, grateful for the change of subject, said, "I can. But I'm not exactly wild on my rides. I prefer to trot along smoothly and steadily. And you?"

"I'm the same. I used to be much more reckless, but over the last ten years, I haven't really had the time for joy rides."

"Why not?" Sibella asked.

"My parents," he said, his voice breaking slightly. "They, uh, they passed."

"I'm so sorry," she said. "I didn't mean to bring up bad memories."

"No, it's okay. Obviously, I wish they were still here, but there's no time to dwell on it. I have duties to attend to now."

Sibella's eyes widened, and all she could manage to say was, "Oh."

This man was no third son of a low-level aristocrat. He was titled. Whoever he was, he was likely sitting on top of an estate and a small fortune. More than enough to get her out of Raphael's household and into proper society. If she could feel genuine affection for him, enough to satisfy his desire for a love-match, he might be the answer to all her problems.

It wasn't surprising that this man had trouble finding a wife, given his stipulations. She'd been the person who was only in a relationship for power and money before —she'd done it to Principe Daniel earlier that year. But this felt different. Every moment pretending to be interested in the principe had been a test. He was an agreeable man, sure, but they'd both known from the beginning that they weren't meant for each other. This man, though, whoever he was, felt *right*.

"I don't want to put a damper on the mood," the man said softly. His voice was like honey in Sibella's ears, low and smooth.

"It's no problem," she said. "Tell me about yourself instead. Do you enjoy travel?"

"I have seen some of the realm, but I much prefer to stay in Esmar. It keeps me connected with the people here," he explained.

Sibella smiled. "I'm the same way. I was born in Askaña, and I nearly moved to Osmain once, but that's the extent of my experience."

"Why did you consider moving to Osmain?" he asked.

Sibella shrugged casually, hoping he wouldn't catch on that she'd only gone there hoping to marry into money. "It's a long story, one that I certainly don't have the time to tell tonight."

"I understand," he said. "I would love to hear about it another time. Do you keep correspondence?"

"Not usually," she confessed. "I have no one to write to."

Sibella thought again about all the times she'd tried writing to her father as a child, but thinking about that only ever sent a sharp pain through her chest.

"You're welcome to write to me," the man said, running his thumb over her knuckles. The heat from his hands moved to hers, and she almost sighed at the comforting feeling.

"Write to you?" Sibella repeated, almost in disbelief.

"Of course! So I can learn more about you, and you can learn about me."

Sibella beamed. "I'd like that."

"I'm glad," he said.

"Where should I address the letters?"

"The mailbox at the château's guest house," he said.

Sibella blinked in surprise. In the first place, because he wanted to use a mailbox instead of sending it straight inside. And in the second place, the château? He must be an honored guest of the roi.

"I know it sounds ridiculous," he said.

"No, I— Well, it's just not what I expected."

"I understand," he said. "And where should I write to you?"

Sibella opened her mouth and quickly shut it again.

There was no way she could disclose where she lived without giving herself away. If this nobleman learned that she was essentially a servant, even to a duc, he would never marry her.

Luckily, she didn't have to respond.

A young man stumbled onto the balcony, holding on to the wall for support. His suit was disheveled, and his mask was barely attached to his face.

"This party's lame," he said, alcohol giving a slight slur to his speech. "I'm goin' home."

Her mystery gentleman quickly dropped her hand and rushed to the side of the drunk man.

"Charlie?" he hissed. "Where have you been? The ball is almost over!"

Charlie. Sibella knew that name.

But the newcomer wasn't done. "I was at a better party than this one, let me tell ya. I met this girl—"

"Charlie! Please! If you want to go home, just go, okay? Go to bed, sleep this off. We'll talk later," Sibella's dance partner insisted.

"I don't wanna talk, Marius. And I don't need your stupid permission to leave this stupid ball," Charlie said.

Marius. The mystery man was *Roi Marius*? Sibella's eyes widened in shock, her heart beating faster and faster. The roi and his brother kept bickering, Marius under his breath, likely to save face, and Charlie loudly in return, but Sibella was frozen in place. She'd been talking to the Roi of Esmar and had no idea. She should have been relieved that such a wealthy and powerful man had shown interest in her, but all she could feel was regret.

She'd spent the entire evening with a man who would never marry someone who didn't give him some kind of political advantage. Sibella wasn't even titled. This wasn't like marrying Daniel, who hadn't known enough about Esmarish nobility to question her legitimacy. There was no way Roi Marius would give her the time of day if he knew who she was. Tears pricked her eyes. This was what she deserved for getting her hopes up.

"I should go," Sibella said weakly. This got the roi's attention.

"No, please. I'm sorry about my brother," he begged.

"It's not him. I just need to get home," Sibella mumbled. Then she bolted, and she didn't look back. She heard Marius call after her, but she pushed forward. As she re-entered the ballroom, she realized she couldn't stay at the ball now even if she wanted to. For one, Marius would surely find her and demand an explanation. And two, upon entering the ballroom, she was greeted by the sight of Leo on the other side of the dance floor, flirting away with a lady in a swan costume.

It didn't take Sibella long to spot Raphael in the crowd as well. In a panic, she ran from the ballroom entirely. Her disguise was good, but it wasn't perfect, and she didn't think she could handle the stress of avoiding her family on top of everything else.

She pushed her way out of the ballroom and walked

to her carriage as quickly as she could without looking improper. In keeping with Sibella's luck, the driver had parked as far away from the door as possible.

The coachman was dozing as she approached, and she rapped on the side of the carriage to wake him.

"Let's go!" she barked.

"Mademoiselle." He yawned. "Back already?"

"Yes," Sibella said, pulling her door open and jumping into the carriage.

"Off we go then," the coachman said without another complaint.

The road was bumpy as the carriage pulled away, but Sibella could hardly feel the jostling over the numbness of despair that settled into every fiber of her being. As the comte's estate faded in the distance, she let all the tears fall that she'd been holding back. Her one chance to find a husband was ruined. Sibella and her mother would never be free.

"My wife and I will arrive on the 42nd day of autumn to further discuss our trade agreement. I am eager to make the acquaintance of you and your brother, Prince Charlie."

Stephan Smirnov, Tsar of Tatria, to Marius Roche, day 8 of autumn

4

Day 8 of Autumn

*M*arius opened the postbox expectantly, but his heart sank when he found it empty. He shouldn't have been surprised. The box had been barren since the ball, but the idea of his mystery mademoiselle finally writing him a letter was all he had to look forward to.

The last few days at the château had not been pleasant ones. In addition to the usual slog of papers and meetings, there had been... an incident. The day after the ball, Marius had been sitting in his study when Amélie barged in with a letter, out of breath from her sprint down the hall.

"Your Majesty!" She panted. "Disturbing news from the estate of the vicomte de Galaxie."

Marius glanced up from his work and Amélie practically shoved the letter into his hands.

YOUR MAJESTY,

I am writing to you with horrible news. My brother, the vicomte de Galaxie, was discovered dead this morning. I arrived at his estate at the time we'd appointed for lunch, and his servants informed me he was still in bed. When they went to check on him, he was discovered dead. It appeared as though he'd been shot through the window by a very skilled archer.

I don't know what to do, or how to get justice for my brother. I have already reached out to the captain of the royal guard, but I need all the help I can get. Please, I'm begging you, investigate his murder.

Your faithful servant,
Madame Pauline Cartier

MARIUS PUT THE LETTER DOWN, his hand shaking. He couldn't get one line out of his head: *very skilled archer.* Could it be? Could whoever killed the vicomte be the same person who had murdered his parents all those years ago?

"Has Général Constantin confirmed Madame Cartier's recounting of events?" Marius's voice cracked.

"He is looking into the situation as we speak." Amélie

nodded solemnly. "As far as I'm aware, the vicomte's wounds are as Madame Cartier described."

Marius shook his head. This seemed like a bad dream. It had to be. After all this time, why would the assassin come back to Esmar? The kingdom-wide hunt for the killer that had begun after his parents' death should have been enough to scare them away forever.

The culprit had never been found, but they had made one final kill after the assassinations of the roi and reine. Or at least everyone assumed the murder had been the work of the assassin. All that had remained of that victim was her wedding ring, covered in blood. But since that terrible day, Esmar had been peaceful. Peaceful enough, anyway. Marius still had his worries, but until now, he hadn't had to fear for the safety of himself or his court.

"Are the guards investigating this case like they would a serial killer?" Marius asked.

"Of course not. Why would they?" Amélie laughed.

"You must admit, this case does bear remarkable resemblance to when my own parents…" Marius trailed off. It still felt weird to say it out loud even after all these years.

"This can hardly be treated as a repeat offense, Your Majesty." Amélie shook her head. "It's been ten years since then."

Marius pursed his lips. "But the weapon—"

"There is no need to concern yourself, Your Majesty. The guard will take care of everything."

Marius could have scoffed right then and there, but he didn't want to argue. Of course the guards would take care of the problem. Just like they took care of his parents' murderer—by sitting on their asses and letting the killer get away.

"In other news," Amélie continued, "I've heard rumors that you were seen dancing with someone at the masquerade ball last night."

Marius snapped his head up. "Who is she? Do you know?"

"No, your Majesty. I was hoping you might. Perhaps she could be a suitable bride for you?" Amélie suggested.

The desk clattered and a few loose papers floated to the ground as Marius pushed himself out of his chair. He was glad to have Amélie on his staff, but her constant insistence that he be married as soon as possible was stressful. And when he thought more about it, he realized he didn't want to share his mystery mademoiselle with anyone.

"I need to get some air," Marius said quietly. Then he stalked out of the study.

He hadn't planned where he was going, but before he knew it, Marius found himself at the guest house at the edge of his property. It was hardly used, and far from prying eyes. The perfect place for private letters to be exchanged. He glanced inside the mailbox, hoping against all odds that he would find a letter there from his mystery mademoiselle. He'd barely been able to focus since the ball. Every time he closed his eyes,

Marius pictured her in his mind. He'd considered who she might be, running through a list of women related to noble families who might have made their society debut the night of the ball, but his attempts kept coming up empty.

He almost regretted asking the mystery mademoiselle to send her letters to the guest postbox instead of sending them straight to the château and to his desk. Whichever messenger she sent might have given him an idea of who she was. But when he'd been on the terrace with her and enraptured by the ease of their conversation, Marius had been reminded of how tired he was of being so formal with everyone around him. If this woman was going to be the only one to treat him as a person instead of an object, he could act like a normal human being and get his own mail.

He hadn't been surprised to find the box empty that day, but he was disappointed. It had been less than a day since the ball, after all, and that was an awfully short turn-around for her to write to him. That was, if she ever wrote at all. Charlie had been so embarrassing that Marius was almost certain she would never reach out to him again. His heart sank. The one woman he'd actually wanted to know better, and it had already been ruined.

Marius closed the box in defeat and turned to return to the château. He spotted Amélie hurrying toward him across the lawn and waited. When she finally reached his side, she was out of breath and red in the face.

"Your Majesty, you must go inside at once!" she huffed.

"What are you doing following me?" Marius asked.

"A kitchen maid saw you leave and alerted me. It is much too dangerous for you to be out here without security," Amélie scolded.

"I believe I can go where I'd like on my own property, Amélie," Marius said.

Her mouth dropped open in surprise. "Of course, you can, it's just… well, it's not safe for you to be alone. I insist you bring a guard with you when you leave the building."

He took a deep breath and simply nodded. This seemed to satisfy Amélie, who saw him safely back to the château. But internally, he was stewing. He was roi, dammit! If he couldn't walk to his own mailbox, what *could* he do?

Marius was tired of feeling like a trinket inside a glass display case. This was his life, and he was wasting it. Until he found his mystery mademoiselle, he couldn't relax.

A plan took shape in Marius's head at that point, and before he knew it, he was digging ragged clothes out of a cluttered drawer. It hadn't taken very much searching through Charlie's room to find his "going out" clothes—which were just standard peasant garments. Charlie didn't like to attract attention on his outings, one good aspect of his dissolute habits.

Every day since, Marius had worn his disguise to

check the mailbox. It had successfully kept the staff from bothering him again, and no one betrayed him to Amélie, but the box was empty every time. And today was no different. With a sigh, Marius closed his mailbox and trudged back to the château. He would be back the next day to check again.

Some sign from his mystery mademoiselle was all he had to look forward to. Marius would wait forever for her if he had to.

Day 12 of Autumn

The door to the shop creaked open on rusty hinges, revealing a dust-filled space. Sibella, who had both of her hands full carrying bolts of fabric, fought back a sneeze. The store was in a nice enough location, in a wealthy area of town within walking distance of her home, but she couldn't remember the last time she had seen the lights of a business coming from inside.

She dropped the bolts in a heap and stepped around them to survey her new base of operations. She threw open the shades, letting sunlight stream into the room. It wasn't in horrible shape. The paint wasn't chipped, and the marble floors were in good condition. She would have to spend a day cleaning to give the place a professional shine, but that wouldn't be too difficult.

Sibella made her way to the small spiral staircase in the corner and climbed to the loft. This would be her workspace, while the downstairs area would be where she met clients. It was pitch-black upstairs, and she wished she had a lamp. She worked her hand along the wall, searching for a window or a source of light. She stumbled as her knee banged painfully into a large piece of furniture. After regaining her balance, Sibella kept going until she felt thick fabric beneath her fingers. She tugged the drapes open, squinting as daylight flooded into the loft.

Her eyes adjusted to the brightness, and her jaw dropped at the view. The window was large, and it faced the street. From the second floor, she had a view of the whole city of Luméte. In the distance, she could even see the glittering grounds of the château. A pang of grief hit her at the sight of it, knowing that Roi Marius lived there. He'd probably already forgotten all about her.

Sibella hadn't written to him. It had seemed like a waste of time. It would take a miracle for him to over-look her social status as a tradesperson. As much as she wanted to speak to him again, it was a foolish idea and would only lead to heartbreak.

Breaking away from the window, Sibella inspected the rest of the room. The only furniture was the work-table she'd ungracefully rammed into a moment before, and a chair that didn't look particularly comfortable. With any luck, she could convince Raphael to spend a bit of money on furnishings.

She turned to descend the stairs—she needed to bring her bolts of fabric up to her workspace. The metal of the stairs made loud clunking noises with each step she took, and she made a mental note to avoid going up and down them if she had customers in the shop. As she stepped down onto the main floor, the door to the shop swung open.

"Knock, knock," Sibella's mother said, entering the space with a cautious smile. Delphine Bellerose-Lavigne looked nearly identical to Sibella. Both women were tall, pale, and had the same shade of golden hair, but the older woman carried signs of stress and age around her eyes that Sibella had yet to develop. Delphine held a large box in her hands, and as soon as she was fully inside, she set it down, shaking out her stiff hands.

"Maman," Sibella greeted her warmly, wrapping her mother in a tight hug.

"Raphael was going on a rant about the comte de Cieux. Apparently, they had some kind of argument after the ball the other night. I'm not sure what it's about, but I thought it might be best for me to get out of his way. If he asks, I came here to drop this off," Delphine said, gesturing to the package she'd brought with her.

"What is it?" Sibella asked, leaning over to peek inside.

"It's a gift to help you get started," Delphine said.

Sibella gently lifted the lid on the box, and her breath caught in her throat. Nestled in the box was the most perfect sewing machine she had ever seen. It was spotless. Not new, but clearly well taken care of. Leagues above the rickety old one in her bedroom at home. And sitting next to it was a sewing kit. When Sibella gingerly lifted it and opened it up, she found a gorgeous pair of silver-plated shears, snips, and a thimble.

"Where did you get this?" Sibella smiled.

"It was mine," Delphine said with pride.

"Maman, I couldn't possibly—"

"Take it, Sibella," Delphine said. She cupped Sibella's face in the palm of her hand, and Sibella leaned into her mother's touch.

"This was my favorite sewing machine from my time as a seamstress," Delphine explained, motioning to the beautiful machine.

"I can't believe I've never seen it before," Sibella said, thinking of all the times she'd helped her mother in their tiny shop in Céleste.

Delphine shrugged. "I put it in storage."

"Why?" Sibella asked.

"Your father," Delphine said grimly.

Despite Rey Nicolas being dead, Sibella felt a twinge of anger at the mention of the man.

Her mother continued, "He gave me the machine during my stay in Askaña. After things didn't work out, I put it away. It hurt too much to think about him, and I knew I couldn't do my best work on anything that reminded me of him. But you can."

Sibella's excitement at seeing the new sewing

machine was replaced with resentment. She'd never known Rey Nicolas, but Sibella hated her father with a burning passion. When Askaña had been overthrown and Nicolas killed in the process, she hadn't grieved at all. The realm was better off with him gone.

"I want you to take the machine," Delphine said. "Your old one is wearing out. You need the best equipment for your shop."

Sibella gave her mother the warmest smile she could muster and gingerly lifted the box. "Thank you, Maman."

"Of course. Anything for you."

Sibella carefully ascended the spiral staircase, Delphine following closely behind with several bolts of fabric in her arms.

"This is a lovely space," she said, looking around. "You'll do good work here."

Sibella set the box down on her worktable and sat in the small chair. Just as she'd suspected, it was horribly uncomfortable.

"What was your first studio like?" Sibella asked.

"Nothing quite this nice." Delphine laughed. "If I'd had this shop, I don't know what I would have done with myself."

A strange silence fell over the women. Delphine said, "I don't think I quite imagined you walking in my footsteps."

"Being a seamstress, you mean? Or being a slave to the almighty duc des Étoiles?" Sibella said darkly.

"Both, I suppose," Delphine admitted, leaning on the worktable. "I had such high hopes for you. I always had these fantasies that your father would accept you. That you could escape a life of labor and do something greater."

"You mean rule Askaña?"

"Or anything you wanted to do." Delphine sighed. "I know it was an impossible dream, but I didn't want you to lead the same kind of life that I did: working my fingers to the bone, always worrying over money and housing, marrying just to keep us afloat. I wanted things to be better for you."

"Yet here I am," Sibella said softly. She hadn't meant to insult her mother, but Delphine had to turn away to wipe a tear from her eyes.

"I really thought the principe would make things different for you," she said.

"I did too," Sibella said, taking her mother's hand gently. "I wanted to get both of us out of here."

"You know it's not as easy as it sounds," Delphine said. "Not when we're bound by marriage to the Lavignes."

"I don't care what that man thinks." Sibella shrugged. "He can go die in a ditch for all I care."

"Sibella!"

"What? It's true."

"He is the only reason we've survived."

"He's a monster," Sibella said, tears pricking her eyes.

"If you need proof, just look at everything he's done to me."

Delphine buried her face in her hands, but Sibella wasn't finished. "He estranged me from society. He only supported me when he thought I might marry a principe. Now that I'm back, I have to work for him for, well, *forever*. I will never have any money of my own. No means to advance, either by marriage or by hard work. I am his prisoner!"

"I know." Delphine sobbed. "I know."

"Then how can you defend him?"

"Because he's all I have."

Sibella shook her head. "No," she hissed, seething with anger. "*I* am all you have."

Delphine went down the stairs without another word, tears streaming down her face. Sibella didn't rise from her chair to ask her to stay, or even to offer an apology she wouldn't mean. She only listened as the sound of her mother's weeping faded and she heard the front door open and close. Sibella was alone once again.

She knew she couldn't continue like this, hiding from Raphael yet clinging to what little he provided. An image of Roi Marius at the ball appeared in the back of her mind. Winning any kind of attention from him at this point was a long shot, but he was the only chance Sibella had of freedom for herself and for her mother. The roi would never agree to marry Sibella once he found out who she was. But who said he ever had to know?

"Your Majesty,
You must forgive my sudden departure from the ball. I did not
feel well and had to rush home. I have been most anxious
about writing to you after the way we left things, but I hope
you can excuse my hesitation.
I will say that I haven't been able to get you off of my mind
since that evening. You were quite the exquisite dance partner,
and I truly enjoyed your conversation. I would like to start a
correspondence with you, if that's still alright. I am very
interested in getting to know you better."

An unsigned letter to Marius Roche, day 12 of autumn

6

Day 42 of Autumn

*M*arius stared out the window in anticipation. Any moment now, the Tsar and Tsarista of Tatria would be arriving at the château, ready to negotiate the renewal of their old trade agreement. It seemed like just yesterday he'd been putting the initial pieces in place for their visit, and now the day had come. Time had begun moving quickly since his mystery mademoiselle had written to him.

When he'd first opened the post box thirty days ago, he'd thought he was hallucinating. He had to have been. But no—a small envelope had been carefully tucked inside the box. The butterflies had appeared in his stomach instantly. After so many days of disappointment, he hadn't realized how convinced he'd been that his mystery woman might never write to him.

Marius's hand had been shaking as he'd pulled the letter out of the box. He broke the seal, unable to wait long enough to bring the letter back inside, and pulled out a handwritten note. He had to know who she was, and why she'd waited so long to contact him.

He read it as slowly as his racing mind would allow, scanning the neat handwriting for any traces of her identity, but he was disappointed to find no signature at the end of the letter. Marius had almost growled in frustration, stalking back to his office and collapsing at his desk. He'd read the letter a few more times, then pulled out some of his finest stationery and penned a response. There was no return address on the envelope. Clearly, his mystery mademoiselle didn't want to be found. Marius had put his return letter in the same mailbox, hoping that by some miracle the note would reach her.

Two days later, he'd received his answer by way of another letter, and they'd been keeping up correspondence ever since. His missives to her got longer the more they got to know each other, and he began to pick up on the personality of his mystery mademoiselle. She seemed to be a traditional lady, delicate and feminine. Marius didn't mind this at all. He also would have been fine if she'd said she liked to ride horses through mud like a madwoman, or go hunting like many gentlemen of the court, but it appeared that she was more interested in simple things. Things that wouldn't clash with the responsibility of becoming reine, which made it all the more possible to see himself by her side.

With every passing letter, the image he had of her became more and more like the type of woman he'd want to marry. There was just one small problem—he still had no clue as to her true identity. He'd thought about involving the royal guard in his search, but their lack of skill in finding the murderer on the loose in Esmar didn't inspire confidence.

In the days since the last murder, two more members of the court had been slain. It was deeply disturbing and made Marius more nervous than before about Charlie's late-night escapades.

Marius had not confided any of these concerns to his mystery mademoiselle. While he trusted her, he didn't trust that their letters were secure. Someone with less than honorable intentions could easily find his letters first. Also, it was nice to not talk about his title or responsibilities for a change. She'd addressed the letters to Roi Marius, but that was the only mention of his rank she ever made. It made him feel almost normal. Marius wished more than anything that he could lead a life without his position being held over his head. His mystery mademoiselle had understood the sentiment perfectly.

Marius watched the world outside, longing for another letter from her. He wanted to check the post box, but until the Tatrians were settled in, he would have to wait. Nothing was more important than the trade negotiations and the benefits the treaty would bring to his people—Marius knew this. But his heart was with the mysterious woman. He needed to know who she was. He needed to see her again.

A flash outside the window brought him back to the present. He squinted as he looked out into the brightness of the day. A pristine white and gold carriage was making its way up the long drive to the château. He could tell from the assortment of expertly crafted golden flowers that adorned the carriage that it was the Tatrians. Tatria was known for the beautiful and rare flowers that grew there, many of them with useful medicinal qualities. It was imperative that the trade agreement be renewed so that the Esmarish would have access to the healing properties of Tatrian medicines.

Marius stood and prepared himself to greet his guests. He gently tucked the lady's last letter into his desk and left his study. When he arrived at the throne room, he was relieved to see that Amélie was already there with a posse of maids behind her.

"Everything is ready for our guests, I assume?" Marius asked.

Amélie nodded. "Yes, Your Majesty. The rooms have been prepped. A few servants have had their daily duties altered to accommodate the needs of the tsar in the event that he requests assistance. Entertainment has been booked. However—"

"Thank you, Amélie," he said.

"There is one thing, Your Majesty—"

"Yes?"

"It's your brother."

Charlie. Marius felt the blood drain from his face. "Is he okay?"

"Well," Amélie said, flustered, "we don't know. He isn't here. We've searched all over the château."

Marius took a deep breath, trying to keep himself calm. Of course Charlie would cause problems. What would the Tatrians do when they weren't properly greeted by the prince and heir presumptive? Charlie knew how much was riding on these negotiations—he'd been informed multiple times by both Amélie and Marius himself. Medical care for the Esmarish people was at stake. It was imperative that everyone in the château be on their best behavior to smooth the way for a renewed alliance.

"Find him, please," Marius said, forcing his tone to stay even.

Amélie nodded. "Of course, Your Majesty. I've already sent a team of servants to search for him. Rest assured, he will return soon."

Marius didn't doubt that. Amélie was nothing if not capable. He was more worried about how Charlie would behave once he was brought back to the château. What if he was drunk or angry? What would the tsar think of that?

Marius's thoughts were still swirling around his head when the large doors to the throne room opened with a groan. He rushed to his dais, trying to make himself look presentable for the Tatrian envoys. Luckily, he was seated before they rounded the corner.

"Your Majesty, may I present to you His Majesty Tsar Stephan Smirnov of Tatria and Her Majesty Tsarista Saffron Smirnova of Tatria," the page announced.

The Tatrians strode confidently into the room. Tsar Stephan was an older gentleman with a graying beard, wielding a cane. He had an air of kindness about him and Marius smiled, hoping it might be easier than he had expected to get along with the Tatrians. But then his gaze fell on Tsarista Saffron. Marius didn't know how their marriage had been arranged, and he could hardly judge a man for marrying a woman who was so young and beautiful, but the age difference was apparent. Tsarista Saffron was perhaps in her late thirties, much younger than the Tsar, with flawless dark hair and pale skin that didn't quite mask the conniving gleam in her eyes.

Marius knew that the pair only had one child, Tsarevna Azura, who had been conceived shortly before the tsar's health began to slip. She hadn't been mentioned in any of the tsar's letters, so Marius wasn't surprised that she wasn't in attendance with her parents, but it would have been nice to meet her. She was only a few years younger than Charlie, but the little that was publicly known about Azura painted her as someone very devoted to her royal duties. If Charlie and Azura had been able to strike up a friendship, maybe Charlie would be more inclined to take his own responsibilities more seriously.

Marius stood to greet his guests. "Your Majesties. It is a pleasure to meet you."

"You as well," Tsar Stephan said.

"I trust your journey was pleasant?" Marius asked.

"Pleasant as being in a stuffy carriage for several days can be," Tsarista Saffron said with a snooty chuckle.

Marius, unsure how to respond, laughed nervously. "Well, welcome to Esmar."

"Thank you, Your Majesty." Tsar Stephan smiled. "To show our gratitude for sharing your beautiful château with us for the duration of our stay, we present to you a gift. May it bring peace and goodwill to our negotiations."

A small Tatrian servant carried forth a bouquet of large pink flowers. Marius recognized them as Aesowiles. They could be dried and ground and made into an illness preventative for many basic conditions, the common cold and influenza chief among them. The flowers could only grow in the Tatrian climate and soil, like so many of their other rare plants. Attempts had been made to grow them in Esmarish greenhouses, but without success. No one outside of Tatria had ever successfully cultivated an Aesowile—or any native Tatrian plant, for that matter.

Marius smiled and motioned for one of his servants

to receive the gift. Amélie stepped forward, graciously accepting the bouquet.

"Thank you for your generous offering," Marius said.

"It is the least we could do," Tsar Stephan said. He stepped forward, admiring Marius. "You look just like your father."

Marius nodded solemnly. "Thank you. It is an honor to carry on his legacy."

"He was a good man," Tsar Stephan said gently.

"Is Prince Charlie here to greet us as well?" Tsarista Saffron interjected, changing the subject.

"He is… ah… on his way," Marius stammered.

"On his way? What could possibly be more important than our arrival?" Tsarista Saffron scoffed. Marius thought it was a rhetorical question, but as she stared into his soul, it became apparent that she wasn't joking.

"Nothing I can think of," Marius said. "I'm sure he will have a perfectly reasonable explanation when he arrives."

"You mean you don't know what he's been doing?" Saffron pressed him.

Marius wanted to disappear. This was falling apart quickly. Somehow, Tsarista Saffron had been able to pick out one of his largest weak spots without missing a beat. Marius fought to keep his voice calm as he said, "Charlie has his own duties to attend to that keep him quite busy, but I trust that he will treat you with the respect you deserve."

Could the Tatrians tell that was a lie? Given Charlie's

tendencies to ignore the responsibilities of his position and indulge his own whims, there was no one Marius trusted less than his younger brother. The tsarista raised her brows and scrutinized him carefully, but she didn't press the point further.

Marius cleared his throat. "I'm sure he will be here soon. I apologize for his tardiness, but rest assured, he is looking forward to meeting you."

Tsar Stephan nodded. "It is no trouble, Your Majesty."

Marius smiled. The tsar seemed like a reasonable man. Perhaps the negotiations would go well after all. Marius stood, descending the steps from his throne to meet the Tatrians on the marble floor. While he stood taller than both the tsar and tsarista, Marius felt much too small as he stood before them.

"I'm sure you are weary from your journey," Marius said. "Take the day to rest, and we will begin our official business tomorrow."

The old man nodded. "Very well. I'm sure my wife will appreciate the time to relax."

From the scowl on Tsarista Saffron's face, Marius wasn't so sure about that. But he held his tongue. The tsarista looked like she was poised to engage in an argument at any time, and Marius had no interest in ruining the negotiations before they'd begun. "If you need anything, please don't hesitate to ask."

"Thank you, Your Majesty," Tsar Stephan said. He

held out his arm to Tsarista Saffron, who ignored the gesture and turned to face Marius.

"I will have my own personal staff, yes?" she demanded.

Marius was nearly stunned into silence by her rude tone. "The servants are all aware of your presence, madame. They will be more than happy to accommodate all of your needs as they arise."

"Accommodate? No, no. That won't work. You see, I need a personal staff. I simply couldn't share a servant with anyone." She laughed haughtily. "There was only space in our travel party to bring one maid from home. I'll certainly need more than *that*."

Marius pursed his lips, thinking of something to say that wouldn't offend the woman. Finally, he said, "I'm sure I could arrange for another maid to tend to you."

"And what about a chef? A dresser? A food taster? My comfort is of the utmost importance," she said, perfecting her posture, crossing her arms, and staring down her nose at Marius.

"Darling," Tsar Stephan said, "don't you think that's a bit extreme?"

Tsarista Saffron looked like she wanted to argue with him, but her husband continued talking over any of her objections. "A personal servant would be most generous, Your Majesty."

Marius nodded, grateful for the older man's intervention. "Consider it done."

"Let's get settled in," Tsar Stephan said, his wife

finally taking his arm. Amélie hurried after them, eager to show them to their chambers. When the Tatrians were finally gone, Marius sighed in relief. That hadn't been a total disaster. Now that he was free until dinner, he could finally check on the mail.

Marius was extra careful not to be seen crossing the garden wearing the set of peasant clothes he'd swiped from Charlie's modest collection. The last thing he needed was to be identified by the Tatrians as he gallivanted around the château. He snuck outside and made his way to the mailbox. He pulled it open in anticipation, only to find it empty.

He tried to hide his disappointment despite the lack of witnesses. How foolish of him to be irresponsible like this when the future of Esmarish healthcare was on the line. Marius sighed, closing the box.

He turned and noticed a figure in the distance, looking straight at him. Someone had seen him dressed as a peasant, snooping around the old guest house. His first instinct was to run, but he knew that wouldn't solve anything. In fact, it might raise more suspicion in his unexpected visitor than remaining where he was. With the Tatrians visiting Esmar, he couldn't afford to have anything swirling around about intruders on the château grounds. His disguise was good from a distance, which was all he needed to sneak around without being bothered by Amélie or the guards. As long as the person didn't come any closer, he would have nothing to worry about. But if they did, he would almost certainly be recognized.

He pretended to be busy, checking inside the small mailbox, which was empty. Damn. He'd come out here for nothing.

"What are you doing?"

The voice startled Marius, and he turned around sharply to find himself face to face with the most beautiful woman he'd ever seen. She wore a pure white dress that made her glow in the sunlight. Lace covered her shoulders, giving glimpses of the fair skin that lay beneath. She clutched a matching parasol in her gloved hands, shading her head of blonde hair from the midday sun.

And her eyes. She had the most stunningly blue eyes. Marius's own eyes were blue, but his were a darker shade that didn't stand out particularly. Hers, on the other hand... they were an icy blue. The only other time he'd seen eyes like that had been at the ball. His mystery mademoiselle had had eyes like that. Marius's stomach flipped. It couldn't be her, could it? He would have to broach the subject cautiously, just in case.

"Hello," he said, hoping that she wouldn't recognize him as the roi.

"I've never seen anyone else out here," she said, eyeing him suspiciously. She made no formal address, no curtsy, nothing.

Marius tried his best to not appear rattled by her presence and appearance. "Yes, well, I'm not here often."

She narrowed her eyes at him, then cocked her head. "Who are you?"

Marius's eyes widened in shock, then his surprise turned to embarrassment. This woman obviously had no idea who he was. And that caused a burst of disappointment to flare up in him because his mystery mademoiselle had known who he was at the ball, despite his costume. She'd addressed every letter to Roi Marius. If this was his mystery mademoiselle, she would almost certainly recognize him again in this disguise. This couldn't possibly be her.

Still, she stared at him expectantly, waiting for an answer as to his identity that he wasn't inclined to give. He would have to think of a lie, and quickly.

"I deliver important documents. For the roi," Marius said, trying to sound confident enough that this woman would believe him.

"You're the royal mail carrier?" She almost laughed at this.

"Uh, yes," Marius lied.

"Aren't you a little old to be running around town delivering mail?"

"No," Marius said defensively. "It's very important work. It could never be entrusted to a child."

As soon as Marius said it, he knew how silly it was to be up in arms about a job that wasn't his. Somehow, though, it was still less embarrassing than admitting the truth about who he was and why he was in disguise.

The woman stepped closer, looking him over. "What's your name?"

"What's *yours*?" Marius countered.

"I asked you first," she said.

"I asked last," Marius shot back, hoping she would drop the subject entirely.

"You're acting very strangely," she said. "Perhaps I should alert the royal guard."

"No!" Marius exclaimed, a little more forcefully than he would have liked. Calming his voice, he continued, "That's not necessary."

She raised an eyebrow as Marius wracked his brain, trying to come up with something— anything—he could say that would assuage her suspicions. He finally said, "I'm Jack."

Not entirely a lie. Jackson was his middle name.

"Just Jack?" she asked, eyeing him suspiciously. It was uncommon for anyone in Esmar, even the farmers and laborers, to introduce themselves by first name only. One used titles if one had one, surnames if one didn't, or even both. Marius was too slow on his feet to think of a fitting surname for his imaginary alter-ego, and he smiled awkwardly, hoping she wouldn't press him further.

"Yep," Marius said. "And you are?"

She smirked. "Sibella."

"Just Sibella?"

She crossed her arms. "Yep," she replied, copying his tone.

Marius almost laughed. This girl was clever.

"What brings you to the château today?" he asked, trying once again to get her attention off himself.

"Business." Sibella shrugged.

"Obviously." Marius crossed his arms. "What kind of business?"

"I'm a seamstress."

"And you sew for the roi?"

Marius had never thought much about his staff before. He had Amélie, of course, and he knew his personal attendants well enough. But he'd never considered the other aspects of his life that were taken care of for him. Amélie had always hired his staff. She'd hand-selected his chefs, his drivers, and apparently his seamstresses.

"I… well. I'm a fairly new business, you see. I was hoping to secure the roi as a client."

"Impressive," Marius said. "You're talented, then?"

Sibella raised her chin with pride. "I'd like to think so."

Marius nodded. "I wish you all the best then. With the roi."

He made a mental note to ask Amélie later about Sibella's pitch to become a royal seamstress and how it had gone. He wasn't sure what the selection process looked like for a role like that, but he wanted to give her the best chance possible. Young, beautiful, and apparently an ambitious businesswoman—Sibella deserved to have a genuine chance at achieving her dream.

"Thank you." Sibella smiled. "I really ought to get going. I don't want to keep you from your work."

Marius wanted to argue that he had no work to be doing, but he smiled back and said, "Lovely to meet you, Sibella."

She began to walk away, but looked back long enough to say, "You too, just Jack."

"My dearest mademoiselle,
You have no idea how happy I was to receive your letter in the
mail. I have also had you on my mind since the ball and have
longed to speak with you again. I would of course be delighted
to start a correspondence with you. Consider your absence
fully forgiven.
I apologize for the way my brother behaved in front of you at
the ball. There is no one in my life so challenging as Charlie,
but he is the only family I have left, and I will always want
what's best for him.
Please tell me about your family. Do you have siblings?
I hope this letter finds you somehow, as your last letter had no
name or address to send it to. If you provide me with details
on yourself, I would be happy to send my letters to you instead
of dropping them off in the mailbox."

Marius Roche to his mystery mademoiselle, day 14 of autumn

"Your Majesty,

There is no need to apologize on Prince Charlie's behalf. I understand completely what it is like to be a sibling. I, myself, have two brothers. I am always both humbled and challenged by them. I've yet to decide if that's a good thing or a bad thing. Unfortunately, though, I spent a lot of time by myself growing up, and as such I participated in more independent hobbies rather than spending time with my family. I am fluent in three languages, and I am proficient in each of the five kingdom's national dances. I have also always had an eye for fashion.

What about you? When you aren't busy running the kingdom, what do you do for fun?"

The mystery mademoiselle to Marius Roche, day 17 of autumn

7

⚮

Day 43 of Autumn

Sibella nearly collapsed as she opened the front door to the Étoiles estate. It wasn't as if the door was particularly heavy, but she was so exhausted from a long day at the shop that it felt like it wouldn't take much for her to pass out.

Business had been growing steadily since the shop had opened. She was now building as many garments as she could manage and the long hours always left her fingers and back sore from hunching over her sewing machine and occasionally poking herself with a pin. The muscles in her arm also objected to the amount of sewing she did, as she had to constantly turn a hand crank to make the machine run. But the money was steady, and Sibella had to do whatever she could to stay in Raphael's good graces. She knew she couldn't rely on

Roi Marius to support her, despite how sincere he seemed in his letters.

Sibella pushed the door closed behind her and started up the staircase to her bedroom. The relative quiet of the foyer disappeared as she reached the first landing and heard the unmistakable sound of shouting emanating from Raphael's study. She could hear her stepfather's deep voice and the softer tones of her mother speaking. Common sense told Sibella to get as far away from an angry Raphael as possible, but concern overpowered her. If her mother was in there with that monster, who knew what might happen?

Sibella inched closer to the study, fighting to keep her breath from shaking as she pressed her ear to the door and tried to listen. She could only pick up bits and pieces of Raphael's rant through the heavy door. "Lazy… selfish…"

"Don't come any closer!" Delphine screamed. Sibella's heart nearly leapt out of her chest at the sound of her mother in distress. It wasn't the first time this had happened.

The last time Sibella had interfered in a fight between them, her mother had made her promise never to do so again. She didn't want Sibella anywhere near Raphael's outbursts. At the time, Sibella had agreed. After all, she had been preparing to leave for Osmain to court Principe Daniel in just a few days and didn't need any bruises that would have to be explained to strangers. But now, as much as Sibella wanted to pretend that Roi Marius was a viable option for her future, she couldn't let herself rely on him. It would always be Sibella and Delphine against the world. She had to protect her mother.

Sibella closed her hand around the pair of sewing shears in her pocket, ready to pull out her makeshift weapon at a moment's notice. She pushed open the door a crack, just enough that the conversation inside became much clearer.

"...getting involved in my business," Raphael spat.

"This is a family matter. You can't just—"

"I most certainly can. This is my home. My money. My title. You are no one. It doesn't matter if *your* reputation is ruined."

"What about you?" Delphine asked, voice shaking.

"I'll do just fine. Arthur needs to learn a lesson. Don't mess with the duc des Étoiles. A lesson you would do very well to learn yourself, you good for nothing—"

Sibella chose that moment to swing the door wide open. Delphine looked at her daughter with a mix of terror and surprise. Raphael, however, didn't bat an eye as he turned to face Sibella. She tried not to cower under his glare.

"Hello," Sibella said, feigning nonchalance. "I'm back from work."

"You," Raphael seethed.

"I don't need to stay long, but I would like to tell my mother about my day. I'll just grab her and we'll be going."

Raphael moved to block the door. "I don't think so. I wasn't done speaking to her."

Sibella's fist tightened around her sewing shears. "I think you are."

"And who are you to tell me what to do in my own home? I ought to throw you out on the street to remind you of where you're from."

Sibella ignored him and took her mother's hand. "Let's go, Maman."

Delphine shook her head, tears in her eyes. "Sibella, please—" Sibella couldn't help but notice the beginnings of a nasty shiner on her mother's eye. No doubt she would be kept away from proper society until it healed.

Delphine's protest was cut off as Raphael slammed Sibella against the wall, his hand to her throat. Stars exploded across her vision as she fought his grip and gasped for breath, trying to shake off the shock of his assault.

"Raphael!" Sibella heard her mother scream.

"Don't ever come in this room again, do you understand me? You're no more than a servant as far as I'm concerned," Raphael seethed, leaning in so close that he peppered Sibella's cheeks with spittle as he raved. Sibella tried to nod, but she could barely move her head with Raphael's hand still on her throat. He must have realized this, but instead of letting her go, he threw her aside. Sibella landed in a heap on the floor across the room. Her hand instinctively flew to her throat as she took shallow, labored breaths.

Raphael stepped over where she lay, all traces of temper gone as he hissed, "I said get out."

Sibella weakly pushed herself to her feet, still trying to catch her breath, and stumbled out of the room before Raphael could attack her again. She heard Delphine asking him if she could leave the room too, but he forcefully turned her down. Sibella started the trek up to her room, the failure of her attempt to help her mother weighing heavily on her shoulders.

Her anger festered as she reached her bedroom. She slammed the door behind her and fell onto her bed, staring up through the window at the stars that dotted the night sky above.

Sibella wasn't sure how long she lay there, looking up at her ceiling and trying to stay still enough that her neck wouldn't ache. When, after a while, she heard a soft knock at her door, she didn't respond. And when the door opened slowly and closed again ever so softly, Sibella didn't react. She knew who it was.

"Sibella, darling, are you alright?" Delphine asked.

"Fine," she ground out. Her throat burned when she spoke, and she decided that was a perfectly acceptable excuse to speak less.

"What were you doing in there?" her mother asked. "I told you to stay out of our fights. I didn't want you to get hurt like this."

Sibella still didn't look at her mother, but she heard her sniffle. She must have been crying. Sibella rolled her eyes. "I'm not sure why you're upset. I saved you from his wrath."

"It's not your responsibility to protect me, Sibella!" Delphine said, her voice rising slightly. She stopped herself, took a deep breath, and continued, "It's my job to protect you, and I've failed."

Sibella, still looking up into the heavens, said, "Yes, you have."

This only made Delphine's tears fall faster, but Sibella didn't care. They wouldn't starve to death in Raphael's house, or be exposed to the elements, and her marriage to the duc at least protected Delphine from proper society's cruelty. But instantly, Sibella regretted everything. Every letter that she'd sent to her father begging for help had been a mistake. If she'd relied only on herself instead of looking for acceptance from a man who never gave it, she and her mother would not be in this situation.

"We can't leave him, Sibella," Delphine said softly. "You know this."

Sibella bit back tears. There had been many times when she'd considered leaving Raphael's home by herself. It would be an easy escape. He would never follow after her, and probably be grateful for her departure. But each time Sibella had run to her room and hastily thrown her things in a bag, she'd found she couldn't do it. She could never leave her mother alone with that man. Sibella and Delphine were a team, always had been, and she had never been able to willingly leave her mother behind.

But this time felt different.

"No," Sibella said. "We *can* leave. You just won't. From now on, I will obey your wishes. The next time I hear you scream, I won't come to your defense. I wish you the best of luck with Raphael. I hope you survive his wrath."

Sibella didn't know which was worse: the throbbing around her neck where Raphael had come close to strangling her, or the ache in her heart from fighting with her mother. But before either of them could continue, a knock sounded from Sibella's door. She clenched her fist in frustration. Was it too much to ask to be left alone?

Without waiting for a response, the door opened. Sibella didn't bother to look up and see who else had intruded into her space. If there were no insults being hurled her way, and Maman was already here, there was only one other member of the household who would be visiting her.

"Do you mind if I speak to Sibella for a moment?" Simon asked.

"Of course," Delphine said with a sniffle. "I'll just be going, then."

The door closed, and Sibella was left alone with her younger stepbrother.

"It's been a while since I've seen him this angry,"

Simon said, sitting gently on the edge of Sibella's mattress.

She reluctantly rolled over to face him. "He didn't go ballistic while I was in Osmain this summer?"

Simon shrugged. "Not really. He and Delphine still had their spats, but he never hit her."

"So it's all my fault."

"No," Simon said firmly. Then, after a moment, he sighed. "He wasn't always like this. He would get angry, but only occasionally, and even then, it was less explosive. But after my maman died, he changed."

Sibella found it hard to imagine a Raphael who didn't terrorize his family, but Simon continued. "It was difficult watching him change, seeing how much damage he could do to Leo and me. We've coped with it in our own ways. I try not to provoke him, and Leo tries a bit too hard to impress him. But you... you're different. You fight back. And even though it's a risky choice, I have to admit I admire you for it."

"Thanks, Simon," Sibella said weakly. She didn't see herself as a fighter at all. She sat up and looked at herself in the mirror. Her golden hair was mussed in a million directions. Her eyes were red and puffy from the tears that had been streaking down her cheeks, and her neck was swollen, the beginnings of a nasty bruise forming. Raphael had done his damage. This was not the face of a warrior.

She fell back down onto her firm pillows with a

thud. Simon seemed to catch on to the fact that she wanted to be left alone, and slowly stood.

"I'm off to Monsieur André's estate, but I wanted to make sure you were okay before I left," Simon said.

"I'll be fine. Thank you for checking on me," Sibella replied. Without another word, Simon slipped out of the room.

Alone with her thoughts once again, Sibella found herself lying in the same spot on her bed, admiring the stars that hung so beautifully in the night sky. They were free, burning as bright as they dared, casting pinpricks of light for Sibella to marvel at.

She had worked too long and too hard to find peace to allow Raphael to crush her soul. Whether or not her mother would come with her, Sibella needed to get away from the duc. If she couldn't find heaven, perhaps she could at least find a place among the stars.

"My dearest mademoiselle,

After the way you danced at the ball, it doesn't surprise me in the slightest to learn that you have studied dance. Unfortunately, I haven't had much time for hobbies in recent years. Before I was roi, I enjoyed studying star reading. I was actually quite good at it for someone my age, but there are some events even the stars can't predict, and my parents' death was one of them.

I am honored beyond belief to be Roi of Esmar, but I'd like to be something more than that as well. I don't know what I'd do now if I weren't roi, but I suppose it doesn't matter. My duties can't wait for what I want."

Marius Roche to his mystery mademoiselle, day 19 of autumn

"Your Majesty,

I am most intrigued to learn about your old habit of reading the stars. I, myself, am very passionate about astronomy, but I have read a few books on astrology as well. It seems to be a fascinating subject, but I have no real talent for it. Perhaps you can show me how to do it sometime?

As for your duties taking up most of your time, I certainly know how it feels to be put into an inescapable box. You are not the first person of noble birth I've met who has confided to me about their disdain for power. My cousin is prominent in Osmainian society and has made it very clear to me that a title isn't worth chasing. I wasn't sure I believed her at the time, but now I think I do.

While there are lots of rewards that come with your kind of power, I can certainly see how balancing your work with your everyday life would be nearly impossible. It's not an easy job to be roi, and I commend you for taking it on."

- The mystery mademoiselle to Marius Roche, day 22 of autumn

8

Day 44 of Autumn

Two days. Charlie had been missing for two days. Marius tried not to worry. His brother was sneaky, and he knew his way around the city better than most men, noble or otherwise. But as Marius sat down for dinner with the Tatrians for the second time, he looked at the chair where his brother should have been and hoped that he was safe. Amélie had assured him that her staff was looking into Charlie's disappearance and that he would be back at the château any time now, but that did only so much to ease Marius's nerves.

Now, as he glanced across the dinner table at Tsar Stephan and Tsarista Saffron, he hoped they wouldn't bring up Charlie's absence. He didn't have any good answers for them, and he certainly didn't want to appear as though he didn't have control of his kingdom or his family.

"Have you been enjoying your stay in Esmar, Your Majesty?" Marius asked.

Tsar Stephan nodded respectfully. "Of course, Your Majesty. You have a beautiful home."

The negotiations had been going well, if somewhat slowly. With any luck, they would be able to officially sign the renewed trade agreement the next day, and then the Tatrians would leave Esmar in peace. Marius hoped they would depart sooner rather than later. Tsar Stephan was perfectly amiable, but his wife, well...

"I love the silver and blue color palette you have," Tsarista Saffron said condescendingly, her nose scrunching as she glanced around the dining hall. "It's adorable."

Marius hated the woman. Discussions had stalled out yesterday because she'd supposedly been struck by a horrible headache, claiming "your little château is too stuffy, it's causing me distress!" and once she'd made it to dinner, she'd sent her food back, requesting traditional Tatrian dishes instead of the Esmarish delicacies that had been served. Marius wanted to defend his kingdom, perhaps snap back at her petty remarks, but he'd kept his rebuttals painfully diplomatic. He needed the trade agreement with Tatria, and if diffusing a few insults was all he had to do, he would certainly try his best.

"Thank you," Marius said, pretending not to notice the veiled insult.

A page ran into the dining hall, huffing and puffing. Marius and the Tatrians looked up at his rapid entrance in surprise.

"Your Majesties, I present to you Prince Charlie of Esmar!" the page said, then took a moment to catch his breath. Marius's stomach flipped and he clenched his teeth. This couldn't be good. Charlie must have bypassed announcing his arrival to any other servants. Otherwise, Amélie would have given Marius a warning.

It didn't take long for Charlie to enter the dining hall. He'd probably just arrived at the château, making the page run ahead of him to make the formal announcement. He looked surprisingly composed considering the duration of his absence, strutting confidently into the dining hall. He had obviously changed out of his rustic clothing, and his shoulder-length hair was neatly combed and pulled back.

"Sorry I'm late, everyone," Charlie said as he sat down at the dinner table. "Very important matters to attend to."

"It is good to finally meet you," Tsar Stephan said.

"And you as well," Charlie said. Marius couldn't help but be impressed. He hadn't ever seen Charlie act so formally. Marius had begun to think that his brother was simply incapable of behaving appropriately in front of dignitaries. He was still angry with his brother for his absence over the past two days, but he couldn't deny that Charlie was behaving decently now. He must have realized how important this meeting was.

"You've made it just before the main course," Marius said.

"Excellent!" Charlie smiled.

"I do hope the menu is more agreeable to my palate tonight," Tsarista Saffron remarked, lifting her glass and taking a sip of wine.

"Now, dear, I'm sure they will have prepared something more to your liking after your concerns last night," Tsar Stephan said.

"What was wrong with your meal last night, Your Highness?" Charlie asked innocently.

"It was just so bland compared to the food back home," Saffron explained. "Back in Tatria, we have so many spices that it's impossible to cook a tasteless meal."

Marius had tasted Tatrian food on several occasions, from different chefs, and every time, it felt like the flavors were trying to wage a war in his mouth. Maybe it was because he had grown up with Esmarish food, but he found that the simple dishes of his homeland were much more refined.

Charlie cast Marius a questioning glance. He shot back a look that he hoped would communicate that Charlie should drop the subject. While it did make Marius uncomfortable to be constantly insulted by Tsarista Saffron—he of course wanted to defend Esmar—he needed to keep his temper even.

Unfortunately, Charlie wasn't so willing to bite his

tongue. "I'd hardly call Esmarish food tasteless, Your Highness."

Saffron looked at him with so much pity that Charlie might as well have been a homeless puppy. "Of course *you* wouldn't, darling."

Charlie narrowed his eyes at the tsarista, no doubt formulating a crafty reply in his mind. Luckily, at that moment, the main courses arrived. The small servant girl laid their plates down quietly, even including one for Charlie. Marius looked at his dinner. It was a traditional Tatrian dish of roasted duck, sitting atop a pungent combination of vegetables, rice, and a sauce that Marius was sure would burn his tongue on impact from the sheer amount of spices in it. His chef had prepared something for Saffron after all.

From across the table, Marius saw Charlie politely thank the servant girl before digging in. Marius took his time with his first bite, cutting his meat slowly before raising it to his mouth. It tasted exactly like all the other Tatrian food he'd tried—so overwhelming that he didn't know what the flavor was even supposed to be.

He eyed Tsarista Saffron from across the table as she nibbled on her food and made a face that Marius had come to know very well over the past few days. It seemed to be Saffron's only reaction to anything, actually. Distaste.

"What is this?" she asked, setting her fork down with a clatter.

"It's exactly what you requested, dear," Tsar Stephan

said calmly.

"No, it isn't. I requested flavorful food like I'd find back home," Saffron said, taking a swig of her wine.

"My apologies," Marius said, trying to smooth over the situation. "My chef isn't accustomed to making Tatrian dishes."

Saffron huffed, then flagged down the young servant. "I want this plate out of my sight. Bring me something more appetizing."

The servant girl silently nodded and picked up the plate. In her haste to remove it, she nearly tripped over Tsar Stephan's cane, which jutted out slightly from the table. She quickly regained her balance and scurried back into the kitchen. A few minutes passed, and Marius continued to suffer as he choked down the Tatrian dish. His only consolation was that Tsar Stephan seemed to be enjoying his meal.

"Where is that servant girl with my food?" Saffron said, glancing around. She pointed at another servant who stood against the wall, ready to assist. "You there. Please bring me a new dish. Apparently doing it on her own was too difficult for that incompetent servant girl."

Marius's anger rose more and more with every word Saffron said, but he kept his tone even and remarked, "My staff are very good at what they do. I'm sure they will find a dinner that will satisfy you."

Charlie, however, didn't bother trying to hide his feelings. He glared at Saffron with a disgust so obvious that Marius found himself trying to subtly signal his brother to give him a warning. He needed Charlie to behave for just one night, then the trade contract would be signed and all of this would be over.

As Marius neared the end of his plate of torture, the small servant girl finally reappeared with a different dish. This one looked Tatrian as well. Marius smiled to himself. His chef had been remarkably quick. He would have to give the man a raise.

As the girl neared Saffron to pass her the new plate, she once again tripped over Tsar Stephan's cane, but this time, she wasn't able to catch herself. She lost her balance and the food went flying, missing Tsarista Saffron by inches. The poor servant girl fell to the ground with a thud as Saffron screeched.

Charlie stood up in alarm and looked at the servant first. "Are you alright?"

"Yes. Thank you, Your Highness," the servant girl said as she regained her footing. Her face was red with embarrassment, but she kept a stiff upper lip as she brushed at her dress.

"Now she's talking in front of us?" Saffron said, aghast. "In Tatria, our staff are silent and efficient. It's clear that Esmar has yet to learn the art of domesticating servants."

"I asked her a question. I should expect her to respond to her prince," Charlie argued.

"I expect another dish immediately," Saffron demanded.

"Of course," Marius said. He motioned to the servant

girl. "Could you go fetch her another?"

The servant girl nodded, but Saffron held out a hand. "No! I don't want that one anywhere near my dinner. I wouldn't feel safe if she brought my food to me."

"Give me a break," Charlie mumbled under his breath.

"What did you say?" Saffron said, turning her attention to him.

"You're being ridiculous," Charlie said, loud and proud. Marius cringed. This wouldn't end well.

"Excuse me?" Saffron said, pushing her chair back and standing.

"Charlie!" Marius hissed, rising from his seat as well. He had to stop this exchange before Charlie made things worse than they already were. But Charlie either didn't hear Marius or didn't care.

"The first dish we were served was perfectly fine. Standard Tatrian food, if you ask me," Charlie said.

"It was disgusting! Your chef should be sent packing. He can't cook!" Saffron seethed.

"He can cook very well, he just doesn't have the repertoire to cater specifically to you because he isn't in your employ," Charlie said.

"Charlie, stop!" Marius tried to grab his brother's arm to snap him out of his rage, but Charlie shrugged him off.

"If you haven't noticed, Your Highness, this is Esmar, not Tatria!" Charlie said, gesturing around the room.

"I've had enough of this disrespect," Saffron said,

suddenly regaining her usual rigid poise. "I can't do this anymore, Stephan. I'm leaving."

"No, please!" Marius protested.

Tsar Stephan rose, albeit slowly and with the help of his cane, to stand next to his wife. "Darling—"

"Prepare the carriage!" Saffron commanded another servant. "We will leave immediately."

"But it's getting close to nightfall," Marius said. "And your bags haven't been packed."

"I wouldn't be forced into this if it weren't for your useless servant and your joke of a prince," Saffron said, sticking her nose in the air. The poor servant had begun to tremble, her training no match for Saffron's rage.

"Don't talk about her that way," Charlie said, ignoring the dig at himself. "Don't talk about *anyone* that way!"

"I am Tsarista, and I will speak however I wish," Saffron said, then turned to leave the dining room. But as she neared the door, she turned her head and declared, "The trade agreement is off!"

"No!" Marius said. "Tsar Stephan, I beg of you, please don't do this. Esmar needs your imports."

Tsar Stephan looked uncertain, but he slowly shook his head. "I believe it would be best if we revisited our negotiations another time."

Marius's world was spinning. He held on to a chair for support, afraid he might collapse if he didn't. What would he do if he lost access to all of Tatria's medicines? What would his people do?

"How soon can we reconvene?" Marius asked the older man.

"Never!" Saffron interjected. "You're lucky we aren't threatening war for the disrespect I've been shown! Tatria will never trade with Esmar again!"

And with that declaration, Tsarista Saffron left the dining hall in a huff.

Marius reached out for Tsar Stephan. "Your Majesty, I truly apologize—"

"Save it," Stephan said, looking Marius in the eye. "I like you. You mean well, and I respect that. But I cannot begin to think about our trade contracts until my wife has calmed down. Give it some time, and we will try again. I will write to you when I think the time is right."

"But—"

Tsar Stephan held up his hand to silence him. "I'm sorry. The tsarista and I will be leaving immediately."

Without another word, Tsar Stephan turned and left the dining hall. Marius considered going after him, but showing such desperation would probably just drive him further away.

He turned to the servants and said, "Please see the tsar and tsarista to their carriage."

The servants scrambled, leaving Marius alone with Charlie. He turned to face his brother. "Are you drunk or are you stupid?"

"I'm perfectly sober, I'll have you know," Charlie said, slumping back down into his chair.

"Stupid it is," Marius said. "I was this close to signing

a trade deal with the Tatrians that would provide medicine to our people for years to come. And you've ruined it!"

"I don't want their medicine," Charlie said, crossing his arms. "That woman was rude and obnoxious, and if that's the best Tatria has to offer, we're better off without their assistance."

"Tell that to your people when they're sick and have no remedy," Marius said.

Charlie just shrugged. "I won't have to. We have plenty of allies. We can buy Tatria's herbs elsewhere."

"That would cost us double what it would if we had been able to negotiate this agreement, but you've made sure it's my only option." Marius sat down next to his brother and said seriously, "I'm disappointed in you, Charlie. Where were you?"

"The better question is, where were *you?* The Tatrians blatantly disrespected you and Esmar and you didn't defend your kingdom at all. What kind of roi does that?" Charlie said, a steely look in his eye.

Marius felt like he'd been struck, anger and shock mixing together. "I did what I had to do for our people. You wouldn't understand."

"You're right," Charlie shot back. "I don't understand how you could let down your subjects like this."

"I didn't ruin the trade deal, Charlie," Marius said. "That was all you. *You've* let your people down."

Charlie's mouth hardened. "I was doing my best. For you. For Esmar."

Marius laughed bitterly. "I can see that."

"I'm serious," Charlie said. "I lost track of the days, and yes, I forgot the Tatrians were coming. But as soon as I realized it, I took the time to pull myself together before I came home. I thought you'd prefer that to me being drunk again."

"I do," Marius admitted. "It's much easier to yell at you when you can actually comprehend what I'm saying."

"Look, I'm sorry, okay? I'm sorry you have no back-bone, and I'm sorry you're a terrible leader," Charlie said. "Next time, I just won't come home at all."

Marius shook his head. A million insults and defenses swarmed in his mind, but he reminded himself that he was roi. He had to be more mature than Charlie. But there was one thing he was sure of: he had to rein in his brother before more damage was done to Esmar's reputation. Marius could already feel pangs of anxiety in his chest, and he had a feeling it would only get worse for both himself and for Esmar if he didn't stop Charlie now.

If he wanted to, he could find reasons to have Charlie stripped of his title and expelled from the château. But he knew in his heart that wasn't what his parents would have wanted. They would have stayed by Charlie's side and supported him no matter what, and so Marius would do the same. And if he was honest with himself, Marius still held out hope for his brother.

He sighed and leaned against the dining table. "There's not going to be a next time, Charlie."

Charlie was silent, but he looked up at Marius with a question in his eyes.

"You offended the Tatrian royals. On purpose. I can't trust you around our allies anymore. From this moment forward, you are banned from society functions. No balls, no dinners, no formal events. And I have to know where you are at all times. I'll be assigning a personal guard to you that will report back to me on your whereabouts," Marius said. "You are welcome to continue making poor decisions, but you won't be doing so in the public eye."

Charlie laughed. "I'm an adult, you can't force me out of society."

"I most certainly can. As roi, I am the head of Esmarish society. If I decide you're not a part of it anymore, you aren't."

Charlie glared at Marius with a look of hatred that shook him to his core. It was terrible having to treat Charlie like a misbehaving child, but he had no choice. He had to put his people first.

"As soon as I see your behavior has improved, I will gladly accept you back into society," Marius said.

"Don't count on it," Charlie spat. "I'm not changing myself just to appease you and the other soulless members of the court." With that, he stood and stomped out of the dining hall.

Marius sank back into his chair and sighed, trying to

calm himself down enough to at least fool himself into thinking he would be able to fix this disaster. He knew that he wasn't the best roi, but he'd never felt himself losing control of his kingdom before. He needed something—or someone—to balance him and push him back to being the best roi he could be.

He'd always prided himself on his foreign diplomacy. He was no stranger to dealing with hostile monarchs. Rey Nicolas of Askaña stuck out in his mind as being a particularly tough negotiator. And he would have secured the deal with the Tatrians despite the difficulty if Charlie hadn't interfered. But perhaps Charlie had a point. Maybe he *was* weak. He couldn't afford for something like this to happen again. He made a mental note to ask Amélie about the possibility of appointing a council of diplomats to help him with negotiations in the future.

But even that idea wasn't enough to keep Marius from feeling like he was missing a vital piece in making himself a better roi. With a start, Marius remembered he had the most recent letter from his mystery mademoiselle in his pocket. He pulled it out and read over it again, feeling a wave of calm wash over him. She seemed to understand him and the demands of his position, yet she still saw him as a human being. She cared about him as a person. He needed to find this woman. His sanity might depend on it.

"My dearest mademoiselle,
It is such a relief to write to someone who understands me so implicitly. Just having someone to tell all of this to has lessened my burden. I sincerely thank you for your genuine concern and for being a listening ear.
Most women I speak to only seem to care about my title or my money, but you seem to care about me, and it is a welcome change. My greatest challenge as of late has been searching for a reine. I want someone who can love more about me than just the crown on my head.
I sincerely hope I find her someday. Maybe I already have?"

Marius Roche to his mystery mademoiselle, day 25 of autumn

"Your Majesty,

I hope that one day you can overcome the constraints that society has set upon you. You are already a great roi. You deserve some happiness of your own.

I'm sure you will find a reine who meets your qualifications. It doesn't seem like much to ask for someone who treats you like a human being, but I suppose that's just the nature of high society. It's hard to truly find a place. A struggle I can relate to all too well.

I hope I'm not misreading your last letter, but are you considering me a candidate to be your wife?"

The mystery mademoiselle to Marius Roche, day 28 of autumn

Day 45 of Autumn

Sibella was tired. She'd spent the last two days doing everything she could to avoid her family, staying late at her shop and going straight to her bedroom when she arrived home. Her fingers ached from the amount of sewing she'd been doing, making the task of carrying her parasol around town a painful one, but it was still better than the horrible sunburn she was sure to get if she didn't carry one. She also had a nasty bruise on her neck where Raphael's hand had been. Luckily, the chill of winter had come early this year, which made it easier to wear a scarf in public until it faded.

She was miserable.

To make things worse, meeting Jack at the château had left her so flustered that she hadn't been back since.

She'd carried her letter around in her small drawstring purse since that afternoon, waiting for an opportune time to stop by the mailbox again. With everything falling apart in Sibella's personal life, she hadn't had a chance to try until now.

She slowly walked the path that led to the mailbox by the seemingly unused guest house, enjoying the autumn breeze that rustled through the hedge surrounding the château. She took a deep breath, savoring the crisp air, just as she was about to round the corner that would put her destination into view.

That was when she heard it. A sickening thud came from the road around the curve, followed by a man's voice crying out for help. Sibella gasped in shock and instinctively pressed herself against the hedge, closing her parasol to make herself harder to spot. She couldn't afford to get involved in whatever was happening on the other side of the hedge, lest she be kept for questioning. She couldn't risk Raphael finding out that she'd been anywhere near the château. Who knew what kind of punishment he'd inflict on her if he found out she hadn't been working?

She stood frozen for a few minutes, willing her heart rate to slow, until there was no more noise. Slowly, she stepped away from the hedge. She glanced around, but there was no one in sight. She shook her head to clear it. It must have been nothing. But as she rounded the corner, her heart dropped down to her stomach and she let out a frightened scream, her parasol falling to the ground.

A man, clearly nobility from his fine clothing, lay dead on the ground before her. There was an arrow protruding from his chest, and blood pooling around the corpse. Foam coated the man's lips, as if he'd been convulsing before his death. Sibella fought to keep bile from rising in her throat at the sight. She couldn't move, couldn't think, shock keeping her feet rooted in place, though she shook violently.

And she didn't notice that there was someone else on the path until he grabbed her by the shoulders and put his hand over her mouth.

"Sibella," he said, his voice familiar, "we have to run. Now, before they shoot us, too."

This somehow spurred her into action, and when he released her and she turned to see who stood behind her, she was both surprised and relieved to see Jack. He carried no weapon and based on the look of sheer terror in his eyes, Sibella knew he couldn't have committed the murder. He took her hand and pulled her away from the body in the road, forcing her out of her stupor. She nodded weakly to show she'd heard him, then together they ran back the way Sibella had come.

She didn't think about where she was going. She only knew that she had to get away from the crime scene before she was discovered with a dead body and considered a suspect. Or worse, if the killer came back for her. Sibella hadn't realized she'd been running to her shop until she found herself at the door, fumbling to get the shop key out of her purse.

Her hands trembled so much it took her longer than it should have to open the door, but as the lock clicked and she finally pushed the door open, she practically fell through into the room beyond. As Jack came in behind her, she slammed the door shut and locked it tight. She peered out the shop window to see if anyone in the street looked suspicious, but the few people who were out at this point in the afternoon seemed too caught up in their own business to be concerned with Sibella. Still, she drew the curtains as an extra precaution.

"I don't think we were followed," she said finally, breathing deeply.

"If we were, they must have been hidden very well. I didn't see anyone around us," Jack confirmed.

Sibella nodded. "Good."

Then she turned on her heel and walked up the spiral staircase that led to her workshop. She needed to get her mind off of what she'd just witnessed, and the familiarity of her workroom was much more preferable than the overly formal and proper downstairs shop.

"Where are you going?" Jack called after her.

"Upstairs," Sibella said plainly. As she ascended the metal staircase, she heard Jack following her.

"What were you doing at the château?" Jack asked.

"The same thing as before," Sibella said, stepping into her loft and taking a seat at her sewing machine.

"Which was—whoa!" Jack cut himself off, and Sibella

was glad he didn't press her further about why she'd been near the château. As he climbed the stairs, he looked around at her simple space. A grin slowly spread across his face. "Where are we?"

"My shop," she said sheepishly. "I know it isn't much, but—"

"I love it," Jack said, crossing the room to look out the window at the château in the distance. "I forgot you had your own business."

"I'm surprised you remembered me at all," she admitted. She was just realizing how strange it was to be recognized by someone outside of her home, regardless of the circumstances from which he remembered her. But as Sibella thought about it, she realized it was odd that she'd remembered him, too.

Jack turned his head and looked into her eyes. Sibella's heart leapt a bit as she met his gaze. His eyes were a beautiful deep blue—serious, yet youthful. The strangest sensation churned in her chest, like she could look at him forever without tiring of it. He was exceptionally handsome, with his fair skin and thick brown hair, so dark it almost looked black.

He said, "I couldn't forget you, 'just Sibella.'"

She took a breath and tried to fight the blush rising to her cheeks. There was something about Jack, something magnetic that she couldn't quite put her finger on. She'd only felt this kind of electric connection one other time in her life, with Roi Marius himself.

She suddenly remembered the letter in her purse

that she'd meant to drop off at the château. What was she supposed to do with her correspondence now, after what she'd witnessed? She supposed she could give her letters to Jack to deliver, but Sibella found the idea of presenting herself as a friend of the roi to be a bit presumptuous, especially to someone who could expose her as a tradesperson and not a member of the nobility. No, she would have to brave it later on and drop off the mail herself. Sibella sighed and turned away from Jack and his ocean-blue eyes.

"I suppose we should talk about what we saw, shouldn't we?" he said, seeming to sense her frustration.

"I don't know that I want to," Sibella replied, the gory image of the body flashing in her mind and making her shudder.

"I think we might have to," he said, leaving the window and putting a hand on her shoulder. This did nothing to help calm her nerves. In fact, it only made her very aware that there was a handsome man close enough to her that she could feel the warmth of his body behind her, a realization that only made her feel worse. She shrugged off his touch and sat at her worktable.

"I came to pick up documents from the guest mailbox, and as soon as I turned the corner, I saw you standing over the body of the comte de Cieux. What happened? What did you see?" Jack asked.

"Nothing! Just the body," she said, suddenly feeling defensive. She tensed as she continued, "I swear. I was about to turn the corner when I heard him get shot and fall."

"Relax," Jack said, laughing a bit. "I don't think you did it."

Sibella sighed, allowing herself to relax. "Who would do a thing like that?"

Jack was silent for a moment, and Sibella looked at him to see if he was planning on responding. He looked pensive, his brows furrowed in thought.

"What?" Sibella asked.

"Nothing, just—I don't know," Jack said.

She narrowed her eyes. There was something wrong about the way his mood had changed so suddenly. His jaw had clenched, and he'd lowered his gaze to the floor. Sibella had a feeling he knew more about the event than he was letting on.

"What is it? What are you thinking about?" Sibella pressed.

Jack took a deep breath. "Are you sure you want to know?"

Sibella considered this. Knowledge could put her in danger, but if she'd somehow been spotted by the killer and they wanted to eliminate any witnesses, she would be safer knowing what she was up against. And the sooner she could put this behind her, the better.

"I want to know what you know," Sibella said after a moment.

Jack leaned against her worktable and said, "Okay. Ten years ago, there was a string of homicides here in

Esmar. Several noble members of the court were murdered in cold blood, usually shot with poisoned arrows. The most notable of these deaths were those of the previous roi and reine."

His hands curled into fists at his sides when he mentioned Roi Luis and Reine Vivienne. Sibella remembered their deaths. It had been shocking, and to happen on Prince Charlie's birthday of all days. Esmar had grieved the loss of their monarchs for three years while Roi Marius settled into his new title. It had been a dark time for Esmar, and Sibella didn't blame Jack for still being upset about it.

He continued talking. "The killer was never found. The final event that people suspected was related to this particular killer was the disappearance of Juliette Lavigne, Madame des Étoiles."

Sibella's eyes widened. Juliette had been the duchesse des Étoiles before her mother had married Raphael. Sibella knew very little about the circumstances of her disappearance, only that it had happened. She'd never thought too hard about it, assuming that the woman had simply decided to leave. With a husband like Raphael, it would have been understandable.

But as she considered Juliette's disappearance now, she couldn't help the quickening of her pulse. She was vaguely aware of her palms becoming sweaty and her breathing turning frantic. If the killer was back after all these years, Sibella could think of only one person who would have had a personal reason to murder Madame Juliette.

"Sibella?" Jack said, dropping down to kneel at her level. "What's wrong?"

"I think I know who the killer is," Sibella whispered.

"What?"

"I know who the killer is," Sibella repeated, louder this time.

"Who is it?" Jack asked.

Sibella said, "My stepfather."

Jack shook his head in disbelief. "Your stepfather? Who is he?"

Sibella pursed her lips. She hadn't intended to tell Jack anything about her true identity. She'd kept herself fairly anonymous until this point, but now she had to tell him—if not everything about her parentage, at least the bit that included Raphael. She slowly unwrapped the scarf she wore around her neck, exposing the bruises on her throat. Jack's eyes widened with surprise when he saw the deep blue and purple marks that Raphael's hands had left behind.

"Sibella..." he said mournfully.

"Stop," Sibella commanded, forcing herself to keep looking at him. "I don't need your pity, I need you to listen to me. My stepfather is the duc des Étoiles."

"You mean—"

"He was Juliette's husband, yes."

Sibella could see the gears turning in Jack's head as he tried to put the pieces of the puzzle together. He blinked a few times, then said, "I have so many questions."

"Ask away," Sibella said.

"Okay." Jack rose from his crouch. "He did that to you? The duc?"

Sibella nodded solemnly.

"Why? Why did he do that? Why don't you leave his house?" Jack stepped closer, inspecting her injury. "Did he make this mark with his hands?"

"Yes. But I can't leave, it's complicated," Sibella said, shrugging away from his curious eyes. "But this isn't about me, it's about the duc."

"I think this is about you, Sibella," Jack said. "Because you don't exist. Not according to proper society, anyway."

"What, you don't believe me?" Sibella said, crossing her arms defensively. She wanted to point out that as far as the snobs of court were concerned, Jack didn't exist either, but she resisted the urge. The people who served royalty usually knew more secrets than anyone, and if Sibella was going to prove that Raphael had murdered Juliette, she was going to need his help.

"The duc doesn't have a daughter, biologically or otherwise," Jack stated plainly.

"I assure you, he does," Sibella huffed. "He doesn't like to acknowledge me as his own, because that would raise questions about my parentage that he doesn't want to answer. My mother is Duchesse Delphine."

"Who is your father?" Jack asked.

Instead of answering, Sibella simply said, "He's dead."

"I'm so sorry," Jack said solemnly.

Sibella shrugged. "He deserved it. I don't think anyone misses him."

Jack fell silent as he considered that.

"Anyway, the duc doesn't like me. He never has. I've never had a social season, and I've never been invited to any events held by the nobility. In public, he pretends like I don't exist, and behind closed doors I'm his servant." Sibella gestured around the room. "This is technically his shop. Every penny I make goes straight to him."

"That's awful," Jack said.

"I'd like for him to pay for what he's done to me and to the roi and reine, but Raphael is slick. He's probably covered most of his tracks. And I don't want to go to the royal guard with a case unless I can bring them irrefutable evidence. Otherwise, they'll just brush me off," Sibella explained. "Unless..."

"Unless?"

"You work for Roi Marius, right?" Sibella said, looking into Jack's eyes.

"Yes," he said, more hesitant than Sibella expected him to be.

"Why don't you bring our case to him so the royal guard can investigate?" she asked.

Jack considered her question but shook his head. "I almost never see the Roi. He is a busy man. And while I'm sure he would appreciate our investigation, I don't think speaking with him would be more successful than going to the guards themselves."

Sibella sighed in disappointment. "Then it does come down to just you and me, doesn't it?"

"You, me, and the duc," Jack replied. "There's no denying his connection to Madame Juliette, and based on the look of your neck, it's safe to say he has violent tendencies."

"Does that mean you'll help me expose him?" Sibella asked, a dangerous flicker of hope flaring in her chest. If she and Jack were successful, this would change everything.

Jack nodded. "Let's catch a killer."

"My dearest mademoiselle,

It seems you understood the intention in my last letter perfectly. I do see you as a potential candidate to be my reine. I must warn you before we solidify our courtship, however. As much as my work seems to be all pomp and circumstance, there is a legitimate danger in being in the public eye as much as I am. I would be lying if I told you that the same threat didn't extend to my future reine.

I've never considered myself a fighter. I prefer to solve problems peacefully if I can. I believe it is better, in any event, to see an issue from all angles before taking action. That can help with some threats, but I will admit it doesn't fix everything. I hope you can understand this.

My decision in taking a wife is not to be taken lightly, and I while I would be disappointed if you lost interest in courting me after considering the potential dangers, I wouldn't be offended."

Marius Roche to his mystery mademoiselle, day 30 of autumn

Day 46 of Autumn

Two more dead.

Marius gripped the letter from the sole heir of the recently deceased baron and baronesse de Lunaire in his hand so tightly that the paper crumpled under his hand. No one had seen anyone suspicious in the area either before or after the murders, but this killing had all the markings of the same killer. The couple had both been found in their garden, poisoned arrows protruding from their chests.

If Sibella was right and her stepfather was to blame for the deaths, then Raphael had to be stopped.

"Where is Général Constantin?" Marius asked, looking up at Amélie, who had delivered the bad news to him while he'd been busy trying to catch up on work. If he thought he'd been drowning before Sibella came along, now he was truly swamped. He knew he should stop seeing her and leave the crime solving to his guards, but when he thought about abandoning the only chance he'd ever had at forming a legitimate friendship with someone outside of the château, he found he couldn't do it. His mystery mademoiselle had yet to appear in person, and until she did, Sibella was all he had.

He had also decided against recommending her sewing services to Amélie, even though he knew his money might be able to help her buy her freedom. Sibella had access to the duc's estate. Having her there to keep an eye on him and gather evidence was imperative to their investigation. He would have to keep her in Raphael's house for now, but if they were successful in exposing him as the killer, "Jack" would see to it that Sibella was given a handsome reward from the roi. A reward she would not meet him in person to receive.

"I informed him of the incident at the Lunaire estate just before I came to see you," Amélie said. "He seemed concerned about it. He's probably on his way here as we speak."

"Good," Marius said, turning his attention back to the documents in front of him. It was difficult to focus on the trivial reports and small requests that landed on his desk when there were bigger issues at hand, but Marius had to keep working. He couldn't stop, or all the worries and feelings he'd been able to suppress since he'd become roi would explode out of him.

"Your Majesty," Amélie said, still standing in front of his desk, her mouth drawn in a hard line that meant she wasn't done with the bad news.

"What is it, Amélie?" Marius nearly groaned.

"No need to get impatient with me," Amélie said. "You'll have plenty of time to work over the next few days. The ball you were set to attend has been canceled, as has the opera."

"What?"

"There is a killer out there, Your Majesty. People are afraid."

Before Marius could even begin to think about the implications of her news, there was a loud knock at the door. Without waiting for an invitation, Général Constantin, the head of Marius's guard, poked his head in.

"I came as soon as I heard, Your Majesty," he said, stepping fully inside and closing the door behind him.

Constantin was remarkably young to be the captain of the royal guard, only a few years older than Marius himself. His family had descended from a long line of military leaders, and Constantin was no exception. He'd started his training earlier than other men were allowed due to his well-connected parents, and after rising through the ranks after just a decade of service, he'd decided to accept the position as Captain of the Royal Guard upon the retirement of Général Felix, the previous incumbent.

"We keep meeting like this, Constantin," Marius

remarked. "It seems I only see you when one of my nobles is found dead."

"I know, Your Majesty," he replied. "Rest assured, my men and I are doing everything we can to unmask this assassin, but it's proven to be very difficult."

Marius said nothing, only gesturing for Constantin to continue. He needed to hear the reasons behind the guard's failure to solve the case.

"There is no discernible pattern among the victims besides their social status, and as such no real way to determine who might be attacked next," Constantin explained. He stood straight with an air of professionalism, but Marius could tell from the slight waver in his voice that this mystery had rattled him. "We have sent out an advisory to anyone at risk discouraging them from employing any temporary staff at their estates. While we suspect the killer has a substantial amount of money, it is quite possible that he or she is tracking and monitoring each victim's routines, posing as a groundskeeper or musician. We are doing all we can to keep your people safe."

Constantin continued, "As for the evidence we've gathered, there are no marks on the weapons that would point to anyone specific. The arrows are well made, clearly purchased by someone with money for personal commissions, but they aren't overly intricate like one would find in the personal armory of someone among the nobility."

"No criminal with any intelligence would commission an arrow or a blade that had their personal mark-ings on it," Marius said. "That's hardly an indication at all."

"Exactly," Constantin agreed. "That's why we've been struggling. Now, when we compared them with the ones used ten years ago, we found they were made by the same fletcher."

"What about the poison?" Marius asked. "The arrows were all poisoned, were they not?"

Constantin nodded. "That is a more interesting discovery."

Marius raised his eyebrows. "Did the poison change with this round of killings?"

The arrows that had killed his parents had been laced with deadly snake venom, and it had worked more effectively than any cyanide or arsenic. Cold grief wormed its way through Marius's veins as he remem-bered the way his parents' eyes had glazed over in front of him, how they'd gone limp and left him just when he'd needed them most. He shook off the feeling. He couldn't allow himself to think about his parents for too long or he might slip back into the depression he'd faced in the first few years after their deaths.

"Yes, Your Majesty. The arrows we've been able to recover from the recent deaths have had traces of girselia on them," Constantin said.

"What?" Marius's eyes widened, unable to hide his shock. Girselia was the most dangerous plant in the realm. Ingesting its deadly bloom could kill a man within minutes on its own, even without the help of an arrow. According to all known historical accounts, it had been the use of girselia that had secured a victory for the Tatrians when they'd fought a war with the much larger Askanese army several centuries ago.

In fact, girselia was among the rare plants that only grew in Tatria.

"You don't think the Tatrians have something to do with this, do you?" Marius asked.

Constantin shrugged. "It's difficult to tell. But given how their visit went, it wouldn't surprise me."

Marius shook his head. That would be an invitation for war, and while Tsarista Saffron had certainly been angry when she'd left, Marius doubted Tsar Stephan was conniving enough to attack Esmar so brazenly. It was more likely that the killer had acquired the plant somehow and was using it to throw Constantin off their trail. But who would do such a thing?

Marius thought of Raphael.

"Constantin," he said. "I would like you to look into a member of the court for me."

"Of course, Your Majesty. What do you need?"

"Keep an eye on the duc des Étoiles. I've heard some less than stellar reports of his character, and I want to make sure we can cross him off our list of suspects."

Constantin bowed his head. "I'll send two of my best men to trail him, Your Majesty. In the meantime, our biggest priority is keeping you safe."

Amélie, who had been listening intently while

Constantin gave his report, piped up. "That was actually going to be my next order of business."

She turned to Marius as she continued, "I believe it would be best for you to stop all public appearances until this threat has been removed. It's getting dangerous out there."

Marius wasn't sure what to think. On one hand, appearing in public would send a message to his people that Esmar was strong, and that he wasn't afraid of an assassin. It could make him appear as a powerful ruler. But on the other hand, the free time Marius would gain from not attending social events would allow him to spend more of his days investigating the case with Sibella.

After a moment of thought, he nodded. "Send my regrets to those whose invitations I've already accepted."

Marius hoped his disguise as Jack would be enough to keep the killer off his trail. It seemed he now had work to do outside the château.

"Your Majesty,
I am well aware of the dangers that exist in being as powerful
as you are, but I am not afraid. I would be honored beyond
belief to accept your offer of courtship! I am humbled at the
feeling that I know you so well when we have barely even met,
and I am relieved that you feel the same way.
I hope that you can find happiness and that I can be the
partner you're looking for."

The mystery mademoiselle to Marius Roche, day 32 of
autumn

Day 53 of Autumn

Jack's voice filled Sibella's mind as she crept out of her bedroom. It was late, and all she could do was pray Raphael and Leo were already asleep as she tiptoed down the stairs that led to Simon's bedroom.

The reason for her sneaking had come a few days ago when she and Jack were throwing around ideas about how to obtain evidence against Raphael. She suggested visiting La Dame Masquée, a tavern across town that Sibella had heard the name of frequently in her household. Jack had agreed but insisted that she also search the estate for anything that might prove his guilt.

Sibella's insides twisted at the thought of snooping in Raphael's personal belongings. If he knew she was sneaking around late at night, looking through his things, who knew what he might do?

She'd ultimately agreed to look around a bit, but outright refused to set foot in Raphael's study. She knew he would punish her worse than she'd ever been before if she got caught in there. All she could do was hope there was enough evidence elsewhere.

The first step in her plan to search the estate was to enlist some help. Without Jack here to investigate alongside her, she would need someone to point her in the right direction.

She had thought about approaching a servant for help but had ultimately decided against it. The servants worked for Raphael, not her, and she had never been close enough to any of them to earn their loyalty. It wouldn't take much prodding from Raphael for any of them to tell him everything. Which meant she would need to ask someone else. And the only other person worth asking was Simon.

She knocked on his door as softly as she could. There was, predictably, no response. He was likely long asleep. Sibella pushed the door open just a bit and whispered, "Simon?"

Silence.

She slipped inside the bedroom and clicked the door shut behind her. The room was so dark she could barely see to put one foot in front of the other, but she pushed forward anyway, her hands outstretched, trying to find his bed. Finally, she felt the plush silk of his bedding brush against her fingers, and she grabbed on to the bed as if it would disappear at any second.

"Simon," she whispered again. No response. Sibella sighed. She hadn't realized he was such a deep sleeper. She reached out until she hit his sleeping body, then shook him violently.

He awoke with a start.

"Wha... what... what the hell?" he mumbled, then fumbled around for a moment, lighting the candle on his bedside table. He squinted at the light as it cut through the darkness.

"Sibella?" he asked, his gaze settling on her. "What are you doing?"

"I need your help," Sibella said, plastering a look on her face that she hoped conveyed her desperation.

"This late? What could you possibly need my help with?"

Sibella didn't want to tell Simon anything if she could help it. The less he knew, the less he could potentially tell Raphael. She was usually one to tell half-truths rather than outright lie, but she had no better option. She said, "Raphael took my good sewing supplies as punishment for speaking out of turn. While he's asleep, I'm going to see if I can find them. I need your help."

"Why me?" Simon protested.

"You know your way around the estate much better than I do. Where would he hide something he didn't want me to find?" Sibella asked.

Simon rubbed his drooping eyes as he thought, then he said, "There is always the cellar."

"The cellar?" she asked. "I thought there was just wine down there."

"There is wine, yes. But in the furthest corner there should be a small closet. That's where he stored everything he didn't want around anymore after my maman..." Simon couldn't finish his sentence, but Sibella understood.

"You think he would hide something there?" she asked.

Simon shrugged. "There's a good chance."

"A chance is all I need," Sibella said.

"I don't have to come with you, do I?" Simon asked with a yawn.

"No. I've got it from here. Thank you, Simon."

Simon didn't reply. He only handed her his candle and slumped back into his blankets.

Sibella left his room as silently as she could. She wound through the hallways of the house, pausing anytime she heard a noise. She was grateful for Simon's candle as she descended the stairs to the cellar. As the faint light illuminated the space, the only thing in sight seemed to be wine.

Remembering Simon's directions, she looked to the back of the cellar. As she approached the far wall, she noticed the outline of a door to the right. She took a deep breath, then tried the handle. Unlocked. That was unusually good luck, but perhaps whatever he had stashed away in the closet wasn't worth securing.

She opened the door, and a foul, musty scent overwhelmed her. She coughed as she stepped into the small room, sending dust flying from a trunk next to her. As she regained her bearings, Sibella moved her candle around, trying to figure out what she was looking at.

Most of the items had clearly been untouched for years, and a lot of it didn't appear to be taking extended storage in the dank cellar well. A rack of rotting dresses sat next to a stack of books with yellowing pages. Trunk after trunk was piled up along the walls. As she pulled one down to check its contents, the lock split open, causing a cascade of jewelry to fall to the floor with a clatter. She quickly scooped the jewels back into the trunk and placed it where she'd found it, hoping she hadn't made too much noise.

Sibella focused, looking for something without a layer of grime over it. Something that would indicate that Raphael had visited this closet recently.

And she found it. Behind a stack of hat boxes was a sheet that looked fresher than anything else hidden away. She lifted it lightly, not sure what she would find underneath. She took a deep breath, then pulled the sheet away.

Underneath was a bow, perfectly intact. Sibella could have sworn her heart stopped beating for a moment. It was a beautiful weapon. Expertly crafted.

Reflexively, Sibella tossed the sheet back over the

bow in a heap. Mind reeling, she held on to the wall for support. There hadn't seemed to be any arrows with the bow, nothing that might be compared to what Raphael left behind at the crime scenes.

She lifted the sheet again to get a second look at it. If she was going to kill someone, this was not the weapon she would use. It was decorative, with swirling designs etched into the wood. Deadly, no doubt, but too distinctive to be good for stealth. This was most likely not the bow he'd used to kill anyone. So why hide it here?

Sibella sighed. This was not enough to get Raphael arrested. It could be used as evidence, sure, but it was well-known that Raphael liked to hunt. It could hardly be considered unusual for a man with that hobby to have a few weapons lying around his home, even if it was kept out of his armory. Still, it was progress.

She searched a little bit more after fixing the sheet over the bow, but there was nothing else noteworthy stashed amongst Madame Juliette's belongings.

Sibella couldn't wait to tell Jack what she'd found. Hopefully they could find a solid motive, then it would be easier to find proof that it had been Raphael all along. She was eager to start compiling evidence to make a case to the royal guard.

Sibella would enjoy sitting back and laughing as Raphael was brought down once and for all.

"My dearest mademoiselle,
I will no doubt find my happiness when I have the perfect
reine to rule beside me.
I know it's been less than a season, but I feel like we
understand each other better than most. I would like to meet
you in person. I think it's time you revealed your identity to
me. I promise, if you tell me who you are, I will do everything
in my power to be worthy of your affection."

Marius Roche to his mystery mademoiselle, day 35 of autumn

12

Day 58 of Autumn

*M*arius let himself into Sibella's shop. She'd given him a key the last time they'd met to plan their investigation, and he was honored that she'd trusted him with it. They'd had a few meetings in the thirteen days since they'd found the comte's body, and each time, Marius was glad to be spending time away from the chaos of the château and with someone who seemingly cared about him. He'd left instructions for Amélie every time he'd snuck out, telling her to leave him alone for the evening. So far it seemed to be working, and no one had caught on that he'd been disappearing.

When the door closed behind him, he heard Sibella's voice from the loft. "Jack? Is that you?"

"It's me," Marius said. "Are you ready to go?"

It felt like a stab to the heart every time she called him Jack. Marius wanted to tell her the truth, to tell her who he really was, but he wasn't sure how revealing himself as the roi would change her attitude toward him. She'd been so honest with him, so down to earth, that he couldn't bear to reveal his true identity now. What if she were offended by his lie? He could lose her friendship entirely, or she could start treating him too formally to try and gain his good favor. He couldn't risk it, not now that it might finally be possible to catch the person who had murdered his parents.

Despite Constantin's assurance that his men were watching the duc, they hadn't seen anything suspicious yet. It was seemingly up to Marius and Sibella to uncover the truth. And she was doing a pretty good job of it on her own. Finding the bow in Raphael's cellar was a promising start.

Sibella descended the staircase. She wore a gray skirt with layers of fabric that looked like the petals of a flower and a matching bodice that fell off her shoulders and accentuated her cleavage. Despite the plain color of the outfit, Marius couldn't help but stare. He'd noticed her beauty before—he'd have to be blind to miss it. But she'd always worn modest clothing, and now that she was wearing something more revealing, Marius couldn't deny that he was attracted to her. The masked face of his mystery mademoiselle materialized in his mind, and guilt nagged at his insides. She had begun writing to him once more, and he didn't want to betray the woman who seemed to understand him so implicitly. He had an obligâtion to her first, no matter how beautiful Sibella was.

The bruise on Sibella's neck had healed well, thankfully. It was probably the main reason for her style change. Marius was still uncomfortable leaving her in that house with a man who was, at the very least, an abuser. But there was nothing he could do without compromising himself. He didn't want to have the duc arrested and leave Sibella without the monetary support he provided, and to give her money himself would expose Marius as a liar.

Sibella plucked her long black cloak off a hook by the door and slung it over her shoulders, then smiled and said, "I'm ready now."

"Let's go, then. Put your hood up and stay close," Marius instructed.

Sibella did as she was told and they left the shop together, locking the door behind them. The streets of Esmar were dark and a cool breeze flowed through the city, sending chills through Marius's body. He hadn't brought a coat of his own, as there hadn't been one in Charlie's drawer of peasant clothing. He hoped it would be warm enough where they were going that he wouldn't catch a cold.

Marius had never visited the poor side of Luméte before, partly because his duties as roi kept him close to the château, but mostly because he wasn't the kind of man who spent time in brothels or taverns. He only knew where the most popular tavern was because of the reports on Charlie's location he received from the guards keeping track of the prince.

As Marius and Sibella navigated the streets, the cobblestones became more uneven under their feet and the buildings seemed to age under layers of dirt and grime. Marius had always tried to do his best for his people, even the poorest of them, and he had to remind himself as he looked around that Esmar wasn't the worst place a poor person could live. Askaña, in particular, was notorious for their horrible standard of living for anyone below the upper crust. So while this side of the city wasn't as glamorous as the shining château and its surroundings, it was still a decent place to call home.

For the moment, anyway. With the trade negotiations with Tatria falling apart, who knew what kind of struggles his poorer citizens could be facing soon? Marius shook himself out of his thoughts. He would have plenty of time to make plans to keep his subjects well cared for once he got home.

"You're awfully quiet," Sibella remarked beside him, her breath hanging in the frigid air as she spoke.

"Sorry," he said. "I just… have a lot on my mind right now."

"Do you need to talk about it?" Sibella asked. "I think I'm a pretty good listener."

Marius wanted nothing more than to tell Sibella his struggles. He desperately needed a confidante. Writing to his mystery mademoiselle had brought him some comfort, but something in Sibella's bright blue eyes practically begged him to tell his secrets. But he couldn't tell her, not unless he wanted their friendship to be ruined. So he shook his head "no", and Sibella shrugged.

"Okay," she said. Marius could feel her eyes searching his face, but he forced himself to look away. He knew if he didn't, he might crack.

"The tavern shouldn't be too much further," Marius said, changing the subject.

"Good," Sibella said, "because you look like you're going to freeze to death."

Marius wrapped his arms around himself, trying to stop the shivers that had been creeping through his body. "I'm fine."

He made the mistake of looking over at her. He'd meant to reassure her that he was plenty warm, even though he wasn't. His fingers were as cold as ice, and the thin cotton fabric covering him did nothing to protect him from the wind. But when he looked at his companion, her look of concern made his heart leap in his chest and he forgot all his words. Her golden hair had turned almost silver in the starlight, and her eyes sparkled, striking as ever. He found himself glancing at her lips, but turned his gaze back to the road ahead before he could analyze them further. He couldn't look at Sibella that way, not when he was so close to finally meeting his mystery mademoiselle. He wondered what would happen when he did see her in person again. Would he still like her as much as he had the first time?

They traversed the final few blocks in silence. As they came closer to the tavern, Marius heard the muffled sound of music coming from within. The windows poured candlelight onto the streets, bathing the pair in a warm glow. She grabbed on to his arm as they neared the entrance and he instinctively pulled her close.

"Keep your head low. We're just going to observe, ask our questions, and get out," Marius instructed, pushing open the door to the tavern.

La Dame Masquée was the most popular tavern in Luméte. Inside was a bustling scene, with rich and poor alike downing drinks at the bar, playing cards at the tables, or listening to the musician who plucked away at guitar strings in the corner. It was crowded inside, and Marius was glad that no one had immediately recognized him in the hubbub. He kept his head down, trying not to attract any attention. The last thing he needed was to be greeted by name in front of Sibella. Unfortunately, that also meant it would undoubtedly be more difficult to spot the duc in the crowd.

He grabbed Sibella's hand tightly as they wove between several patrons and their escorts on the way to the bar. They'd discussed this plan the last time they'd met at Sibella's shop and had ultimately agreed to come to La Dame Masquée to search for more evidence. They would talk to the bartenders—and the owner, if they were lucky—to see if Raphael had done anything suspicious while in their establishment. If anyone knew a nobleman's secrets, it would be the person who served him.

They finally reached the bar and Sibella raised her hand to flag down one of the bartenders, who slammed down a stein in front of an older gentleman before acknowledging her. The bartender was a middle-aged woman who was obviously trying to look much younger. She wore a low-cut bodice and bright red lipstick that drew the eye to her face.

"How can I help you, darling?" she asked.

"I need information," Sibella replied. The woman eyed her suspiciously, but leaned closer to listen to Sibella's request. Sibella took a deep breath before she continued and said, "What do you know about the duc des Étoiles?"

A look of recognition crossed the woman's face, but Marius couldn't quite place the intent behind her eyes. This woman certainly knew of the duc, but that wasn't necessarily surprising. The real question was, did she have any information about him that would be useful?

"I'm afraid I won't be of much help," the bartender said. Sibella reached into her purse and held out a few coins to the woman. They sparkled silver, and the bartender's eyes widened. Marius himself couldn't help but be a bit impressed. Bribery hadn't been a part of the plan, but it seemed Sibella wasn't interested in wasting any time.

"Tell me what you know about the duc," Sibella repeated.

The woman took the coins and quickly pocketed them. "He's here often. Sometimes he'll rent a room upstairs for the night, but usually he plays cards with his friends. I've only seen him do anything truly interesting once. He got into a fight a while ago. I almost had to ban him and the other man from my establishment."

"Who did he fight?" Marius asked without thinking.

The bartender looked at him. She cocked her head to the side as she eyed him—did she recognize him? Marius hoped she wasn't about to reveal his identity then and there. Thankfully, she didn't. Instead, she said, "He fought the comte de Cieux. It was after one of their card games."

Marius's blood ran cold. He flashed back to the body that he and Sibella had stumbled upon outside the château. The comte.

"Do you remember what they were fighting about?" Sibella asked.

The woman shook her head. "I was behind this bar the whole time. I couldn't hear anything specific. They were too far away."

Marius was slightly disappointed at the lack of details. The next person he and Sibella would need to investigate would be whoever else had been at the card table that night. If they could establish a solid motive for the murder, it might help their case against the duc.

"Who else was at the table that night?" Marius asked.

The woman shrugged. "How should I know? They all scattered when the fight broke out."

Another dead end. Of course.

"Do you know anything else about the duc?" Sibella said.

"Not really," the bartender replied. "He isn't the kind to get drunk and overshare."

Of course he wasn't. That would make everything too easy.

"Thank you for your time," Marius said. The bartender smiled, then turned her attention to the other patrons crowding the bar.

"What now?" Sibella asked, looking at Marius.

He glanced around the tavern, unsure. He had no real way of knowing who they needed to approach next. Since the bartender didn't know anything else, they were on their own. As he looked, however, hoping for anything that could help their case, a certain patron stuck out from the crowd. He was standing near one of the card tables, watching a game. He was tall and lean, with long brown hair, and he looked suspiciously like… Charlie. Marius's eyes widened at the sight of his brother on the other side of the room.

Sibella put a hand on his shoulder. "Jack? Are you alright?"

"I'm fine," he said, pleading with his eyes for her to not ask any questions. "Please excuse me for a moment. I'll be right back. Just wait here."

"Okay," Sibella replied, unsure.

Marius crossed the tavern, pushing past people as he went. His eyes scanned the crowds and found the guard he'd assigned to trail Charlie standing in the corner. He was in disguise, unremarkable to the untrained eye. Marius hoped the guard would keep his mouth shut about seeing Marius at the tavern. While having a guard keeping an eye on Charlie was a relief, that wouldn't stop an assassin with a poisonous arrow. He needed to somehow convince his brother to stay out of trouble, at least until he and Sibella completed their investigation. When Charlie finally spotted him, the shock on his face was obvious. His brows rose and his mouth fell open. He sputtered, "Marius?"

"Charlie!" Marius said as he reached his brother's side. "I'm glad to see you."

"What are you doing here?" Charlie asked. "Are you following me?"

"Of course not. I'm here for my own reasons."

"Which are?"

Marius hesitated, unsure how much to tell Charlie. He didn't seem to be drunk yet, despite the flask of whiskey in his hand, and he might be of some help. But Marius wasn't about to publicly discuss his plan to catch the duc, either.

"Fine, don't tell me." Charlie rolled his eyes.

"I'll tell you all about it, but we need to get out of this tavern first," Marius said.

"Why? What are you trying to hide?" Charlie looked around the tavern. He spotted Sibella pretty quickly, as she had been watching their conversation from afar. A wicked grin crept across his face. "Stars above!"

"What?" Marius said.

"You've got a mistress! Perfect Marius isn't so perfect after all," Charlie said, chuckling smugly and taking a swig of his drink.

"This isn't what it looks like," Marius said, trying to defend himself before Charlie ruined everything with Sibella. "She isn't my mistress, she's just—"

"Your friend, right? Let me guess, your friendship includes a lot of other *benefits*."

"Charlie!" Marius exclaimed, his cheeks turning hot from embarrassment.

Charlie shrugged. "Don't try to deny it, brother. I can see you blushing."

"I'm not—I mean—ugh!" Marius threw his hands up in exasperation. "She's just helping me with something, okay?"

"Why don't I introduce myself, then? We can hear the truth from her." Charlie moved to push past him.

In a panic, Marius grabbed his brother's arm. "No! Don't introduce yourself! She can't know who you are, or she'll figure out who I am."

Charlie laughed. "She doesn't know who you are? How?"

Marius didn't answer. He didn't want to get into the story about Sibella's identity any more than he wanted to explain why he was in the tavern. Instead, he said, "She thinks I'm a commoner."

"You? A commoner?"

"It's a long story," Marius said.

"I'm going to need to hear it. You know that, right?" Charlie laughed.

"I know. Just not now, or here," Marius said firmly.

"So what do you want me to say to her?" Charlie asked.

"Nothing. You're not talking to her. You're going to go home right now."

"Well, I have to say something. She's coming up behind you now," Charlie said, pointing beyond Marius where, sure enough, Sibella was pushing her way toward them.

Marius whipped back around to face his brother and growled. "Just go along with what I say."

"Jack?" Sibella asked, "Who is your friend?"

Marius turned to face her. He must have been gone long enough to raise her alarm. Otherwise, why would she have interfered? If she was concerned, though, she hid it well. She came across as being mildly curious.

"Sibella, this is…" Marius hesitated, but thankfully, Sibella didn't seem to notice. "My brother. Pierre." Charlie glared at Marius. He must not have liked that name.

"Oh! I didn't know you had a brother," Sibella said, looking at Charlie. "You look familiar. Have I seen you somewhere before?"

Charlie shook his head vigorously. "No. I'm sure you haven't. How do you know, um… my brother?"

"I told you I would explain it later, *Pierre*," Marius said pointedly. "I need to see Sibella home safely."

Charlie interjected. "But—"

"If you're home when I get back, I'll explain everything."

"Wait," Sibella said, then looked at Charlie with mischief in her eyes. "Do you come here often? To the tavern, I mean?"

"I do," Charlie admitted. "Why?"

"Jack," Sibella said, grabbing his hand for emphasis. "Maybe we should tell him what we're doing here. He could help us."

Marius didn't even have time to consider her point before she began dragging the two of them out the door. The warmth from the tavern that had kept Marius from freezing disappeared, and the cold wind that hit them upon entering the street made him start to shiver. Sibella looked around, then led them into a quiet alley.

"We'll need to keep our voices down, Sibella," Marius reminded her.

"I know," she said. "Pierre, can we count on you?"

Charlie nodded, and Sibella recounted their story up until then. Most of it, anyway. She left out some choice bits, including the discovery of the comte de Cieux's body. She somehow connected the dots of their meeting in a way that was so convincing that Marius himself was tempted to believe her. When she'd finished talking, Charlie shook his head. From shock or disbelief, Marius couldn't tell. Either way, by that point, Marius was so cold he thought his fingers and toes might start falling off.

"So what do you need me for, exactly?" Charlie asked.

"I need you to be our eyes and ears inside the tavern," Sibella explained. "If you see anything or hear anything that supports our theory, please tell Jack as soon as possible."

"I'm going to be honest," Charlie said, "I'm usually not of sound mind when I leave the tavern. I don't know how reliable my information would be."

Sibella looked at Marius for help. He just shrugged. He'd known that Charlie wouldn't have been much help. It was interesting, however, to see Sibella and Charlie in conversation. His two worlds were colliding, and he didn't know what to make of it.

"I'll keep an eye out for him. I want you to succeed, but I can't make any promises," Charlie continued.

"That's fine. Any help is appreciated," Sibella said. "Thank you, Pierre."

She then turned toward Marius. "You're shivering! Let's get back to my shop before you turn into an ice cube." Marius could barely nod his assent, his teeth chattering.

"I'm gonna go back to the tavern. See you around, *Jack*," Charlie said, snickering as he made his way back inside. Marius was too distracted by the cold to instruct Charlie to come home, and then he was gone.

"Here," Sibella said, taking off her cloak to wrap it around Marius.

"No," he protested, holding out his hand to reject her

gesture. He couldn't take her cloak, or she would be just as cold as he was. Besides, what kind of a gentleman would that make him?

Sibella pursed her lips. "I know it's a woman's cloak, but it's not that feminine, and you look like you're going to freeze to death at any moment."

"It's not that it's a woman's cloak, Sibella." Marius laughed.

"Then take it!"

"No."

Sibella didn't say anything else. Instead, she moved toward him so quickly that Marius didn't have time to react, and slung the cloak around both of their shoulders. It was ill-fitted, and it didn't close in the front like it should have, but between Sibella's body heat on one side and the wool across his back, he felt a thousand times better than he did before. The cloak smelled like vanilla, a warm scent that reminded him of music and laughter. Together they began the trek back to Sibella's shop.

"Sibella—"

"Shhh," she said. "I don't want to hear any more of your protests."

"I was going to say thank you."

"Oh," Sibella said quietly, giving him a small smile. "Well, you're welcome."

It was a lovely thing to see Sibella smile, and Marius found himself unable to look away from her. Her eyes contained more sadness and heartache than anyone else he'd met in his life. She was tragic and beautiful at the same time, but seeing her happy, however fleeting, had unlocked some secret part of Marius's soul. He wanted her to smile more. What's more, he had a desire to be the one who made her happy, who could help her forget her pain for however brief a moment. He suddenly became aware of how close Sibella was standing next to him as they walked under the cloak. He could feel her breaths, strong and steady, and the touch of her skin where their arms met.

"You're sure you want to go back to the shop? Not the duc's estate?" Marius asked.

"I'm sure," Sibella said. "I'll just tell him I was working late tonight if he asks. I'd rather do that than risk his wrath by going home at this ungodly hour."

"Do you even have a place to sleep at the shop?"

Sibella shrugged. "I'll make it work. I always do."

When they finally reached the shop, she pulled her keys from her purse, opening the door. Warmth and light from the fireplace inside flooded through the doorway, but Marius hardly felt different. He tried to tell himself it was just the cloak keeping him warm, but he knew the truth. It was Sibella. Her presence had left him with an undeniable heat.

"When will I see you again?" he asked, leaning close to her.

She took a sharp breath, then said, "The day after tomorrow? Right after the shop closes?"

Marius nodded. "I'll be here." With that, he shrugged off the cloak and turned to go.

"Wait," Sibella said. He couldn't help but look back at the sound of her voice.

"Take the cloak," she said, holding it out to him. "You need it tonight. Just bring it back when you come again."

Marius smiled and accepted her gift. Time seemed to slow as his hand brushed hers. He said, "Thank you. Again."

"Good night," Sibella said, stepping into her shop and gently closing the door.

The walk back to the château felt shorter than usual. He tried thinking about important matters as he walked —Charlie, the Tatrians, the investigation, his mystery mademoiselle—but his mind always found its way back to Sibella. The cloak smelled like her, a warm vanilla scent that wouldn't let him think of anything else. There were a million things he should have been worrying about, things he should be planning, but he couldn't help it. In his heart, there was only Sibella.

"Your Majesty,
I apologize sincerely for my absence these last several days.
Please don't take it as any kind of disinterest on my part.
I would like to reveal my identity to you, but I'd prefer to do so
in person. Seeing as we found each other in person first, this
seems like a natural way to find each other again. Where and
when should we plan to meet?"

The mystery mademoiselle to Marius Roche, day 50 of
autumn

13

Day 60 of Autumn

It had been a crisp, chilly morning when Sibella finally returned to her small room at the duc's estate. She'd had a fitful night of sleep in her shop after her outing with Jack, lying on the hard floor in front of her fireplace with only a bolt of fabric for a pillow. When she woke up the next morning, every muscle in her body was sore, and she had flecks of ash from the fire in her hair. She'd crept into the house carefully that evening, only to find out that Raphael hadn't even noticed her absence, much less thought to question her about it. Even her mother hadn't said anything about her being gone, which hurt more than Sibella would have thought it would. She hated to think her mother might care less about her after the last fight they'd had.

Even now that she'd had a good night's rest in her own bed, she wasn't looking forward to another day of sewing. While she loved the craft, knowing all of the money she earned was going to Raphael was enough to kill her passion. The only thing she had to look forward to was her meeting with Jack. Well, Jack and, of all people, Roi Marius. They'd finally agreed on a time and place to meet, and while Sibella was nervous to reveal herself to him as a tradeswoman rather than a noblewoman, she couldn't help but hope that he would at least listen to her concerns about the duc, perhaps look into his crimes. Sibella smiled at the thought of Roi Marius having Raphael arrested. Jack had claimed the roi wouldn't be of much help, but she had to try. Jack would be so happy if she could report back that Roi Marius would be aiding their investigation.

Sibella pulled her hair back with a blue satin ribbon, tying it in as nice of a bow as she could manage without help, then opened her bedroom door. She was shocked to see Leo on the other side, looking as annoying and impatient as ever.

"I knew I heard you up and about," he said smugly.

"I'm on my way to work. As I always am this time of day," Sibella said, trying to shove past him. Leo blocked the narrow hallway, his arms outstretched to keep Sibella from going anywhere.

"That's funny," Leo said. "I didn't see you yesterday."

Sibella stopped short, feeling like all of the air had been sucked from her lungs. So, someone had noticed her absence after all. Sibella forced her tone to be even when she replied. "You must have just missed me. I went to the shop earlier than usual."

"Earlier?" Leo said, a smile spreading across his face that made Sibella's skin crawl. "That's interesting, since you were out so late the night before."

Sibella was glued to the floor, too shocked to move. She'd been seen at the tavern. This was worse than she ever could have imagined—especially if it was the duc who had spotted her. He would surely demand answers.

"What are you talking about?" Sibella said, deciding her only hope was to play dumb.

"You know where you were. And don't pretend like you weren't there. I saw you myself," Leo said. "You were at La Dame Masquée."

"That's impossible," Sibella said. "You must have gotten me confused with someone else."

"So that wasn't you standing at the bar wearing that gray dress and black cloak?" Leo asked, arching an eyebrow.

"Of course not," Sibella lied, but she knew her calm exterior was melting. He'd found a weak spot and he seemed to know it.

"I would say I'm surprised by your behavior, Sibella, but I can't. I always knew your *mother* was a money-hunting whore, but this is a new low for you," Leo spat.

Tears welled up in her eyes. She wanted to defend herself. She wanted to defend her mother. But she couldn't find the words. And unfortunately, no matter how misguided it was, there was some truth to his statement. Her mother had only married Raphael for the financial stability and the title he had offered, and Sibella had gone off to Osmain to marry Principe Daniel for nothing more than his crown.

"You were at a tavern notorious for prostitutes, and then you don't come home that night? That seems a little too coincidental, if you ask me," Leo continued. "I hope you weren't planning on using the money from your *clients* for anything other than supporting this family. After all, my father would be devastated to hear you're keeping secrets from him."

"Leo, please. I'm begging you, as your sister, don't tell Raphael you saw me. I promise you, it's not what you think," Sibella said, her hands trembling.

"If you weren't selling yourself to patrons of the tavern, what were you doing there?" Leo asked, looking at her pointedly.

Sibella shrank in on herself. She couldn't possibly tell Leo the real reason, and she wasn't quick enough on her feet to come up with a lie that would successfully get him to leave her alone. Embarrassed and afraid of what might happen, Sibella stood there, unmoving and silent.

Leo emitted a satisfied cackle. "That's what I thought. You're worse than I imagined."

"What's it going to take for you to keep this between us?" Sibella said quietly, defeated.

"Nothing," Leo said, finally moving out of her way. He smiled, but Sibella eyed him warily.

"Nothing?" Sibella repeated.

"Nothing you do will stop me from telling him," he said.

Sibella could think of a few things that would stop him from running his big mouth in front of Raphael, but all of those solutions would land her in jail for one violent crime or another. What would happen to her mother if Sibella was forced to leave? Would Raphael keep Delphine, or send them both packing? Anger and despair swirled within her, but she held back her tears. She didn't want to give Leo the satisfaction of seeing her cry.

"If you were just going to tell him anyway, why confront me? Wouldn't you like to see the surprise on my face?" Sibella said, her voice wavering.

"That's true. Perhaps my silence *can* be bought, then. For a little while, anyway."

"What do you want?" Sibella asked, frightened of what he might say.

"Give me the profits from your escapades."

Sibella glared at him while he smiled. At least it was money and not something more demeaning, but Sibella didn't have many coins. In fact, the only money she had left was the remains of the money Principe Daniel had given her. She had a choice to make. She could either give Leo the money and be out of resources entirely, or she could let him tell Raphael what he had seen and likely be turned out on the street. It was a decent amount of money, but certainly not enough to live on.

She slowly opened her purse and pressed a few silver coins into Leo's outstretched hand.

"That's all you've got?" he asked.

"Yes."

"Prove it," Leo said, snatching her purse off her wrist. Her arm wrenched at a strange angle and pain shot through it as he ripped the bag out of her grasp.

"Leo! Stop!" Sibella said, grabbing for her purse to no avail. Leo opened it, dropping the rest of her coins into his hand.

"That's what I thought. You little liar. Holding things back from me," he said, the silver jingling in his palm. As soon as he'd gotten the money, he let Sibella's purse fall to the ground. Thankfully, the coins were all that had fallen out. She couldn't even imagine the chaos that would have ensued if Leo had found the letter she had written to Roi Marius inside.

Sibella literally bit her tongue to keep from lashing out at Leo, and he looked down at her without any sign of pity or remorse in his eyes. "Pleasure doing business with you."

"You won't tell anyone you saw me?" Sibella asked again, grabbing his arm in desperation.

"You're in the clear for now. But if I ever see you out again, or if things start to get boring around here, I won't hesitate to turn you in."

She nodded. That was truly the best she could hope for with Leo. It made her wish that Simon had been the one to spot her at the tavern. He would have teased her about it endlessly, but he wouldn't have stolen her money or threatened to tell his father.

Without another word, Leo turned on his heel and left Sibella alone in the small hallway.

~

THE WORKDAY PASSED AGONIZINGLY SLOWLY. She'd been swamped with so much work she hadn't even had time to drop off the letter for Roi Marius. She met with a few clients for fittings, but the rest of her time had been spent working on commissions, leaving her alone as the hours dragged by with nothing but the whir of her sewing machine and her thoughts. Every minute was torture as she toiled and fretted over the endless horrible possibilities that awaited her. What if Roi Marius lost interest in her? What if Leo told Raphael she'd been in the tavern? Would Raphael beat her? Kick her out? Or do something to her mother instead?

In her daze, she hadn't even heard the soft jingle of the bell above the door signaling that someone had entered the shop. She only looked up when she heard a sharp knock behind her. She turned to see Jack standing at the top of the staircase, leaning casually against the wall like he'd been watching her work. His deep blue eyes seemed to sparkle as he looked at her curiously.

Sibella cleared her throat. "Jack. My apologies, I didn't hear you."

"You'd better be careful, or anyone could walk right in," he said, smiling.

"Anyone? Like you?" Sibella stood, putting her hand on her hip.

"I wouldn't say I'm just anyone," he said, pushing himself off the wall and crossing the room to meet her. Her heart fluttered in her chest as he drew near. He was as handsome as always, and as much as she hated to admit it, she was attracted to him. And not just for her usual superficial reasons. What she felt for Jack went beyond money or desire for power, neither of which he could ever provide. She *trusted* him. He was the closest thing to a friend she'd ever had outside of her family, and it was both strange and somehow comforting to know that he had her back.

"Did you bring back my cloak?" Sibella asked.

"Of course," he said. "Although I was tempted to keep it for myself."

"You liked it that much?" Sibella asked, grinning.

Jack nodded and looked into her eyes. "It reminded me of you."

Hearing that, Sibella could hardly breathe. He'd thought of her while he'd been gone. She couldn't fight the blush that rose to her cheeks. She tried to tell herself that it meant nothing, that he was just being a sweet friend, but rational thought seemed to be blocked from her mind by the fresh-linen scent of him.

"I, uh—" Sibella's voice cracked. "We should get to work."

"Right," Jack said. "Can we go downstairs? It's getting dark, we should sit by the fire."

"It does get cold at night this time of year," Sibella agreed, stepping down the staircase with Jack following closely behind. Once they reached the first floor, she threw a few blocks of wood onto the hearth and lit a small fire.

"Have you found anything new?" he asked as Sibella tended to the growing flame.

"I haven't seen Raphael since the last time I saw you," she admitted, sitting down and holding her fingertips out to warm them. "To be honest, I haven't been home much."

"Does he usually avoid you like this?" Jack asked, joining her.

"Unless he's on a rampage, yes," Sibella said. "He would prefer it if I didn't exist, so he likes to pretend I don't."

"That's awful," Jack said, shaking his head.

Sibella shrugged. "I'm used to it." She'd been ignored by her real father for years. When Raphael had turned out to be a raging asshole, she hadn't even been surprised that her own father would have left her in the care of a man like him. It hadn't taken long at all for Sibella to find herself in constant survival mode in her own home.

Jack appeared to be lost in thought for a moment, then said, "When my parents died, I thought it was the worst thing that could happen to a family."

"Then you met someone with an even worse sob story, right?" Sibella said sarcastically.

"No, I just—well, yeah, to be honest," Jack said, sheepishly running his hand through his hair.

"You don't even know the half of it. But if you want a true tragedy, I'll give you one. I *am* one," Sibella said. "I could tell you the entire ballad of Sibella Bellerose, but I'm not sure you want that. I'm not even sure I want that. Besides, it's not like there's anything you could do to change it. I'm stuck with the life I was given."

Sibella hadn't realized how emotional she'd become until she finished speaking and deflated on herself, biting back tears. She'd tried so hard for so long to better herself and her mother—to belong, to be loved. But it seemed like the way to a happy life was always one step forward, then two steps back. First with her father, then with Raphael, and now with both Principe Daniel and Roi Marius. A sturdy and comforting hand grazed her shoulder, but she didn't bother to look up. She knew it was Jack, being his usual caring self.

"I want to hear every detail about your life, Sibella," he said. "I know you don't like to share things. I can feel the walls you put up to shield yourself from pain. But I'm not here because I want to make your life worse. I'm not here to hurt you."

"I know," Sibella said weakly.

"If you decide you want someone to listen, I'll be around." Jack was too good to be true. There was no way anyone actually wanted to hear about Sibella's string of heartbreaks. Yet he seemed to actually care… and that was the most unsettling thing of all.

Sibella shook her head and shrugged Jack's hand off, trying to get her mind back on the business at hand. "So, the murderer."

"Oh. Yeah," Jack said.

"Has Pierre overheard anything at the tavern?"

"Pierre? Oh, no. I don't know. I haven't seen him since that night, anyway. I'd hoped he would come home after we saw him, so that I might explain the situation a little further, but he didn't. He probably drank too much or found someone he wanted to sleep with. Or both," Jack said.

"Does he do that a lot? Get drunk, I mean?" Sibella asked.

"More often than I'd like," Jack admitted.

"He's a little young to be out drinking so much, isn't he?" Sibella noted. He'd looked several years younger than Jack. But more than that, his comfortable presence at a tavern full of Luméte's elite didn't make all that much sense. Where did he even get the money to buy all the alcohol he consumed? Based on Jack's humble wardrobe, Sibella would wager that Pierre regularly gambled and drank away their household funds.

"He's eighteen," Jack confirmed. "He's been going out since he was sixteen, though."

"And you raised him in such a way that this behavior is acceptable?" Sibella asked, and then immediately regretted it. She had no right to judge Jack's situation, just as he hadn't looked down on her for her problems with Raphael. Embarrassed, she buried her head in her hands. "I'm sorry."

"Don't be. Honestly, I deserved to hear that," Jack said. "But now you can at least take comfort in knowing that both of our lives are complete messes."

"How is that supposed to be comforting?" Sibella asked, nearly laughing at the absurdity of it.

"I'm not sure," Jack admitted. "It sounded better in my head."

They sat in comfortable silence for a while after that. Sibella had nothing to say that would provide any sort of comfort, and she sensed that Jack was in his own head, worrying about something he had no interest in sharing. He stared straight ahead at the fireplace, eyes glazed over as though he were off in his own world.

"Jack?" Sibella said after a while. He didn't respond, or even acknowledge that he'd heard her. She shook his arm. "Jack!"

"Huh? Oh, sorry," he said, snapping to attention.

"Are you alright?" Sibella asked. She was curious as to what he had been thinking about, but didn't want to press him.

"I'm fine," Jack said, smiling in a way that was probably meant to be reassuring, but instead left Sibella more concerned for him than ever.

"We keep getting distracted," she said. "Let's get back to the matter at hand. Maybe if we look at the records of the previous victims, we could figure out a connection, or a motive."

"That might be helpful. Then we could investigate those individuals to try and gather evidence against the duc," Jack said. "Do you have some paper to take notes?"

"Not much, but yes," Sibella said. She stood and went to the corner where she kept small slips of paper to record the measurements of her patrons. She grabbed a quill and some ink on her way back to where Jack was waiting by the fire.

"Okay," she said. "I hope you know more about the nobility than I do. I'm afraid I won't be much help. I know some of their titles, but I don't even know what most of them look like."

"That's alright," Jack said. "I know many of them, thanks to my line of work."

There was something else there, just under the surface of what he was saying. Sibella was certain he was hiding something from her, but she didn't have the faintest idea what it could be—some government secret that he'd heard in passing, or gossip that he couldn't share. Sibella shrugged it off and readied herself to write.

"Start with listing everyone we know he killed. We'll look for connections later," she instructed.

"You already know the last few. Madame Juliette, Roi Luis, and Reine Vivienne. There were about ten murders in total, from what I remember, all well-known aristocrats. Even the former duc des Étoiles—the current duc's father—was one of the earlier victims," Jack said.

"Wait," Sibella said in shock. "He murdered his own father and was never arrested for it?"

"I'm sure the death was investigated, but I suppose they didn't find anything."

"He knows how to cover his tracks," Sibella said, nearly groaning at how difficult Raphael was going to make it to prove his guilt. "Who else?"

"Olivier and Lea Dupont, the only known first cousins of the royal family," Jack said, counting off the victims. Sibella furrowed her brow. It must have been tragic for Roi Marius and Prince Charlie to lose not only their parents, but their cousins as well.

"There were some lesser nobility killed, too. Some were barely even titled," Jack explained. "Monsieur and Madame Boisclair were about as low in precedence as one can be and still be a member of the nobility, yet they were also killed. Their fortunes and land were significantly smaller than anyone else on the list. It certainly wasn't enough money to kill over."

"That doesn't make any sense," Sibella said, thinking out loud. "If Raphael was trying to kill off more prominent members of society, they never would have been targets."

"Unless it was for personal reasons," Jack said.

"That's not possible," Sibella said. "From what I've seen, Raphael doesn't generally consort with anyone he considers beneath him. If what you say is true, and the

Boisclairs were barely even nobility, there's almost no chance that Raphael would give them the time of day, much less murder them."

"Okay," Jack said. "So it wasn't about rank, and it wasn't personal. What could the pattern be, then?"

"Could they have owed him money? Maybe they were the other people at the table the night he got into the fight at La Dame Masquée?" Sibella suggested.

Marius nearly laughed at the idea. "The Boisclairs kept to themselves. Aside from major social functions, they were never spotted outside of their estate. And while their fortunes are meager, they would certainly have enough to pay back gambling debts if they somehow *did* end up owing Raphael money."

Sibella considered this for a moment, staring at the names she'd jotted down. "Were all of the murders planned?"

"I believe so," Jack confirmed. "They were all killed by an assassin with poisoned arrows, and never at public events. It was always either in the privacy of their own homes or estates, or somewhere without many other people around."

"Like Vicomte Galaxie," Sibella said, remembering his untimely death earlier that season. She'd overheard Simon and Leo gossiping about it soon after, while everyone was still in shock.

"That's right."

"Maybe we're going about this the wrong way," Sibella said, looking up from the paper. "We've been focusing on Raphael's connections to the victims rather than the victims themselves. If we can figure out what *they* had in common—other than rank, of course—that will help us figure out a motive. Do you know of any connection between Roi Luis and the Boisclairs?"

Jack fell silent for a moment, deep in thought. Sibella bit her lip as she wracked her brain, but she knew she would come up empty. She didn't know much about Esmarish nobility now, never mind those who had been in power when she was younger and still living in Céleste. If either of them knew anything, it would have to be Jack, with his work at the château.

"I think, and don't quote me on this," Jack said, "there may have been a distant family connection."

"How distant are we talking here?" Sibella asked, preparing her quill to write, just in case he said something noteworthy.

"The royal line has been sparse for generations," Jack explained. "Most of the monarchs have only been able to have one or two children, and that's left the line of succession looking pretty bleak. After Roi Marius and Prince Charlie, the next person currently in line would be a third cousin who doesn't even live in Esmar."

"Interesting," Sibella mused aloud. "So, if you had to guess... how many of those killed would have been within, let's say, ten places of the throne while they were alive?"

Sibella didn't need his confirmation. She had a gut feeling she'd just figured out the solution. But she still felt a twinge of satisfaction when Jack said, "Four or five. But most of the others killed were in the line of succession as well, just outside of those initial ten. All except Reine Vivienne and Madame Juliette."

Sibella bit her lip as she considered this hitch in their theory. The two women hadn't been in line for the throne at all, but there was such an undeniable pattern with the rest of the victims that Sibella wasn't sure what to make of it. Raphael wanted the throne. That had to be it.

"I'm not sure why they would have been killed," Sibella admitted. "Maybe Juliette discovered what he'd done and he silenced her. Maybe Reine Vivienne was pregnant with another heir. Either way, I think we've found our motive." Jack looked into her eyes, having clearly understood her point. Fear simmered under the surface of his expression. Sibella had to admit, it was disconcerting to realize that Raphael wanted the throne. He was such a terror to her and her mother with the power he had over them in their daily lives. What would he do from the throne of Esmar? Even worse, Sibella realized with a twist of her gut, Roi Marius was almost certainly a target as well.

"We have to warn the roi," Sibella said, standing. "His life is in danger!"

"Leave that to me," Jack said, taking hold of her hand. She was sure he meant it to be reassuring, but all his touch did was tangle her emotions. Jack's touch was the poison and the antidote at the same time, spreading both fear and serenity to Sibella's very core. How was it possible that she'd felt such a connection with Roi Marius at the ball, but now she was drawn to—of all people—a *mail carrier*?

"I will personally see to it that he is properly warned of the situation the moment I leave here," Jack promised.

Sibella nodded weakly. This was better, anyway. It would be a disaster if Roi Marius discovered she wasn't nobility before she could try to snare him into marriage. Besides, she trusted Jack. She knew he would deliver the message.

"How is he? Roi Marius?" Sibella asked before she could stop herself. "I mean, when you met him, what was he like?"

Jack gave her a look she didn't know how to interpret and he hesitated before answering. "He's fine, I guess."

"Just fine?" Sibella pressed. "Was he kind to you? How does he treat people on his staff?"

Jack looked unsure how to respond, but he eventually said, "He cares about his staff very much. I think sometimes he gets overwhelmed, but he tries his best to be good to them."

Sibella sighed in relief. This was excellent news. How he treated his staff was a good way to tell if he would be open to the idea of marrying Sibella despite her lack of money or title. Hope coursed through her, but it dissipated as quickly as it came when she looked at Jack. Roi Marius didn't matter as much when she looked at the man before her, and she wasn't sure what to make of that.

Jack tugged at her hand, urging her to sit back down with him, and she slowly lowered herself down in front of the fireplace.

"I can't think about this case any more right now or I might go crazy," he said.

"It is a heavy subject," Sibella agreed, noticing that Jack still hadn't let go of her hand. She knew she should pull away, but when he looked into her eyes, she found she couldn't. The light from the fire danced around the room, illuminating his handsome features.

"I need a distraction," Jack said softly. Without thinking, Sibella's eyes darted to his lips. She couldn't help it. She needed a distraction as well, and she wondered how it would feel to lean forward just slightly, to press her lips against his, to forget about everything in the world for a little while.

But he didn't try to kiss her, and she sat there, too terrified of her own desire to act on anything.

"Talk to me, Sibella," Jack commanded softly. "Tell me about your life, about your sewing, about your dreams. Anything, until every worry I have is replaced by a thought of you."

Sibella could feel Jack's kindness tearing her walls down, but as they talked and laughed that night, she found to her surprise that it didn't scare her nearly as much as she thought it would. Maybe she'd finally found someone worth being vulnerable for.

"My dearest mademoiselle,
I am glad to hear you're open to meeting in person!
Meet me at Café Cosmique just after sundown in ten days.
Hopefully that should be enough time for this letter to
successfully reach you.
I won't be wearing anything that distinguishes me as nobility.
With a murderer still on the loose, I don't want to put a target
on our backs. If you do the same, I'm sure we will still find
each other.
I am very much looking forward to seeing you again. The first
time I met you, you took my breath away. Now that we are
officially courting, I'd imagine that feeling will be tenfold."

Marius Roche to his mystery mademoiselle, day 55 of autumn

14

Day 65 of Autumn

Marius sat restlessly at his desk, polishing his reading glasses and straightening his cravat compulsively as Amélie briefed him on pressing issues. Thankfully, she wasn't one to prattle on needlessly, and she'd wasted no time getting straight to the point as soon as she'd entered his office.

"The Osmainians have written back regarding our request for the resale of their Tatrian imports," she said, producing a letter from the large stack she was holding and slapping it down on the desk in front of Marius, jolting him back into focus.

"And? Will they help us?" he asked, placing his reading glasses back on his face and peering over the document from Imperatore Antonio.

"Some," she said, the relief evident in her voice.

"Their trade agreement cannot be re-negotiated yet, so all they can provide us with are their surplus supplies at the end of each year. They aren't going to charge us more than the Tatrians would, but we will have to cover the cost of transporting the goods from Osmain to Esmar."

Marius sighed and massaged his temples. "We will have to ration access to the plants if we're only getting Osmain's scraps, but this is good news for the moment. Obviously, we will have to try to renegotiate with Tatria again in the future, but for now I'm satisfied."

"Excellent, Your Majesty. And, oh, it seems Principe Daniel has attached a personal letter for you as well," she said, pulling out a still-sealed letter and placing it down gently on his desk. Marius smiled at the reminder of his friend, but his happiness quickly turned to nervous excitement at the thought of letters… and letter-writers. Tonight, at sunset, he would finally meet his mystery mademoiselle once more.

He hoped he would like her now as much as he had at the comte's masquerade ball. He wasn't quite sure what he'd do if the connection was no longer there, without the mystery causing excitement. What if he didn't wish for her hand anymore once he saw her again? He'd been preparing himself to propose marriage to his mystery mademoiselle since they'd started exchanging letters, but now that he was about to be in that moment, he was hesitant. And he wasn't sure why.

Marius needed a reine, and judging from everything

they had exchanged, his mystery mademoiselle should have been a perfect candidate. But he couldn't shake the feeling that something wasn't quite right. Still, he'd committed to meeting her, so he would go. Perhaps she would dispel all of his doubts and steal his heart once more.

"Rey Hugo of Askaña seems to be open to an alliance," Amélie reported. "We received a letter from him as well. You'll have to write him back soon, of course…" While he'd been thinking about his evening plans, Amélie had already started discussing their next order of business. Marius couldn't focus on anything she said. He was exhausted. He'd been spending so much time with Sibella that it had started to put him behind in his duties, and he had locked himself in his office that day to try to catch up. If he wanted to keep seeing her, he would have to get things settled at the château first.

And he did want to spend more time with Sibella. More than anything. He almost wished she knew the truth about who he was so he could seek her counsel. He was becoming more and more certain each day that Sibella would still see past his title if he were to reveal himself, but his new worry was that she would never forgive him for deceiving her for so long. A nagging voice in the back of Marius's mind reminded him that a friendship built on lies wasn't a real friendship at all, which only made him feel worse.

Besides that, there was the growing attraction he felt for her. He'd been trying to push it to the side, but every time he saw her, he couldn't deny the desire that welled within him. He almost wished he could propose to Sibella, but between the lies he'd been feeding her and his courtship with his mystery mademoiselle, he knew it was a horrible idea. He only hoped that after he married the mystery mademoiselle, he could continue a friendship with her. He wasn't sure how that would work, but he supposed he'd have plenty of time to think about that later, after he'd secured the hand of his mystery mademoiselle.

Once again, Amélie ripped Marius out of his thoughts. This time, she slammed something down onto his desk, and he jumped back in surprise. She'd dropped her entire stack of papers in front of him, all of them appearing to be official documents requiring his approval on various issues. If Amélie noticed that she'd startled him, she didn't show it.

"Here are your proposals for the day, Your Majesty. Shall we go over them together?" she asked.

"Not tonight, Amélie," Marius said, taking off his glasses and rubbing his eyes. "Come find me tomorrow."

"But tomorrow you have to attend the ribbon cutting ceremony of the new schoolhouse!" she protested.

"After the ceremony then, Amélie. I can't look at these papers any more right now," Marius said, standing up to leave. He stretched his legs, stiff from sitting all day.

"Your schedule is clear until the end of the night. I saw to it myself," Amélie argued, crossing her arms and planting herself in place. "We will stay here and work through these until you're back on schedule."

"You're more than welcome to look through the documents yourself, but I need to rest. Please don't send any servants for me tonight. I need to be alone," Marius said, giving his usual excuse for when he wanted to sneak out. He pushed past his advisor to reach the door.

He stopped when he heard Amélie say, "I hope you're not getting into any trouble. Don't think I haven't noticed your recent absences."

Marius sighed. He'd tried to be careful, but it was impossible to hide from Amélie. She knew everything there was to know about the inner workings of the château. But as strict as she could be, Marius knew Amélie was the closest thing he'd ever find to a second mother. She'd been at his side since his parents had died, pushing him in the right direction.

"Don't worry. I'll be back later tonight," he said, giving her a smile that would hopefully get her off his back.

"With the recent troubles, are you sure this is a good idea? I could send some guards with you to make sure you're not left defenseless," she offered.

"No. Thank you, Amélie," Marius said, darting out of the room before she could argue any more. He couldn't have guards following him to the café. He intended to blend in, not stand out as royalty. To the average patron in Café Cosmique, he would just look like another commoner.

Marius changed his clothes quickly, and headed out of the château as the sun was beginning to set. The world seemed to be bathed in a golden glow as orange and pink clouds streaked the sky. It was a beautiful sight, but he didn't have much time to stop and stare. His mystery mademoiselle was waiting for him.

When he reached the entrance of Café Cosmique, Marius found his hands were shaking slightly. It was the moment of truth, and he wasn't sure if he could take it. But he pushed open the door, nonetheless. A young woman wiping down a table looked up and smiled at him in greeting.

"Good evening, monsieur," she said. She hadn't bowed or acknowledged him as Roi Marius. Good. That meant his disguise was working. He glanced around the cafe, but no one seemed to be paying him any attention. The café was bustling, with most tables full. Waiters buzzed around, refilling glasses and delivering mouth-watering meals.

Marius took a seat at a small table for two near the door, looking around anxiously, but he didn't see anyone even sitting at a table alone, much less anyone who could have been the woman he'd met at the masquerade ball.

The sun gradually set, and the skies faded to a deep blue, the stars beginning to twinkle in the darkness. Waiters occasionally stopped by Marius's table, asking if he was hungry and would like to order food, but he declined. His mystery mademoiselle had to come. She wouldn't abandon him like this. Would she?

The waiter brought him a glass of water and Marius slowly sipped at it, watching as the cool liquid turned to room temperature and the cup gradually emptied.

The patrons of the establishment left one by one, and the staff had begun to clean the tables as they neared closing time. It was clear: his mystery mademoiselle wasn't coming. His waiter stopped by one last time.

"Are you sure you don't want anything to eat? Our chefs are closing the kitchen for the night," he said.

"No. Thank you, though. I suppose I should probably head out myself," Marius said with a sigh. He'd wasted an entire evening waiting for a woman who hadn't shown herself. With a sinking feeling, Marius realized he'd probably never hear from her again. Perhaps she'd found herself another husband, or maybe she'd decided that she didn't care to take on the responsibility of becoming reine. Either way, she had removed herself from the picture. He made a resolution to himself then and there that he wouldn't check for any further letters from her.

"I'm sorry your companion didn't arrive," the waiter said. "There's another patron here who I believe was in a similar situation."

Marius's eyes widened. Could it be?

"Are they still here?" Marius asked urgently. But his question was answered as Sibella stepped out from around a corner of the café that had been obscured from his view. She wore a beautiful pale blue dress that shimmered as she walked. The cut of her gown showed off the swell of her breasts and the gentle curve of her figure, and Marius found himself staring at her as she neared.

"Sibella?" Marius said. He knew *she* wasn't his mystery mademoiselle. He'd considered that possibility before and it had led him nowhere. She couldn't be the woman he'd met at the ball because that woman had known him on sight, enough to address the letters to his name when he hadn't even introduced himself.

"Jack!" Sibella exclaimed, clearly surprised to see him. "What are you doing here?"

"I could ask you the same question," Marius replied.

"I came to meet a client," Sibella said, taking her worn black cloak off a hook next to the door and slinging it over her shoulders. "What's your excuse?"

"Official royal business," Marius said, only half-lying. "It's curious that neither of our appointments showed up, isn't it?"

Sibella stopped for a moment and looked into his eyes. There was more pain in them than he'd expected to see. This meeting must have meant a lot to her, and he'd just made light of her pain. Without a word, she turned to leave.

"Sibella, wait!" Marius called after her, running into the street to catch up.

"Jack, please. I need to be alone," she said, walking so

fast that it was almost a run. Marius struggled to keep pace with her and still think of what to say.

He stopped short to catch his breath, then cried out, "Sibella!"

To his surprise, she stopped walking. Then she whipped around to face him, silent intensity radiating from her.

"I'm sorry your client didn't meet you. I can see you're upset. I'm not exactly happy myself," he said, stepping closer to her. She didn't immediately start walking again, which Marius took as a win.

He continued, "Here's the way I see tonight. The first half of it was a waste."

"All of it," Sibella interjected.

"No. The first half. Because the night is only halfway done," he said, without thinking. He wasn't sure what his plan was, but he knew that right now, he would much rather be with Sibella than anywhere else. Especially when the alternative was to return home alone to a barrage of questions from Amélie.

"What are you talking about?" Sibella asked, crossing her arms.

"It's not even midnight yet. Still early enough that you and I could salvage the evening," Marius said. "What do you say?"

Sibella cocked her head to the side and narrowed her eyes. He couldn't tell what was going through her mind and the uncertainty made him uneasy.

After far too much silence for his liking, she said, "What did you have in mind?"

Marius hadn't thought that far ahead. He knew they could always go back to Sibella's shop, but he wasn't sure how much being reminded of work would upset her, given she'd just been stood up by one of her clients. He shrugged.

"I want to go somewhere I haven't seen before," he said. "Somewhere with a view of the stars."

Then Sibella did the most surprising thing of all. She smiled. It was a beautiful sight, and despite the chill in the air, Marius was warmed to his core.

"Okay," she said. "I think I might know of somewhere we can go."

~

THE ESMARISH royal observatory was situated at the edge of town on a small plateau that overlooked the city. The building was already closed for the night, leaving the grounds empty. It had been a long walk for Marius and Sibella, but well worth it for the view. The twinkling lights from the streets below seemed so tiny from there, and even the spires of the château looked small.

"Wow," Marius said, breathless from the view.

"I know," Sibella said. "I used to come here all the time before Raphael saddled me with my shop. I don't have the time to make the trek up here much anymore."

She turned toward a set of marble steps that led up

to the observatory and took a seat on one of them. Marius followed, and together they looked out across Lumète.

"How did you find this place?" he asked.

Sibella shrugged. "I like astronomy. I found the observatory first, thinking I'd like to use their telescopes, but after a while I just used it as a place to avoid being around my family. When they closed for the night and I still couldn't bring myself to walk back home, I would sit on these stairs for hours, contemplating life and making plans for myself."

She sighed and continued, "None of them ever came true."

Marius looked up at the stars, which seemed to be even brighter than usual tonight. "What was your favorite plan?"

She shrugged. "It'll never happen."

"That doesn't make it less important," he insisted.

Sibella looked at him with those bright blue eyes that made Marius weak. She looked impossibly beautiful in the starlight, yet there was still an air of mystery about her. He felt the urge to move closer to her, and the few feet of distance between them suddenly seemed too far. He wanted—no he *needed*—to touch her, to feel her skin beneath his hands.

Marius stopped that line of thinking before it could go too far. Just earlier that evening he'd been abandoned by the woman who had been courting him through letters since the beginning of the season. These powerful feelings for Sibella were clearly just his way of coping with the loss of his mystery mademoiselle. Weren't they?

Sibella appeared lost in thought for a moment, then said, "I trust you, Jack, at least as much as I can trust anyone."

Marius laughed slightly and said, "Wow. Big praise."

"If you really want to know what I had planned for myself, I'll tell you. But it's not important. The dream I have for my life now looks very different than it did back then," she said, turning to face the sea of stars on the horizon.

As glad as he was to hear that she trusted him, guilt gnawed at Marius's insides. He'd lied about his identity for so long. Could he really be trusted? Sibella needed someone in her life who could be fully honest with her. She deserved someone who would support her, and who she could feel comfortable sharing every detail of her life with. And while Marius wished he was that person, he couldn't be. Not unless he came clean about himself first.

Now was the time to tell the truth. "Sibella, I—"

"Jack," she said, scooting closer to him until their legs touched. She was so close to him, her eyes pleading. "Tell me I'm not crazy. Tell me you feel it too."

She was so close he could reach out and run his fingers through her long, golden hair. He wanted her more than anything, and if he was honest, he'd wanted her longer than he liked to admit. He knew, deep down in his soul, that his growing attraction to Sibella was the reason he hadn't felt quite right about meeting his mystery mademoiselle.

At the end of the day, he wanted Sibella to be his bride.

Marius thought his heart might burst with the realization. On one hand, he was glad to know where his heart belonged. But on the other, he knew he had to be honest with her about his deception before he attempted to court her. That was, if she still wanted to see him at all after he confessed his lies. He tried not to think about that possibility. He knew it would shatter his soul.

"Do you mean whatever's between us?" he asked, relieved when she nodded. Marius wanted to wrap his arms around her and never let go. If she felt the same way for him that he felt for her, then that was one less thing to worry about.

Sibella reached for his hand, and Marius didn't fight it. Her fingers were cold in the crisp autumn air, but he didn't mind. Despite the copious amount of work she did with her hands every day, they were smooth and soft, and Marius found himself running his thumb along the back of her hand.

"Sibella, I need to be completely honest with you," Marius said nervously. The excitement of her returned affection and the anxiety of revealing himself as a liar were mixing into an unpleasant knot in his stomach, but he pushed forward anyway.

"I haven't been able to stop thinking about you since I met you. I'd like to court you, but I'm not sure if I'm worthy," Marius said, trying to ease himself into it.

"I don't care how much money you have, or that you aren't titled," Sibella said, taking her free hand and running it up his chest. "I only care about you and me, in this moment."

He was trembling. From the cold or from fear he couldn't tell, but when Sibella glanced at his lips and breathed in slowly, he realized it was something else entirely. Anticipation. He leaned forward as she did, and any rational thoughts he'd had disappeared, replaced with a need for Sibella as his lips brushed lightly against hers.

Her lips were soft, and their touch disappeared all too quickly, but one kiss wasn't enough for Marius. He wrapped his arms around her, pulling her close, savoring the taste of the beautiful woman in front of him and breathing in her familiar scent of vanilla.

Sibella kissed him with a passion he hadn't expected, running her hands along his back and through his hair. Marius groaned and lightly pushed his tongue into her mouth, a boldness she met with fervor. This was paradise, yet he would never be satisfied. With every kiss, he needed more. He wanted her underneath him in his bed. He wanted all of her.

Marius used the low-cut neckline on Sibella's dress to his advantage, reaching around her cloak and underneath the shimmering fabric of her bodice to cup her breast in his hand. She gasped in surprise, but a moment later she repositioned herself, straddling his lap. There was a rush of warmth in his manhood. He was almost certain she could feel it hardening as she smiled against his lips.

Marius ran his hands under the folds of her skirt and up her thighs, exploring Sibella's body. He wished he could touch her between her legs, but between their position and his last shred of self-restraint, he managed to hold off. Instead, he pushed the fabric of the top of her dress aside, allowing one of her breasts to fall free. Without hesitation, he took the exposed tip of her nipple between his fingers while he kissed every inch of her exposed skin. His lips grazed her neck, then moved to her collarbone, and finally landed where his hand had just been.

His tongue gently caressed her skin and Sibella let out a small moan, the sound making Marius's already waning self-control crumble even faster. He took her nipple between his teeth, and she gasped.

"Oh, Jack," she said weakly, tilting her head back.

That moment was all it took for Marius to snap out of his daze. She'd called him Jack. Not Marius. As much as he was enjoying this new intimacy with her, he had to stop. This wasn't fair to either of them. He couldn't be Jack forever. He had to tell her the truth, and he had to tell her now.

Marius blinked slowly and pulled away from Sibella, shaking his head. "Wait. Stop."

She looked at him, eyes full of confusion and growing hurt. "What do you mean?" she asked.

"We can't do this, Sibella. I mean, I can't do this to you," Marius said as she stood up sharply.

"No, no, no," she mumbled, readjusting her clothing to cover herself once more.

Marius stammered, "I mean, you're amazing. It's not you at all, the problem is me—"

"I'm sorry," she said, her eyes sparkling with tears.

"That sounded better in my head," he said, standing as gracefully as he'd spoken.

"I need to go," she replied, looking at him one last time, her face exhibiting enough pain that it broke Marius's heart. Then, without another word, she ran.

Marius hadn't seen Sibella run since they witnessed the comte's murder, and she was quicker than he'd remembered. By the time he realized what was happening, she'd already rounded the corner and was out of sight. He ran after her, trying to catch up, but she was nowhere to be seen. He tried following the path they'd taken to get there, but it was no use. Sibella was gone, and it was his fault.

He shouldn't have tried to sugar-coat anything. He should have just come straight out and said loud enough for the city below them to hear that he was a liar and that he'd been masquerading as a commoner. It would have hurt a lot less than being left alone in the cold streets he didn't know nearly as well as he should. Marius wandered through the city, looking around for any landmarks he recognized that would help guide him home. The roads were dark and empty at this time of night, and he shivered with every step he took.

Marius wasn't going to give up on Sibella just because she'd run away. He would have to explain everything to her soon, but tonight wasn't the time. It would be extremely difficult to find her again in the darkness, and if he did, it likely wouldn't end well. He would stop by her shop the next day and clear the air, but in the meantime, he had to find his way back to the château.

It took hours of wandering around in circles and backtracking down dark side streets, but eventually Marius made it back home. By the time he closed the door behind him, he felt like his hands and feet were going to freeze off. The warmth of the château was a relief, and he spent several minutes just inside the doorway thawing.

When he did move, he went quickly and with purpose, sticking to the shadows and avoiding commonly used hallways. He didn't want to see anyone at the moment, but more than that, if he was spotted, his servants would certainly tell Amélie about him sneaking in long past midnight, prompting a lecture he didn't want to hear. He knew Amélie was protective because she cared about him, but his heart was hurting enough. He couldn't cope with his head of staff adding fuel to the fire.

Luckily, he reached his bedroom without being seen.

He stripped off Charlie's peasant clothes and threw them on the floor in a huff. As he glared at the pile of rags before him, he made a vow to himself: Jack was dead, and he would never come back. From now on, everything Marius did would be as himself.

"Would it be possible for Principessa Luciana and I to visit you for our honeymoon? She has not seen much of the realm and would like to meet you in person. I would also like to see you again, my friend."

Daniel DiAngelo to Marius Roche, day 86 of summer

15

Day 65 of Autumn

Sibella couldn't contain the tears that streamed down her face as she navigated the streets back to Raphael's estate. She'd had a feeling Jack would run after her, and she knew he could catch up to her if she tried to flee, so she'd hidden in the bushes outside the observatory until he'd passed. Once he'd run past her, Sibella started her slow walk home.

She knew the way so well that she barely needed to pay attention to where she was going. Instead, her thoughts scrambled around in her brain, combining into an overwhelming sense of despair like she had never felt before.

Deep down in her soul, she had known that Roi Marius would only break her heart. A man like him would never love someone like her, and the odds of him choosing her as his reine had been slim to none. She'd tried to prepare herself for the inevitability, and while it had kept her from being disappointed, it hadn't prevented her from being upset.

She'd expected him to at least show up to their dinner, speak with her for a little while, and then, after learning she wasn't titled, abandon her and never write to her again. Somehow, that would have hurt less than writing to her for an entire season and wasting her time entirely. But as much as the situation with Roi Marius made Sibella's heart ache, it was nothing compared to Jack.

Jack was the exact opposite of every man Sibella had tried to attract in the past. When she'd courted Principe Daniel, she hadn't tried to get to know him. She hadn't wanted to. His personality hadn't mattered. He could have provided her with a crown and ample resources to provide for herself and her mother, and she'd decided that was all she needed to know. Even Roi Marius, who had surprised her with interesting conversation and a warm disposition, had only been a means to an end. She might still have been interested in him if he hadn't been wealthy, but she doubted it. The truth of the matter was that she was looking for a provider, which Jack was not.

Jack, a mail carrier without a title or riches. Of course he would be the one man who had managed to steal her heart. She'd kept it under lock and key for so long that she'd started to believe she'd never have a need for love, but Jack had changed everything. She thought they'd had a connection.

She cursed herself for revealing her feelings to him. The last time she'd bared her heart to someone, she'd been just a child, begging her father for affection, recognition, *anything*. Since his rejection, Sibella hadn't let herself care. It was the only way to protect herself.

For a fleeting moment, when Jack had pressed his lips against hers, she had let herself believe that this time might be different. That maybe, just maybe, she'd found someone who wouldn't hurt her. But she'd been wrong. The weight of his rejection was worse than anything she could have imagined. She hoped he would leave her alone after tonight. Sibella didn't think she had the strength to pretend to just be his friend after what had happened.

As she neared Raphael's estate, she wiped the tears from her face. She didn't want to show any signs of being hurt if anyone was around to see her. Leo and Raphael would take it as a sign of weakness, and her mother and Simon would want a lengthy explanation of what was wrong. If she was lucky, everyone would already be asleep, and she could sneak into her bedroom undetected.

She'd left her bedroom window locked, not expecting to be returning so late in the night, so Sibella climbed the entry stairs and unlocked the front door. As she pushed it open, she could already hear muffled yelling coming from upstairs.

Raphael and her mother, yet again. Sibella shook her head. After the last time, she'd promised never to get involved in their fights again, despite the danger that Raphael posed to her mother. And after the disaster of an evening she'd endured, she didn't have the energy to even listen in.

Sibella closed the door behind her with a thud and began her slow climb up the stairs. She didn't know how much rest she could get between worrying for her mother and her anguish over Jack, but her body was begging for sleep. Even the stairs left her muscles aching. Midway up the staircase, the yelling ceased. Good. Maybe she could relax after all.

As she neared the top of the stairs, though, it became clear that this was not the case. Raphael appeared, a scowl on his face, and stood over her menacingly. Sibella tried to ignore him, hoping that he would let her pass in peace. After all, she hadn't done anything that he would consider to be wrong. He'd never cared before when she'd disappeared for hours at a time.

She tried to step past him, but he wordlessly moved in front of her, blocking her path. She could feel the rage emanating from him and tried not to let herself feel any fear as his gaze bored into her.

"Good evening, Monsieur," Sibella said casually, flashing him the most pleasant smile she could manage.

"Were have you been?" Raphael said, eerily calm.

Something was wrong. Why did he suddenly care where she had spent her time? It wasn't as if she'd been parading around town, telling everyone her relation to the duc and sullying his good name. This had to be something else. With a start, Sibella realized what it must be: he knew about the investigation. He had to know that she had figured out his crimes. Why else would he be so angry?

There would be no getting out of this one, Sibella could feel it. This fight would not be swept under the rug like every other problem her family had buried. This one was finally going to break them all.

"I was at the observatory," Sibella said, seeing no reason to lie so quickly into their little dance.

"That's not the only place you've been recently, is it?" Raphael growled, moving closer to try to intimidate her. Sibella didn't shake, or even recoil. She looked him in the eye, even as she could feel his hot breath on her face.

"I've been many places. I enjoy taking strolls in the afternoon, so I've been all over the city," Sibella said, crossing her arms.

"And did I give you permission to walk anywhere?" Raphael asked.

"I don't believe I need your permission to leave my shop, Raphael," Sibella said, trying to keep her tone as calm and even as possible.

"*Your* shop?!" Raphael suddenly exploded. "It is not yours! Everything you have is mine. This house, your job, your food, your money, everything. Provided by me!" Sibella didn't say anything. There was no point while he was on a tirade.

Raphael grabbed her arm roughly, and Sibella bit her tongue to keep from crying out in pain. "I own you!" he shouted. "You are nothing without me!"

Sibella wanted to lash out in return. She wished she could spit in his face and wrench her arm away, then give him a taste of his own medicine. But she was defenseless. She didn't even have her sewing shears with her. It wouldn't take much effort on Raphael's part to overpower her.

It occurred to Sibella she still hadn't seen her mother. Fear crept its way through her body for the first time since she'd arrived back at the estate. What if Raphael had hurt Delphine so badly that her life was in jeopardy?

"Where is my mother?" Sibella asked.

"She's recovering from the shock," he said.

"What did you do to her?" Sibella responded, her voice rising despite her best efforts to control it.

"I told her what you'd done. She didn't believe me," Raphael said, ignoring her question entirely. So he *did* know about the investigation. He'd somehow figured out that she'd been snooping around his estate. She didn't know why she was surprised. He seemed to have eyes all over the house.

Sibella held her head high, mustering all her courage, and said, "So what are you going to do now? Kill me like you killed everyone else?"

Raphael's grip on her arm grew even tighter. She

could barely feel her hand anymore, and Sibella knew he would leave a bruise.

"I would love to kill you, Sibella," he spat. "But I'm afraid I don't know what nonsense you're referring to."

"Don't play dumb," Sibella spat back. "I know everything. I know you killed Roi Luis and Reine Vivienne. I know you killed the comte de Cieux. I know you killed Madame Juliette!"

Raphael's features softened at the mention of his first wife's name, an expression which was almost immediately replaced with surprise. He didn't look guilty. If anything, his expression was laced with grief. If Sibella didn't know any better, she might think…

The realization hit her. Raphael didn't know anything. Not only did he not know that she'd been trying to solve the mystery behind the assassinations, but he also wasn't the murderer.

Sibella knew immediately that she'd made a horrible mistake.

His face contorted into an expression of anger more intense than Sibella had ever seen before. Knowing he wasn't the killer didn't ease her fear upon seeing this newer, deeper rage. What would he do? Would he hit her, or simply yell more?

In a split second, without another word, Raphael threw her backward. Sibella caught her heel and fell back down the marble stairs she'd just climbed. The world moved in slow motion. She flung her arms over her head as she hit a step. She tried to catch herself and couldn't. A sharp pain flared up in her wrist. If she'd been able to register anything besides the world spinning, she suspected she would have heard a sickening crack.

By the time she rolled to a stop at the bottom, she was dazed, and she hurt everywhere. She didn't need a doctor to know that her wrist was shattered. She wouldn't be able to sew for weeks, assuming her bones healed properly at all. Her livelihood was gone. Now that she wasn't able to fulfil her end of her bargain with Raphael, what would he do?

Another thought occurred to her. If he wasn't referring to her sneaking around with Jack, what *had* Raphael been talking about?

At that moment, the front door swept open, loud laughter ringing through the entryway. Her brothers. Sibella couldn't bring herself to sit up, or even move. She knew. Leo had sold her out. He'd told Raphael everything. That was why her mother didn't believe anything he'd said. Because it wasn't true.

"What's going on?" Simon asked.

"It looks like the whore finally got what was coming to her," Leo said with a snicker.

Sibella pushed herself up with her good arm, holding her injured hand to her chest and wincing from the pain. She didn't want to fight Leo, but she had to at least pick herself up off the ground. She couldn't let him believe that what he'd done had broken her, even though it very well still could.

A scream pierced the silence, Delphine crying out Sibella's name from the top of the stairs. She'd finally emerged from wherever she'd been fighting with Raphael.

"Don't go any closer, Delphine," Raphael commanded, holding out his arm to stop her from running to Sibella's aid. "This girl has been all over Luméte, selling herself to kind gentlemen and ruining her name and reputation. As everything she does is my responsibility, she will be punished accordingly."

"I… didn't… do… anything," Sibella ground out the words, trying and failing to keep the pain out of her voice.

"She's lying, Papa!" Leo interjected. "I saw her myself."

"Leo can be out at night, but I can't?" Sibella argued, slowly pushing herself to her feet. Every muscle in her body screamed in agony. It would take her days to recover.

"So you were there? You don't even deny it?" Sibella's mother asked, shock and concern in her eyes.

"Maman, I swear. I was out, yes, but I was on official business. And I was most certainly not there to seduce anyone," Sibella said.

"And what was this official business?" Raphael asked.

Sibella glared at him. "I've already made my accusations clear. I've been investigating the string of murders that include the death of your own father and wife!

Forgive me for suspecting you, but you must admit, it doesn't look flattering."

"Papa," Simon said softly, stepping forward and looking up at his father, "what is she talking about?"

"Nothing," Raphael said gruffly. "Her assumptions are incorrect, and I don't want to hear another word about it."

"Yes, Papa," Simon said, lowering his head.

"As for you, Sibella," Raphael continued, descending the stairs menacingly. "You are no longer of any use to me. It is clear you will only ever bring trouble to this family, and I will not stand for it. As of tonight, you are no longer a member of this household. You will leave immediately."

"No! Raphael, please!" Sibella's mother cried out, grabbing his arm in an attempt to beg, but he slapped her hand away.

Sibella was cold. She was numb. All she could feel was an overwhelming sense of dread. How had everything fallen apart in one night? She was going to be injured and alone on the freezing streets of Esmar with no prospects, no money, and no hope. A tear slipped down her cheek, followed by another, and then another. What would happen to her maman?

"Let her at least stay until the morning," her mother cried. "She will need to pack a bag, after all, and it's so cold out there."

"Perhaps she can go back to that tavern she likes so much," Raphael said. "Since she no longer lives in my home, how she chooses to waste her life is none of my concern."

"What about the shop?" Sibella asked hoarsely, finally finding words.

"It will be closed immediately. A shame—it was just starting to turn me a profit," Raphael said.

Sibella kept her head high. She didn't know how she would survive if she didn't. If this was truly the last time she was going to see Raphael, she wanted to walk away making sure he knew that no matter what he tried, he would never destroy her spirit.

"And my maman?" Sibella asked.

Raphael shot his wife a look of disgust. "She will remain here. I can't have people asking questions."

"That's very kind, Raphael, but I'd like to stay with my daughter," Sibella's mother said.

"That was not a request, Delphine," Raphael snapped. "You will stay here with me."

Through the tears streaming down her face, Sibella's mother finally made eye contact with her daughter. Sibella nodded once to tell her to stay. One day, she would come back for her. Once she found a place to live and a way to make money, she would help Delphine escape Raphael's clutches and they would live happily ever after—together. But for now, as abusive as Raphael was, it was still safer for her to remain in his care. At least here she would have food and shelter. Sibella didn't have that security.

"I suppose I'd better go," Sibella said, standing as

straight as she could manage and walking to the door. She opened it and was halfway gone before she turned back to face the pathetic excuse for a family she'd been living with for the past seven years.

She gritted her teeth and stared at the faces of her brothers and stepfather. "I would say it's been a pleasure, but it hasn't. You can all rot in hell!"

~

At least Raphael hadn't confiscated her keys.

While her shop wasn't the most comfortable place to sleep, it did have a roof and a fireplace that would keep her from freezing to death. She would have to figure out some other arrangement in the coming days, as Raphael wasn't likely to keep the building leased for long. She had until the end of the year at best.

Sibella lit a match and tossed it into the fireplace, watching the flames grow slowly. Once her fingers had thawed from her late-night walk, she rose from the hearth and found scraps of fabric. She wrapped her wrist tightly, gritting her teeth to keep from crying out in pain as she worked. She hoped that would help set the wound. She had no money to see a doctor, so she would just have to hope it healed well on its own.

A sharp rap at the window jerked her to attention. She approached it cautiously, grabbing her trusty shears off a nearby table just in case she needed to defend herself. Not that she could do much damage with her dominant hand out of commission, but she would have to try.

She wasn't exactly sure who or what she expected to see on the other side of the glass, but Simon wasn't it. Raphael must have sent him to kick her out of the shop. She sighed and went to the door, opening it only a crack.

"I'm not leaving, Simon!" Sibella said.

"That's a shame," he replied. "Because I've worked out a lovely solution to your homelessness problem."

Sibella considered this for a moment. It wasn't like Simon to lie. He had always been the more truthful and trustworthy of her brothers, and much kinder than Leo. She swung the door open, letting in a draft that sent chills through her exhausted body.

"I'm listening," she said.

"Come with me," Simon said, holding out his arm to Sibella. "You can come back for anything you've got stored here another day."

She slung her cloak back over her shoulders and stepped outside cautiously, then took his arm and asked, "Where are we going?"

"You remember my fiancé, yes?" he said, leading her down the dimly lit street.

"Monsieur André? I've never met him, but yes, I recall the engagement," Sibella said.

"I spoke to him about the situation. He was quite shocked to receive a call this late in the evening, but he agreed to help you. He has plenty of room, and he would be happy to host you until you're stable enough to live on your own," Simon explained. Sibella stopped cold, a smile spreading across her face. She threw her arms around her brother, careful not to hurt her injured wrist.

"Thank you, Simon," she said, relief overwhelming her. "You are the best brother in the world."

"I couldn't leave you to the wolves, Sibella," he said. "Besides, your mother asked that I help you. She pulled me aside after you left, and we devised this plan together. She thought you might be hiding at your shop."

Sibella broke their hug. "I'm sorry I told you to rot in hell."

Simon only laughed as they resumed their walk to Monsieur André's home. "I'll pretend you only meant that for Leo and Papa."

Sibella grinned. "That would probably be for the best."

She felt a rush of hope. Maybe she would be okay after all.

"I would be happy to host you and your new bride at my château. You know you are always welcome in Esmar."

Marius Roche to Daniel DiAngelo, day 5 of autumn

16

Day 80 of Autumn

arius didn't enjoy sitting on his throne. He hardly ever used it for appointments with his subjects, reserving it instead for formal meetings with visiting royalty. He'd tried telling himself that he wanted to appear humble before his people, but the truth of it was that it had never felt like the throne was meant to be his. It had been ten years since his father had died, but Marius still felt like an impostor.

As much as he longed for some reprieve from the constant pressures brought on by his position, in the fifteen days since he'd last seen Sibella, he'd had nothing else to do but pour his energy into his duties. Marius hadn't checked the mailbox to see if there was anything there from his mystery mademoiselle, either. Not only was he offended that she had abandoned him, but he no longer wanted her like he'd once thought. When he lay down at night, Sibella's face was the only one he saw.

Any time Marius paused his work, she was there in his mind. When he finally found sleep at night, she was there in his dreams. He'd tried finding her, of course. He'd gone to her shop several times in the days following their last encounter, but it had been closed every single time, even during regular business hours. There had been no sign of life inside, either. He'd begun to worry that the duc had done something to harm her, but then he'd seen it. Sticking out from underneath the shop's welcome mat was the dirty and worn corner of a piece of parchment.

Marius picked it up and scanned over the words.

Jack,

If you're somehow reading this, I ask that you stay away from me. After what happened between us the other night, I am much too embarrassed to even think about seeing you again. The investigation is off.

Marius had known loss, but this was different. To know that she was gone and choosing to live her life without him was worse than if she had been forced away.

The only thing that gave him any kind of reprieve from the constant ache in his heart was work. He shut himself away in his study, taking meals at his desk, and only allowing entry to Amélie who—to her credit—hadn't asked him any questions about his sudden obsessive return to his duties.

Now though, as Marius sat on his cold silver throne, he came to the sad realization that he couldn't hide behind his work any longer. The Osmainian carriage had arrived mere minutes ago, and with it had come Principe Daniel and his new wife, who would be staying in the château for an undetermined span of time. Marius was happy to see a friendly face, but he didn't know how long he could keep a happy façade for his guests.

It seemed that he would find out sooner rather than later, though, as the principe and principessa rounded the corner and entered through the open doors to the throne room. They weren't preceded and announced by a page, and Marius was relieved by this. He didn't want to waste time with formalities when he'd known Daniel all his life. The principe and his wife walked with linked arms as they neared the throne, and when they reached the foot of Marius's dais, they both lowered their heads respectfully.

"Marius!" Daniel said, smiling brightly. "Your kingdom is as beautiful as I recalled. It is wonderful to see you."

Marius smiled genuinely in return. No one could breathe life into a room like Daniel, and even Marius's heavy heart lifted a bit. "I'm so glad you're here," he replied. Please, introduce me to your wife."

Daniel gestured to the principessa, a tall, slender woman with medium brown skin and striking blue eyes that reminded Marius of Sibella's. He had heard Luciana's story before, thanks to Daniel's desperate letter for help. Luciana was Askanese royalty, had even been reina for all of one day before her kingdom had been overthrown by a group of rebels, whose leader Hugo now held that kingdom's throne. Marius wasn't sure how Daniel and Luciana had ended up together in the end, but it seemed that her marriage into the Osmainian royal house had been enough to get the new Askanese government to leave the young couple alone. In the end, Daniel's request for Marius to harbor the survivors of the coup had been unnecessary.

"May I introduce to you Principessa Luciana DiAngelo of Osmain." Daniel's eyes sparkled as he introduced her, like he was still dazzled by the knowledge that she was his. Marius couldn't help but feel a pang of jealousy at this. He was, of course, elated that his friend had found happiness, but Marius wanted more than anything to have someone look at him with pure adoration the way Principessa Luciana looked at Daniel.

"It's an honor to finally meet you, Your Majesty," Luciana said brightly in perfectly proper Esmarish. "My husband speaks highly of you."

"I'm glad to hear that," Marius said. "And please,

there is no need to be so formal with me. Call me Marius."

Luciana nodded, then switched back to Osmainian so Daniel could understand them. "Of course. I'd also like to thank you for your willingness to help my friends escape the Askanese coup earlier this year."

"It would have been my pleasure." Marius laughed. "Although, I am somewhat relieved I didn't have to get involved." He stood and descended the stairs to join Daniel and Luciana. He couldn't stand the feeling of being literally put on a pedestal, like he was meant to be more important than those he considered his equals.

"I also apologize that I had to miss your wedding earlier this year," Marius said.

"It's not a problem," Luciana said, smiling. "We had a small ceremony anyway."

"How have things been in Esmar?" Daniel asked. "And where is Charlie?"

"Never a dull moment, I'm afraid," Marius replied. "As for Charlie, I have no idea. I haven't seen him in days."

"That's a shame," Daniel said. "It's been so long since I've seen him."

"I'd imagine you'll run into him at some point during your stay," Marius said, although he secretly hoped Charlie would stay far away from this pair of royals after the disaster with the Tatrians.

"The Esmarish social season is still in full swing, is it not?" Luciana asked.

"It is, though I have to admit, it's been a strange season. I'm afraid I haven't attended many events this year, as I've been very busy," Marius said, deciding to leave out the fact that many events had been canceled out of fear of the mystery killer. He didn't want them to worry for their safety, despite the fact that Daniel and Luciana weren't anywhere near the Esmarish line of succession.

"That's a shame," Luciana said. "Daniel sponsored my cousin for the season, and I'm curious to see if she's found a husband yet."

Words flashed in Marius's mind. His mystery mademoiselle had said something about having a cousin who lived in Osmain. Osmain was on the opposite end of the realm from Esmar, and Osmainian relations were rare. Marius couldn't hide his surprise at this coincidence, which Luciana must have taken as him being interested in hearing more about her cousin.

"I would love to pay her a visit. We have some... things to discuss. The last time I saw her, it wasn't a very friendly conversation," Luciana explained. "I know where she usually lives, but I'm not sure I'd like to pay a call there. Her stepfather is a particularly nasty man, and I hope to never see him again."

Marius smirked. The man she was describing almost sounded like Raphael. But that was impossible. Sibella had never mentioned having family in Osmain, much less royal relations. Another coincidence. It had to be.

"Who is your cousin?" Marius asked. "I don't know

much about the personal lives of many of my noblemen, but I'm sure my royal advisor could look into contacting her for you."

"Her name is Sibella," Luciana said. "Sibella Bellerose."

Marius's heart stopped. The air in the room tightened. He could barely breathe. This could no longer just be a coincidence. Sibella, the woman he'd thought he'd known so well, was the cousin of the principessa of Osmain. How could that be? His head spun, questions popping furiously into his mind. If she had such a wealthy, connected family, why had she not gone to them for help getting away from Raphael?

"You've probably been introduced to her as Mademoiselle Bellerose," Luciana continued, but Marius held up a hand to request her silence. Luciana raised her eyebrows and looked at Daniel quizzically.

"You mean Sibella, stepdaughter to the duc des Étoiles?" Marius asked. He needed to sit down.

"Well, yes," Luciana said with a smile. "I take it you have heard of her?"

Heard of her. Oh, he'd done more than that. He'd laughed with her, kissed her, and given his heart to her. Yet when he answered Luciana, all he said was, "Yes."

"How is she?" Daniel asked. "I haven't heard much from her since we parted company. I even invited her to our wedding but didn't get a response. The last update I received from her was at the beginning of the season.

She'd attended a masquerade ball and seemed to have enjoyed herself."

The masquerade ball. His mystery mademoiselle.

Suddenly, all the pieces fell into place. His mystery mademoiselle hadn't abandoned him at the cafe. She'd been there the entre time, he just knew her as Sibella. But how…?

Charlie. Charlie had stumbled onto the patio at the party and called him by his name. That was how Sibella had known to write to him by name, but why she hadn't recognized him when she'd met him as Jack—because she wasn't in Esmarish society enough to know what he looked like beneath his masquerade costume. The walks she'd taken near the château hadn't been to try and secure royal clients. They were to deliver letters to him.

Marius nearly collapsed at his greatest revelation: he'd fallen in love with the same woman twice.

He must have been silent for too long, as Daniel put a steadying hand on his shoulder. "Are you alright?"

"No," Marius said. "I need your help. Follow me."

He had only known Luciana for a few minutes, and he'd never had very deep conversations with Daniel, but if he had any chance of winning Sibella back, he had to put aside his pride and finally be honest. He led them out of the throne room, away from prying ears, and into his study. Pulling open the drawer that contained the letters he'd received from Sibella over the course of the season, he picked up one and held it against the note she'd left Jack. The handwriting on the most recent letter was messier than usual, but definitely written by the same person when held side by side.

Marius told them everything, asking all the questions that had been threatening to burst out of him. Once he'd finished, Daniel and Luciana looked at each other, then back at him.

"Wow," Daniel said. "I told Sibella she'd be able to find a respectable husband in Esmar. I didn't expect her to do this well."

"To answer your main question, Marius," Luciana said, suddenly all business, "her father was my uncle Nicolas. Born in secret, and yes, after he took his vows. As far as I know, besides Sibella's immediate family, Daniel and I are the only other people who know of her relation to me. She doesn't advertise her parentage often. I think she might be slightly ashamed."

That explained the similarity in their eyes that he'd noticed earlier. In many ways, Luciana and Sibella seemed like two sides of the same coin. They were both respectable women from the same family, but one had been given a throne—the other, a sewing machine.

"As for why she wouldn't stay in Osmain with us, that would have to do with my father," Daniel said. "She leaked information to the Askanese that brought danger to our doorstep. All has been forgiven now, of course, but I think she'd be too embarrassed to turn to us for help."

The more Marius found out about Sibella and her situation, the more everything made sense. It occurred to him that Sibella was not exactly the tradeswoman she appeared to be, and that her distant royal relations would make marrying her acceptable to high society. Not that Marius needed society's approval to follow his heart.

"I have to get her back," Marius said, desperation leaking into his voice. "If you'll excuse me, I need to leave you for a little while. This has been a lot to take in all at once, and I need to go find her immediately."

"Wait!" Luciana said. "Are you sure that's wise?"

"Maybe you should wait until tomorrow," Daniel suggested. "It's starting to get late, and you have a lot to explain once you do find her. You'll want to choose your words carefully."

"You should go first thing in the morning. We can keep you company tonight to keep your mind off her," Luciana agreed. "Show us around your home."

After a moment of battle between his head and his heart, Marius nodded in agreement. They were right. Given his history with saying the exact wrong thing in serious situations, he needed to take this slowly and tactfully if he wanted to make Sibella his. Otherwise, she might run from him again.

And more than anything, he wanted Sibella to be his.

17

Day 80 of Autumn

Sibella was useless. Without being able to sew, she didn't know what she was good for. Her hands felt empty, even as she lifted a warm cup of tea to her lips and took a sip, the soothing liquid spreading a feeling of calm throughout her body.

"How is your wrist feeling today?" her companion asked from across the table.

Thomas André was perhaps one of the kindest men Sibella had ever met, though that wasn't an impression anyone would get from looking at him. He was tall and broad, with exceptionally large muscles that Sibella knew must have taken him a lot of work to cultivate. Though untitled, Monsieur André was the heir to a large fortune that had bought him access to the social circles where he'd met Simon.

"The same as yesterday," Sibella said. "I need it to heal more quickly so I can get back to work."

"Take your time, Sibella," Thomas said casually. "I know you feel like you're taking advantage of me and my hospitality, but as long as your presence here makes Simon happy, I'm happy."

"Thank you," Sibella said. "And that is part of it. But I just feel lost. Like I have nothing left to do for myself until this stupid injury heals."

She glanced down at her wrist, now set with a splint and wrapped tightly to make sure it healed properly. Thomas had wasted no time finding her a medic for the injury, and on top of everything else he'd done to clothe her and house her, the care seemed like more than she deserved.

Thomas shrugged. "Maybe take this time to figure out who you are without everything you've had thrust upon you. Who would you be if you weren't always forced to sew for others?"

She didn't reply, but he had cut to the heart of the problem. That independent version of herself didn't exist. She'd only ever truly felt like herself with one person: Jack. He hadn't shown his face since she'd left him at the observatory, not that she had gone to any of their usual meeting spots to look for him. She hadn't checked to see if the note she'd scribbled down using her significantly less-coordinated left hand had been picked up from underneath the store's welcome mat, and she wasn't going to check. She was embarrassed beyond belief that she'd put her heart on her sleeve for him and he'd discarded her so quickly. As much as she longed for him, it was better to stay away.

As Sibella sat deep in thought, there was a knock at the door to the drawing room. Her head snapped to attention when she saw Simon there, a boyish grin on his face as he surveyed the scene before him.

"Hello," Simon greeted them cheerfully. Thomas was out of his seat in an instant, embracing his fiancé and placing a quick peck on his cheek.

"I didn't expect a visit from you today," Thomas said, blushing slightly.

"It's wonderful to see you, love," Simon said to Thomas. "But I need to speak with my sister for a bit. Can I come find you after?"

Thomas raised his eyebrows in question, but said, "I'll be in my bedroom when you're finished here."

Thomas closed the door softly behind him, leaving Sibella and Simon alone. She began to rise from her chair, but Simon held out a hand to stop her, instead taking the seat that Thomas had just vacated.

"Is everything alright, Simon?" she asked, running through every possible scenario that might have happened. What if her mother had been hurt as well, or Raphael had found out where she was?

"Everything is fine," Simon assured her, swiping a spare teacup and casually pouring himself a drink. "But something has been on my mind since that night. I have a few questions that I need you to answer."

Sibella didn't need to ask what night he was referring to. It had strengthened their relationship as siblings so much, and made such an impact, that Sibella suspected they would refer to her getting kicked out of Raphael's estate as "that night" forever.

"Ask away," Sibella said. "Although I can't promise I'll answer anything fully."

"I wouldn't expect you to," Simon said. "But this isn't about you. I don't care about whatever bullshit accusations Leo and Papa tried to pin on you. I need to know about my maman."

"Your maman?" Sibella repeated dubiously.

"You mentioned her," Simon said, suddenly serious. "You think Papa killed her?"

"I used to," Sibella admitted. "Now I don't think so. I know what loss looks like, and he didn't look guilty."

"I just can't get past it," Simon said, idly lifting a spoon to stir his tea. "I feel like there was something more to my maman's disappearance than what I know."

This got Sibella's attention. Raphael had been their only suspect, and if he was innocent, that meant the real murderer was still at large. But if the killer was going to come after her for witnessing the aftermath of the comte's murder, she was sure they would have by now. She and Jack were no longer working together, so she assumed that his hunt for the killer was over. So the way she saw it, none of it was her problem anymore. But still, Sibella was curious.

"What do you know?" she asked, hoping she sounded innocent enough.

"I could ask the same thing of you," he said, eyeing her in a way that made her want to crawl under the table. Not accusatory, just with far too much interest for her liking. Sibella wasn't used to having anyone's attention focused on her.

"I told you I wouldn't promise to answer everything. Just know I was trying to enact justice for her death. That's all," she answered. She smiled to herself as he sat back down in his chair, seemingly satisfied with her answer. There was a silence, and Sibella didn't dare interrupt Simon as he sat, lost in his own thoughts. He raked his fingers through his mousy brown hair and sighed.

"My mother didn't exactly have it easy," he said.

"I'm sure she didn't with Raphael for a husband," Sibella replied without thinking. She was worried the insult would stop Simon from talking, but it didn't.

He laughed a bit, then continued, "Papa hasn't always been as terrible as he is now. Back when Maman was around, he was different. Still arrogant and prone to fits of rage, but there were never screaming matches like there are now between him and Delphine. He liked Juliette, at least as much as he can like anyone."

Simon had said something similar earlier in the season. It still surprised Sibella to hear it. She'd always assumed Raphael incapable of any emotion but hate. While she was mildly interested in the old Raphael, it wasn't all that important. Sympathizing with him wouldn't undo any of the hurt he'd caused Sibella or her mother.

"I'm not exactly sure how my parents met," Simon admitted. "Probably some kind of nefarious blackmail scheme, given my maman's background."

A blackmail scheme? A mysterious tragic past? She couldn't deny that it sounded eerily similar to the way her own mother had ended up marrying Raphael, but she stayed quiet. She wanted to hear every second of the story.

"The current roi's grandfather, Roi Charles, had several affairs." Sibella didn't know much about Marius's grandfather other than that Prince Charlie had been named for him. She listened intently as Simon spoke. "He wasn't known as the most affectionate husband to his reine, and he took many mistresses. As far as the history books say, no children were ever born from these women, but that's not true. There was at least one."

"Madame Juliette," Sibella breathed. Suddenly it made sense why the killer would have wanted Juliette out of the picture. She could have had a claim to the throne if the line of succession was thinned out enough.

Simon nodded. "She was raised in society as a distant cousin of the royal family, while in reality, she was Roi Charles's oldest child and should have been the next Reine of Esmar. Of course, her illegitimacy ensured she couldn't be in line for the succession, and she eventually found an acceptable match in my papa."

Juliette's story sounded like the life Sibella should have led if Nicolas hadn't disowned her. Who would she be if she'd been raised in the Askanese castillo instead of the slums of Céleste? Sibella had many questions to ask Simon about his mother's life, but the only one that came out of her mouth was, "Was she happy?"

Simon considered that for a moment, setting down his teacup. "I'm not sure," he admitted. "I believe, like most people, she lived her life in a gray area of compromises and forgotten dreams.

"Anyway, I'd hoped you might know something, anything, about her disappearance. I know she's probably dead, and at this point that's what I'd prefer. It would break my heart to discover she'd just abandoned us all those years ago," Simon said.

Sibella took his hand and squeezed it reassuringly. "I'm sure she loved you more than anything, Simon. If I learn anything else about her, you'll be the first to know."

He nodded, then stood. "Thank you, Sibella. For looking into her disappearance. It means a lot to me."

Sibella smiled weakly, not able to tell him that her motives hadn't been as pure as that. Perhaps if the mystery of the assassin was ever solved, they could find out what had become of Juliette. Simon deserved the closure.

"I'd better go find Thomas," he said, smiling as if they hadn't just had a serious conversation about his dead mother. "I'm sure he'll be waiting for me."

"Have fun," Sibella said, smirking.

She took another sip of her tea as he left her alone. She was glad to know more about Madame Juliette, but it had brought her right back to the empty, lonely feeling she'd been trying to avoid. Jack had been her partner in the investigation for so long, and there was nothing she wanted to do more than tell him about what she'd just discovered.

Sibella sighed. She was a survivor. She always had been, and she always would be. One day, she would probably look back on this chapter of her life and laugh, but that didn't ease today's pain of being broken and alone.

18

Day 81 of Autumn

*M*arius held his hand steady as he climbed the front steps of the house at the estate of the duc des Étoiles. He couldn't allow himself to tremble now, not when he was so close to finding Sibella. He'd brought one of his guards with him just in case the duc tried anything violent, but that didn't make him any less nervous.

He wasn't frightened of the duc as much as he was afraid of what Sibella might do when he told her everything. He took a deep breath and knocked on the door, anxiety coursing through him. What would Sibella say when she finally saw him in his expensive silks and finely tailored garments? Would she listen to him, or would she run away again?

When the door finally swung open, a butler stood on

the other side. Upon seeing Marius and, more notably, the crown on his head, he bowed. "Your Majesty!"

"Good afternoon," Marius said politely. "I've come to call upon Mademoiselle Bellerose."

The butler's face twisted as if he didn't know what to say. "She isn't here, Your Majesty. Might I bring you to the duc instead?"

Marius sighed. If Sibella wasn't here, and she no longer ran her shop, Marius didn't know where else to look. If a conversation with the duc was what he had to do to find Sibella, he didn't have much of a choice.

"Yes, please," Marius said.

The butler led him to the drawing room, then disappeared to find the duc. Marius's guard stood by the door, watching. He hadn't wanted any of his private conversations to be witnessed, but his guard wasn't likely to repeat anything he'd seen or heard while on duty. Men didn't get the privilege of a position at Marius's side unless they were fiercely loyal to him and able to keep their mouths shut.

It didn't take long for Raphael to appear in the doorway. He bowed respectfully, clearly shocked to be receiving a visit from the roi himself.

"Your Majesty," he stammered. "What brings you to my humble estate today?"

Marius motioned to the chair across from him. "Please, sit."

"Of course," Raphael said, eagerly taking his place. Marius got an uneasy feeling being so close to the duc.

The man was putting on a happy face for Marius, but it was obviously only a façade. Marius had become very adept at noticing when people were only interested in him because of his title, and Raphael was no exception. He was positive that if he'd just been Jack, the royal mail carrier, Raphael would never have given him the time of day.

"I see no reason to make idle chit-chat. I'm on a mission today," Marius said.

"And what might that be?" Raphael asked pleasantly.

"I'm looking for your daughter."

Raphael laughed uneasily. "Your Majesty, there must be some kind of mistake. I don't have a daughter, only two sons."

"Not even a stepdaughter?" Marius pressed.

"No," Raphael said, shaking his head. "But my sons are excellent company, if you'd like an introduction."

Poor Sibella, Marius thought. To be so unloved by someone that they could so easily pretend she didn't exist... Living with him must have been torture. Marius's heart hurt, but it also sparked something else in him. Anger.

"I don't care about your sons," Marius said. He'd never been so direct before, and it felt strange to be blunt. This must have been how Charlie had felt when he'd stood up to the Tatrians. It was freeing, in a way.

Raphael stammered. "Your Majesty, if I may—"

"No, you may not. Now are you going to bring her to

me, or should I alert my guard that you are getting in the way of my search?" Marius demanded.

Raphael's jaw dropped. "You wouldn't… you can't… I am not inhibiting you and I resent the implication that I would ever do such a thing. I believe you're in the wrong home, Your Majesty. I suggest you take your search elsewhere."

While the duc's words were polite, his tone was anything but. He was dancing on a line of courtesy, and Marius could tell that the deplorable man that Sibella had described, who seemed to live just under the surface, was getting closer to making an appearance. Marius didn't back down, though. No amount of the duc's anger would keep him from finding her.

"Mademoiselle Bellerose. Sibella. Where is she?" Marius asked.

"Your Majesty, what could you possibly want with someone so insignificant?"

"I won't ask again," he said, avoiding the question and looking pointedly at the duc.

He hoped Raphael saw the severity in his expression.

"I don't know, Your Majesty," Raphael said, shrugging. He looked entirely too smug for Marius's comfort.

"What do you mean you don't know? Do you at least know when she'll be back?"

"Never, I hope." Raphael actually laughed.

It was Marius's turn to look shocked. "What do you mean?"

"Mademoiselle Bellerose no longer resides here," Raphael said.

Before he could continue, two gentlemen appeared in the doorway, both similar in appearance to Raphael. One of them had sharp features and a nasty expression that mirrored the duc's, but the other seemed to have a kinder disposition.

"Your Majesty, I'm sure you've seen them before in passing, but these are my sons, Leo and Simon Lavigne," Raphael said, suddenly upbeat again. The two gentlemen bowed respectfully. "It seems they've just returned from their morning ride."

"It's an honor, Your Majesty," said the one introduced as Leo.

"Nice to meet you, gentlemen," Marius said, then turned back to Raphael, unfazed by the new company. "You kicked her out of your home? Why?"

"I believe you would get along splendidly with my boys," Raphael continued.

"Enough!" Marius bellowed, surprising even himself with the volume. "Tell me what has happened to Sibella!"

"Sibella, Your Majesty?" Leo sneered as he said her name. "You mean the money-grubbing whore who used to live here?"

"The what?" Marius hissed.

"I'd be careful of her if I were you, Your Majesty," Leo said, oblivious to Marius's rising anger. "She has been spotted in parts of Luméte that aren't fit for a lady."

Leo had to have seen Sibella at La Dame Masquée and had sold her out to Raphael. That was the only place she'd been that could be considered unfavorable. Leo was the reason she was gone. But even worse, the night he saw her had to have been the night Marius had brought Sibella to the tavern. Leo must have spotted her while they were there. Guilt blossomed in his chest. Whatever misfortune she'd fallen into thanks to her stepbrother was at least a little bit his fault as well. If he hadn't taken her there, none of this would have happened.

But if he hadn't, he might not have developed such strong feelings for her, either.

"So, none of you have any idea where she is?" Marius asked. "You just sent her into the streets, homeless?"

"She has been a burden on this family for years. It was time she left," Raphael said. "But why is this a problem for the roi? How do you even know about her?"

Marius stood and looked down at Raphael. "If you don't feel inclined to answer my questions, I certainly won't be answering yours."

He walked to the door, pushing past Leo and the still-silent Simon as he went. His guard followed closely behind and Marius stepped out of the house, lost. If Sibella had been sent away, alone and with nothing, she had almost certainly died in the cold.

Marius figured he would have to stop by La Dame Masquée and see if she'd gone there to seek shelter. He didn't know what he would do if she wasn't there. He couldn't believe she was dead, not when he'd just real-ized how badly he needed her.

"Your Majesty!" a voice called out from behind him.

Marius stopped and turned to see Simon walking quickly down the stairs toward him. "Please, listen to me. I'm sorry about my papa and Leo."

Marius raised his eyebrows in both question and surprise. Was this another trick by Raphael to get him to befriend his sons?

Simon practically ran to his side and said in a voice so low only Marius could hear, "I know where she is."

19

Day 81 of Autumn

Sibella's shop had become dark and imposing in the days since she'd been gone. She had barely visited at all since she'd begun living with Thomas, but today she had to return—to get her sewing machine at the very least. Simon had arranged for her to go to her shop today to pack up her things, promising that someone would already be inside to help her. And indeed, Sibella could see a fire in the hearth from the window, indicating that her assistant had already arrived.

She unlocked the door and gazed upon what was left of her short-lived business. One day, she might try to reopen it somewhere else. Somewhere she could keep the profits from the operation herself, instead of giving it all to Raphael.

"Hello?" she called out as she stepped inside, the entrance bells jingling as the door opened fully. She shut it softly behind her, then looked around for any other signs of life. Besides the fire burning in the fireplace, the shop seemed entirely abandoned. Quiet.

"Hello!" Sibella said again, moving to the staircase and slowly making her way up the stairs, careful of her splinted wrist. "Is anyone here?"

The upstairs was better lit, which Sibella took as a promising sign. There must be someone there. When she took the final step and entered the loft, she saw a figure by the window, looking out of the glass at the sparkling château in the distance.

Sibella knew it was him before he turned around. There was that dark brown hair that she'd run her fingers through while he'd kissed her, the same arms that had pulled her closer to him, embraced her and sent shivers down her spine.

"Jack?" Sibella whispered.

He turned around, and it was only then that Sibella noticed what he was wearing: a pale blue velvet coat and silver satin pants, with fancy shoes that only an extremely wealthy man could afford.

"No," he said. "I'm not Jack."

Sibella's breath caught in her throat, and she stopped dead. Something was off here. This couldn't be the assistant Simon had sent to help her pack, could it? All signs pointed to him being... but that was impossible. Wasn't it?

"You're-you-are you—" Sibella stammered, failing to get the words out. But it made sense—the way he'd just *happened* to be at the cafe when her meeting had fallen through, the way he seemed to know too much about the royal family.

"I'm Roi Marius," he finished for her.

Sibella gaped at him, tension filling the air, heavy and thick, as if the world was going to implode on her. All this time she'd been getting to know a man—*falling* for a man—who didn't exist. On top of all the embarrassment she had already suffered from his rejection, now she had to come to terms with the fact that the only person who might have ever cared about her had been lying the entire time.

It was no wonder he'd turned away her advances. He knew better than anyone that marrying her could never bring him any kind of political advantage. It would do him no good to encourage a relationship that he could never allow to go anywhere.

All the letters, the whole investigation, it had been for nothing.

Because it had been fake.

And apparently, Simon had known at least a little bit about it. At least enough to set up a private meeting.

Sibella's throat tightened, and she brushed a stray tear off her cheek, trying in vain to push her feelings down. This man had already taken enough of her dignity. She wouldn't let him have any more.

His brow furrowed as he eyed the splint on her

wrist. "What happened to you? Are you alright?" he asked.

"Am I a joke to you?" Sibella said, ignoring his question completely, her voice wavering against her will. "I never meant anything to you, did I?"

She should have known that Jack couldn't have been real. The affection he'd shown her was too kind, too gentle, to be true. Good things like him just didn't happen for girls like her. She thought she'd sunk to her deepest low already after he'd pushed her away at the observatory, but she was wrong. This pain was the rawest she had ever felt.

"Sibella, please. Let me explain," he said.

"What is there to explain?" Sibella said. "You're a liar."

He nodded, hurt in his eyes. "I know. You don't have to forgive me, but I'm begging you to listen."

"Why are you even here?" Sibella sneered. "Did Raphael put you up to this? Leo? Or is it just you and Simon in on the plot to humiliate me?"

"What?" He hesitated for a moment. "No. Every mistake made here was mine alone. Neither the duc nor Simon know about Jack. In fact, the duc didn't want to help me find you. Simon arranged this meeting so that I might tell you the truth, and he did it with no questions asked."

"The truth?" Sibella eyed him suspiciously. What could he possibly say that would ease all the pain he'd caused?

"You have every right to hate me, but I have to at least try to make things right. I didn't know at first that you were the mystery mademoiselle I met at the ball. I thought since she'd—since *you'd*—addressed those letters to me personally, that she knew who I was the whole time. So I never considered that you could be the same person as, well, you."

"So that makes it alright, then? It's fine to mislead a humble seamstress into thinking she's finally found someone worth caring for, but it's not okay to lie to a well-born lady in your court?" Sibella said, her voice cracking.

"No!" he said. "No, that doesn't excuse it."

"So how long have you known that you'd met me twice? Did you lie about that too?" Sibella asked.

"Of course not. I just realized it yesterday," he said, and there was genuine hurt in his voice.

"So you only lied about everything else. I understand," Sibella said, crossing her arms defiantly.

He sighed. "Jack was an invention. I created him to spare my image. I didn't want my staff knowing that I was sneaking off to the mailbox to keep up our correspondence. There would be questions. I made up Jack so there would be no rumors. But then once I became Jack, I realized that I was free. You didn't speak to me because I was the roi, you spoke to me because you wanted to know me.

"After so many years of being nothing more than a title, you were my only chance at a real connection with another person. Yes, I used our investigation as a way to find the truth about the murder of my parents, but I kept going to see you. *You.*"

"You aren't a joke, Sibella. I've never been more serious about anyone in my life. The reason I stopped things that night at the observatory was because I didn't want you to be with Jack. I wanted you to be with *me,* and I wanted to tell you everything. The guilt was eating me alive. I want you, Sibella. As myself."

Sibella drew in a breath as he took a step closer to her. Every instinct in her body was telling her to run, to escape before she got hurt even worse, but she forced herself to stay there, to look into his eyes. She would get lost in their deep blue forever if she could, but she knew that wasn't an option for her. He wasn't hers.

"It's too bad I'm just a seamstress, then," Sibella said.

"You think I care about that?" he replied, laughter in his voice. "I'm the roi. I can choose whoever I want to keep company with. Besides, you're not just a seamstress. You're the daughter of a duc, and—according to your cousin—the lost Princesa of Askaña."

"My cousin?" Sibella said. "You've been in contact with Luciana?"

She wasn't sure what surprised her more: the casual exposure of her deepest secret, or that he'd somehow obtained that information from *Luciana,* whose home was on the opposite side of the realm.

"She's spending her honeymoon in the château as we speak. But that's not important," he said. "What I'm trying to say is, I believe you are a perfectly acceptable candidate to be my wife."

"Your wife?" Sibella repeated, her eyes growing wide. Not so long ago, those words would have been everything she ever wanted to hear. But could she become his reine now, after everything he'd done?

"Don't answer me tonight," he said. "I don't want you to make a decision as large as this one in haste, especially considering the lies I've told you."

Sibella was still speechless, even as he took another step closer. He was so close, in fact, that she could feel the warmth of his body and his fresh linen scent tempting her to let go of all her hurt and anger and fall into his embrace.

"I'm truly sorry that I caused you pain," he said. "I hope you can find it in your heart to forgive me."

She shook her head and said weakly, "I don't know you, Jack. Wait, no. Marius? Your Majesty? I don't even know what to call you."

"Call me whatever you want, as long as you're in my life," he said, resting his hand on her waist and leaning toward her seductively, getting so close there were only inches between them. For a brief moment, Sibella thought he might kiss her, and she wasn't sure whether to lean into it or run. But he didn't. He simply stood near her. She found herself firmly rooted in place under his touch.

Could she forgive this man so easily after he'd been deceiving her the whole time they'd known one another? How much of what he'd told her about his past and his struggles had been real, and how much of it was a lie? And how could she think about that now when he was standing so close to her that she could barely breathe?

Just as her anger began to turn to passion and her hurt to desire, he pulled away and headed for the stairs. She was left breathless both by their almost-kiss and his sudden departure, and all she could do was stare after him as he left.

"I'll stop by Monsieur André's home tomorrow to officially ask for your hand," he said. "I promise, Sibella, if you choose to be my reine, I will make sure you're loved and cared for until the day I die."

Then he disappeared down the stairs. Sibella listened until she heard the door close behind him, then finally let the tears fall. Her heart was torn. She'd never thought it would be possible for a roi to ask for her hand, yet he had. But that same man had also deceived her, and she didn't really know him at all. But she would have to make up her mind, and soon, because she wasn't going to run away from him again.

Tomorrow, she would have an answer ready for Marius's proposal.

20

Day 81 of Autumn

It was much harder to enter the château unceremoniously without the anonymity that being Jack had brought, but Marius knew that if he had any chance of winning Sibella back, he could never be anyone but himself again. All things considered, the situation could have gone much worse. She might still turn down his proposal, but he'd explained himself well enough before leaving to give their relationship a fighting chance.

Marius tried to ease his worries by telling himself that even if Sibella rejected him, he would find someone else eventually. But that didn't help. He didn't want anyone else, and he wasn't sure that his shattered heart would recover if she refused to become his reine.

He found himself walking quickly to his office, not

even stopping to acknowledge the servants he passed in the hallway. He needed to work. It was getting late, and Luciana and Daniel would have almost certainly retired for the evening. Principessa Luciana was Askanese and still rose and slept with the sun as per their custom, and where Luciana went, Daniel followed. Marius had to get his mind off Sibella or he would drive himself crazy, and if his guests were unavailable, working was the only way to do it.

He barely had time to sit down at his desk before Amélie descended upon him like a hawk. She pushed the door open without announcement, not even a knock, and stomped up to his desk in a huff.

"Marius!" she admonished. "Where have you been all day? Another member of the court turned up dead while you were gone. We've been worried sick!"

Another murder. He didn't think he could bear to ask who had been killed this time. A shiver ran down his spine as he remembered how dangerous it was to be out in the city without protection. He would have to bring a guard with him to Monsieur André's home tomorrow. He just hoped the guard's presence wouldn't make Sibella angrier than she already was.

"We?" Marius asked, trying not to think about the danger. What if the victim had been Simon, or even Sibella's mother? The list of people between Raphael and the throne was growing thinner by the day, and at this point, there were only about four people left. Three, now. "Please tell me you didn't tell the principe and principessa about the murderer!"

"Of course not." Amélie scoffed. "I meant myself and the prince."

"Charlie?" Marius's jaw dropped at the news. "He's here?"

"Indeed," Amélie confirmed.

Marius hadn't seen Charlie in days. The last time he'd been home, he'd stumbled in drunk late at night without saying a word to anyone, passed out until the early afternoon, then left again that evening. He hoped Charlie was still awake this late. He wanted to see him, especially if he was sober enough to be worried about Marius.

"Your brother spent the evening entertaining the Osmainians. They seem to have gotten along swimmingly, no thanks to you," Amélie said. That was a relief. At least Charlie hadn't ruined another alliance.

"Where have you been?" Amélie asked again.

"I don't want to share anything just yet in case my intentions fall through," Marius said. "But tomorrow, things could change for Esmar."

Amélie cocked her head to the side. "Well that either means you've found a way to fix the trade agreement with Tatria, or you've found a potential reine. Which is it?"

Marius sighed. He trusted Amélie. She'd been his advisor since he'd become roi and she'd served his father before him. She could certainly be trusted to know that there was a possibility of Sibella becoming Esmar's reine. Besides, if Marius did turn up with Sibella on his arm and the château wasn't looking its best, Amélie would run around in a stress-induced rage and Marius would never hear the end of it.

"You can't tell anyone until I announce it myself. Promise me," Marius commanded.

"Of course, Your Majesty," Amélie said, bowing her head.

"Fine. I know I've been gone a lot recently, and I know it's unlike me. But I think I might have finally found someone worthy of being my bride," Marius said, nerves and excitement both coloring his voice.

Amélie's serious expression turned into one of joy as a smile slowly crept across her face. Marius couldn't remember the last time he'd seen her smile. It was such a rare sight that it almost made him uncomfortable.

"Marius," Amélie said with motherly pride, "that is fantastic news!"

He noticed that she didn't call him "Your Majesty". She'd never used his given name before, even when he'd been a child and had simply been "Your Highness". It threw Marius off, but he couldn't help but be happy that his advisor felt so close to him.

"She hasn't said yes yet, so don't get too excited," Marius said, but it was hard to fight a smile of his own, seeing how happy Amélie was at the prospect.

"Why wouldn't she say yes?" Amélie laughed. "You're Roi of Esmar! Any woman would be lucky to have you."

Marius chuckled and shook his head. "I'm not sure she cares that I'm roi. Things between us are… complicated. But rest assured, if she says yes to my proposal, it will be because she wants me for myself, not my title."

"That's all I've ever wanted for you," Amélie said, shocking him by wrapping him in a hug and squeezing tightly.

"Amélie." Marius wheezed. "Can't… breathe."

She let go immediately, straightening her glasses and clearing her throat. "My apologies. I'm simply overjoyed! This will mean a lot to our people too, you know. We need some good news after so much tragedy this past season."

The thought of Sibella bringing comfort to the people of Esmar after all the murders was pleasant for all of two seconds before it made him pause. The murders were something to consider. If he brought Sibella out of seclusion and into the limelight, could her life be in jeopardy? He wanted her to be his wife more than anything, but he would much rather she be alive. Marius couldn't bear to put her in any more danger.

"Speaking of the tragedy," Marius said, still blushing from Amélie's unusually effusive support, "have you found any new leads? I want it taken care of quickly."

"I know, Your Majesty," she said, back to business. "Constantin has been looking into several families with ties to Tatria. The girselia on the arrows is concerning, seeing as that is not a plant that Tatria trades away. It must have been brought to Esmar by someone who had harvested it in Tatria themselves."

Marius nodded. That would narrow down their search considerably. From now on, he couldn't sneak around. He would have to work with Constantin and keep pushing him to find their killer.

"Very good," Marius said. "Please let me know if they learn anything else."

"Of course," Amélie replied, nodding. She paused, and in a moment that was unlike her, she seemed to look past his duties and see the person underneath. "I think you should go find your brother. He'll want to see you."

"That would be a first," Marius said. He couldn't remember the last time Charlie was even remotely neutral about seeing him, let alone happy. But Marius did want to talk to his brother, and if he was in a decent enough mood, then Marius needed to seize the opportunity. He'd been so distant from Charlie for so long—it was time for something to change.

"I think he might surprise you," Amélie said with a knowing smile. Then she bowed and left the room.

Marius wasn't far behind, and he wound his way through the halls of the château until he reached Charlie's chambers. Not knowing what was happening on the other side, Marius knocked lightly on the large wooden door. He waited and waited, but the door didn't open. He had knocked softly. Perhaps Charlie hadn't heard him. Or maybe he wasn't in his room at all. Or maybe—

The door opened.

Charlie, dressed in clothes eerily similar to Jack's usual garb, stood on the other side of the doorframe. He had dark circles under his eyes and his chestnut brown hair was tousled in a very un-princely manner. He was a mess, and Marius couldn't help but feel partly responsible for the way his brother had turned out.

"Marius. What are you doing here?" Charlie asked somewhat defensively, no doubt expecting Marius to come in and lecture him. From the tone of his voice Marius could also tell his brother had already had a few drinks, but he wasn't yet drunk.

"I came to see you," Marius said. "I haven't spoken to you in a while."

"Oh," Charlie said, swinging the door further open and gesturing inside his bedroom. "Well come in, I guess."

Marius smiled and entered his brother's space. It was immediately clear to him that Charlie didn't care about what was customary. While most of the château was decorated in shades of blue and silver, Charlie's room was filled with what seemed like every color imaginable. There was no order to the room, no plan, and Marius wasn't sure whether it made the space feel homey or chaotic.

The room was somewhat cluttered, despite the chambermaids cleaning it daily. His bed was unmade and a set of clothes was wadded up on the floor next to a mahogany table that held an empty glass and a bottle of champagne. His books weren't lined up neatly on his shelf, instead thrust onto it in every direction. Some were upside down, while others had their spines facing toward the wall, leaving the pages exposed.

"You can sit, you know," Charlie said, plopping down onto a red velvet couch in the center of the room. Marius looked around for the nearest chair, a monstrosity made of a gaudy orange brocade. He eased himself onto it slowly and was surprised to find it was actually quite comfortable.

"It's good to see you back at the château," Marius said pleasantly, trying not to sound passive-aggressive.

"It's good to be back."

"What made you decide to come home?" Marius asked, genuinely curious. It was possible that he was just here for the night and would be gone again the next day, but based on Amélie's nudging, Marius suspected it was a more permanent residency.

Charlie shrugged. "A few things."

Marius thought for a moment that was all Charlie was going to say, which would have been disappointing but not exactly surprising. Marius didn't want to press him for any details for fear of causing him to shut down, so he stayed quiet. But Charlie shocked him when he opened his mouth to say more.

"For one, all those nobles turning up dead freaked me out," Charlie said.

"So the word did get to you about them," Marius

responded. "I'm glad you came back. You'll be safer here than anywhere else."

"That's what you were investigating with that girl, wasn't it? You think the duc des Étoiles killed our parents." He pointed at Marius as if he'd just unraveled the greatest conspiracy ever.

"Well, yeah," Marius said. "I guess you didn't need the explanation I'd promised after all."

"I still need some." Her summary wasn't exactly comprehensive. Who is she, and why were you pretending to be poor?"

"She's…" Marius's voice caught in his throat. He didn't know. Who was Sibella? She was royalty, but she was also just a seamstress. She was both the strongest person he knew and the most vulnerable. And her relationship with him was still to be determined. Depending on what she decided tomorrow, she could be his friend, a stranger, his enemy, or his wife.

"I'm not exactly sure how to describe her," Marius admitted. "Just know I admire her greatly. As for my alter ego, that was a lapse of judgment on my part. Rest assured, both Jack and Pierre are no longer with us."

"Good," Charlie said with a slight laugh. "I don't think I could keep pretending to be someone I'm not."

"So who are you, Charlie?" he asked without thinking.

The silence was deafening as Charlie reflected on Marius's question. He hoped he hadn't offended him, but it was clear by the way his brother stared into space that he was genuinely thinking about his answer.

Finally, he responded. "I don't know."

Glancing over at the bottle of champagne on the table, Charlie reached over and poured himself a glass. He took a sip, then said, "I think I need some time away from the party crowd to figure out the answer to that question. That's the main reason I've decided to come home. But, to be honest, I think I'm still looking for the place I belong. And I'll know who I am when I find it."

Charlie looked into Marius's eyes with a solemnity Marius had never before seen on his brother's face, and it shook him to his core. Charlie was still young, just barely a man. He still had plenty of time to figure out who he was. But something behind his pleading blue eyes made Marius feel awful about the lost soul his brother had become.

Perhaps if he'd been able to guide him more as he grew up instead of working so hard to become a worthy successor to their father, he could have made sure Charlie knew his worth. They could have become a team, helping each other in the wake of their parents' assassination. But instead, Marius had spent the years pawning off his brother's care on various nannies and servants, never giving him the attention he desperately needed to develop into the prince he was destined to be. And now, looking at the pain in Charlie's expression, guilt gnawed at Marius for what he'd done.

"Charlie, I'm so sorry. I'm sorry I wasn't there to help you as you grew up," Marius said, his voice shaking.

"You weren't perfect, but neither was I," Charlie replied. "You had so much pressure thrust upon you, and all I had to do was support you, but I even failed at that."

Marius sighed and shook his head. He knew that was as close to an apology as he'd get for the way Charlie had behaved the past few years. "Don't blame yourself for my shortcomings as a brother."

Charlie just shrugged. "I guess we're both pretty awful, huh?"

"I suppose so. But I'm going to try harder. I know you're grown now, and you don't need my guidance, but I can still support you."

"That means a lot," Charlie said, smiling. "I promise you, I'm going to do better. Things are going to turn around for me, you'll see."

Their conversation turned lighter after that, and Marius was surprised to find that Charlie was more charming than he'd expected. When he finally stood up, a long time later, Charlie did too, preparing to walk his brother out. But instead of leaving, Marius turned back to face him, and for the first time since before his parents died, Marius embraced his brother.

And to his surprise, Charlie hugged him back.

21

Day 82 of Autumn

*M*arius hadn't slept. All night, Sibella had been the only thing on his mind. He'd tossed and turned in his bed, one that was much too large for a single man. His bedchamber was cold and empty, and he didn't think he'd ever be able to rest again without Sibella there to keep him warm. Once the sun began to peek through his window, signaling the start of another day, Marius had barely been able to keep himself from making his way to Monsieur André's estate right then, even though he'd originally planned to leave in the early afternoon.

Luckily, Daniel and Luciana were early risers. And when Marius stumbled out of his bedroom—looking less than perfect—to find them sitting in the drawing room, the Osmainians seemed more surprised to see

Marius than he was them. Luciana had been at the piano bench when he'd entered, and Daniel was sitting and writing in a worn leather book. Neither of them had commented on their diversions, and instead helped him keep his mind off Sibella until it was time to make the trip into town.

Now, as Marius made the seemingly endless walk from his carriage to Monsieur André's door, a flurry of nerves exploded in his stomach. This conversation, no matter how it went, would change the course of his life. That alone was enough to make him anxious.

Flanked by guards on either side, he climbed the steps that led to the front door. He hated that he had to be accompanied by constant reminders of his status, but he had to be cautious. He hoped Sibella would understand, but it didn't stop him from raising his hand to one of his guards as the man moved to knock on the front door on Marius's behalf.

"Wait," Marius said. "I should do this myself."

The guard nodded and stepped aside. Marius took a deep breath, then knocked on the door. When it opened, it wasn't Sibella as Marius had been picturing in his mind, but a housekeeper who quickly dropped into a curtsy so low, Marius thought for a moment that she'd fallen.

"Your Majesty!" the old woman said in shock. "What can I do for you today?"

"I need to see Mademoiselle Bellerose immediately."

"Of course," the housekeeper said, opening the door

and gesturing for Marius and his guards to enter. She led them to a drawing room, where he instructed his guards to keep watch outside of the room, but not to enter. He wanted this conversation to be a private one. And more than anything, he wanted Sibella to still see him for something other than just the crown on his head, however unlikely that might be.

As soon as he was settled, the housekeeper hurried off to find Sibella, leaving Marius alone with his thoughts. He didn't know what to do with himself in the ensuing silence. He paced the room with such intensity that he worried the rug would wear through. Waiting was torture. His mind was a mess, and Marius had no clue what Sibella might like to see when she first entered the room. Should he stand? Should he sit? He fumbled around in his pocket until he found the gift he'd brought for her. He held the necklace up to the light, admiring the way the diamonds in the star-shaped pendant sparkled like tiny stars themselves.

The necklace had been one of his mother's, and after she'd died, Marius had picked it out of her jewelry box to save for his future bride. The only change he'd made to it was commissioning an artist to engrave his name into a small space along the edge of the pendant that hung off the delicate chain. As was customary for Esmarish marriages, if Sibella accepted his proposal, she would be expected to wear the necklace every day, and Marius would receive a piece of jewelry for himself to wear, with Sibella's name on it. While this wasn't the necklace his mother had worn with his father's name on it, it comforted Marius to know a memory of his mother would be passed down.

As he paced, Marius wondered if he should have the necklace ready to present as she entered, or if he should save it until the moment was right. After several minutes, he settled on the latter. He would have to be strategic about this, and it would be better to feel her out before jumping into anything.

Sibella entered the drawing room, not saying a word. She opened the door without as much as a squeak of the hinges and shut it with just as much grace and ease. If Marius hadn't been intently staring at the door in antici-pation, he wouldn't have seen her slip inside at all. She was as beautiful as ever, wearing a fashionable pale blue gown that perfectly matched her eyes. The dress must have been a gift from Monsieur André, as Sibella hadn't worn anything quite as eye-catching since the ball where he'd first met her. Her golden locks were tied back in a tight updo, making her look more elegant than Marius had ever seen her before. She still wore the splint on her wrist.

Sibella's gaze found his instantly, but not for long. As soon as he began to feel weak at the sight of her, she looked away, cold and aloof. He was suddenly unsure of what to say, how to start. He'd rehearsed his speech in his head a hundred times but having her there in front of him left Marius feeling like there was cotton in his mouth. Sibella didn't help either, saying nothing and letting their uncomfortable silence stretch on.

When he didn't feel like he could take it anymore, he finally said, "We should sit."

Sibella remained silent. There was no hint at a smile on her lips and no twinkle in her eye. But she left her post by the door and sat on the ornate couch by the window, where she proceeded to look out at the street below instead of at him. Disappointment was already clawing at Marius. If she was this upset with him before their conversation had even begun, how could he hope for her to accept his proposal? He sighed. If he was going to be brutally rejected, he might as well get it over with. He plunged his hand into his pocket, grabbing the necklace.

Before he could get it out, Sibella said, "We never did find out who did it."

Surprised, Marius stammered, "Did what?"

So much for asking her now, Marius thought, once again letting the necklace settle in his pocket.

"The murders," Sibella said, finally tearing her eyes away from the window to glare at him. "We never found the people who killed your parents."

Marius couldn't help but notice the venom in her voice when she mentioned the roi and reine being his parents, but he didn't acknowledge the obvious jab. Instead, he said, "It wasn't the duc?"

"No. He denied it. Not that denial equates to innocence, but I could tell from the disgust and hurt on his face that he didn't do it," Sibella said, then sneered at him. "Although I could be wrong. I've been wrong about people before."

Marius sighed. Ordinarily, he would have been more than invested in this development, but he couldn't get over the stab to his heart each time she insulted him. He would have done anything for her, but she couldn't even bother to be kind to him after all the groveling he'd done. A dark thought manifested in Marius's mind. If she was this averse to his presence, perhaps he shouldn't bother asking for her hand at all.

"Well, that's a shame," he said, again not letting on how her cruelty affected him. "I would have liked to catch the person responsible."

Silence fell over them again. Sibella stared straight ahead, clearly deep in thought. The muscles in her jaw clenched and unclenched, but the few times she opened her mouth to speak, she shut it again. She was achingly beautiful despite her anger, and Marius silently cursed himself for being so willing to dote on her, even now.

After a moment of silence, words finally came out of Sibella's mouth when she opened it. "I have an idea."

Marius raised an eyebrow. "About?"

"How to catch the killer," she said, adjusting her skirts and the splint on her wrist, anything to look away from him. Marius leaned forward, interested to hear what she proposed and how she'd come to it. She didn't make him wait long for the answer, finally looking at him once more. Her eyes were as blue as the sky, full of hope and fear, and Marius felt the words coming before she actually uttered them.

"We use our wedding as a trap," she said.

Our wedding. *Our* wedding. Marius could have cried from joy. He hadn't even had to ask for her hand, she was giving it to him willingly. A stupid grin spread across his face. He tried to stop it, tried to keep the conversation business-like for Sibella's sake, but he couldn't. Not when the future with her that he'd longed for was within his reach.

"So, you'll do it?" Marius said, smiling. "You'll marry me?"

She shrugged. "You're the roi. Only a fool would turn down a marriage offer from you."

It wasn't exactly the declaration of undying love that Marius had hoped for, but it would have to do for now. He knew that she could see him for more than his title. She'd done it before. He was certain now that they'd find their way back to happiness, in time. He would just have to earn her forgiveness *after* the crown was on her head rather than before.

"I'm so glad to hear that, Sibella. You have no idea," Marius said. He would have thrown his arms around her if he didn't think it would only push her further away. He had to give her time. Let her choose to come back to him instead of trying to coax her. If her acceptance of his proposal was any indication, Sibella would only love him on her own terms.

"I'd like to do this as quickly as possible," Sibella said.

Marius nodded. The faster he could secure Sibella as his, the better. "A proper royal wedding on such short notice would be unconventional, especially since our entire courtship has been in secret. It would also take a lot of work, especially with the end-of-season ball also coming up and the new year beginning. But I'm sure something can be arranged. What's your plan to catch the killer?"

"Do you honestly think someone trying to pick off anyone in line for the throne would allow any chance of you producing heirs?" she asked. "Where better to assassinate you than in a public space where they could easily slip away into the crowd afterward?"

Esmarish weddings, especially those of aristocrats, were large events that were open to the public. It was likely that almost all of Luméte's residents would be in attendance for the ceremony. It would certainly be a large enough crowd that an assassin would feel comfortable making an attempt on his life.

"I see your point," Marius said. "So, what do we do?"

Sibella shrugged again. "You've got a lot of guards. We give them specific instructions to lock down the event once it starts. We let the killer try to shoot us, then catch them on their way out."

Marius would like to think he could rely on his guards, but it wasn't as simple as Sibella made it seem. While his guard was excellent when it came to personal protection, they were terrible at investigating crimes and catching criminals. There was every chance that this plan would backfire. But the assassin had killed people in their own gardens, so nowhere was safe. If he was going to marry Sibella and risk his safety anyway, he might as well try to catch the assassin at the same time.

"We will sit down with the général of my guard when we get back to the château, and make a formal plan," he said.

"The château?" Sibella asked, looking at him with apprehension.

"Of course," Marius said. "You'll need to take up residency there immediately. Between the security concerns if you stay here and the wedding plans being rushed ahead, it's necessary."

"I understand," Sibella said, sitting up straighter, almost as if she were already adjusting to the new burdens being placed on her. Marius wished he could take her in his arms and kiss away her worries, assure her that she would be a fantastic reine and that he would support her every step of the way, but he stayed where he was. He didn't know how Sibella would react to such tenderness.

"If you need time to pack your bags, I can send a carriage for you later this evening," Marius offered gently.

She shook her head. "There's no need. I don't have much to pack."

Marius remembered how callous Raphael had been when he'd described how he'd thrown Sibella out of his home. Cast out, left alone, without any of her personal belongings. He glanced once again at her wrist. He never had learned what happened to it, but he suspected it had something to do with her stepfather.

When Sibella stood, excusing herself to pack a bag of what little she had with her, Marius reached out and gently took her injured hand in his. "What happened to your wrist, Sibella?"

She pursed her lips and said only, "Raphael."

Marius stood as well, stepping closer to her, his eyes begging her to tell the whole story. "You can tell me anything, Sibella. There will never be any secrets between us again."

"He pushed me. I fell," she said plainly. She then threw off his hand and exited the room, saying, "Give me five minutes, then we will go to the château."

Marius wasn't exactly satisfied by this answer, but it was too late to ask her to elaborate.

As the door closed behind her, Marius realized that, in all of his excitement, he'd forgotten to give Sibella the necklace.

"The trail to the person who murdered Roi Luis and Reine Vivienne has run cold. We aren't giving up on the search, but I don't expect we will be able to find the person responsible unless they kill again. We will discuss this more when I return to the château."

Général Felix to Marius Roche, year 729

Day 83 of Autumn

 arius was the last one to arrive at the meeting, despite being on time. When he arrived in his council chamber, the casual chatter he'd heard from the hall dissipated into silence as Amélie, Constantin, and Sibella all trained their eyes on him.

"Your Majesty," Amélie said, standing and curtsying quickly before taking her seat again.

"Good afternoon," Marius replied, sinking into his chair at the head of the table. He scanned the faces of his companions for any trace of emotion, but they all appeared calm and collected, ready to formulate the plan that would expose his parents' murderer once and for all. He'd expected that from Constantin and Amélie, who took their jobs so seriously it was a miracle they didn't combust from how tightly wound they were.

But the sight of Sibella sitting in the reine's chair left an ache in Marius's heart. She was still quiet, their carefree banter gone. That was what Marius had feared about telling Sibella his true identity, when he pictured the worst-case scenario. He wasn't sure if she would ever be able to let herself fall in love with him again, but he had to hope. She'd done it twice now, what was once more? At the very least, he hoped they could find their way back to the friendship they'd had in the beginning.

Marius took his seat. "Thank you all for taking time out of your busy schedules to meet me here today. I know there's much to attend to, with the wedding coming up so quickly."

"Indeed," Amélie quipped. "I have no doubt I'll have an extra gray hair or two by the time your vows have been exchanged."

"*If* the vows get exchanged," Constantin piped up. "I understand you believe the assassin will be targeting your wedding?"

"There is every reason to believe Roi Marius is a target," Sibella said. "Even if nothing happens at the wedding, isn't it better to set a trap for the murderer just in case they do decide to attend?"

"I assure you that there will be no threat to your safety at this wedding," Constantin said. "We will increase security if that's what needs to be done, and search every person in attendance for weapons. What-ever you need."

Sibella shook her head. "What we need is to catch the culprit before anyone else gets hurt. This investigation has been dragging on for far too long."

Marius almost smiled at Sibella as she spoke. Her tone was pleasant despite the bite of her words. No doubt she would be invaluable down the line, when it came to negotiations with the other kingdoms of the realm.

"I have a few ideas about how we might be able to corner the assassin, should they make an attempt on your lives at the wedding, but it seems too dangerous a plan to consider in earnest," Constantin argued. "Your Majesty, what if something goes wrong and you get injured—or worse, killed? I don't think inviting death to our doorstep is the way to solve this."

"What is the way to solve this, then?" Marius asked, more forcefully than he'd intended. "Because I don't think simply 'investigating' is enough. It hasn't worked for the past ten years, so forgive me if I doubt it now. I want to bring this criminal to justice. If it's risky, so be it. I can't let my subjects live in fear any longer."

Glancing at Sibella, he couldn't help but notice the uncertainty in her eyes. She tried to hide it by crossing her arms and plastering on a pleasant enough face, but there was no hiding the knowledge that her suggestion was potentially deadly. Still, she didn't suggest calling it off.

Marius hoped that this plan wasn't the only reason she had agreed to marry him. He wasn't sure why she would do that, but his anxieties wouldn't stop nagging at him.

"What do you suggest we do to set up this trap?" Constantin asked.

"Easy," Marius said. "Search attendees as they enter, plant guards through the crowd that will watch the attendees for signs of danger and stop anything before it happens, but also station at least two guards at each of the four exits to monitor everyone exiting the court-yard. If we're lucky, the killer will be caught as they're searched. They'll be arrested before they can even enter the crowd and be a disruption to the wedding."

"What if our guards fail and there is an assassination attempt?" Constantin argued.

Marius had to admit, the thought of one of the poison-laced arrows flying toward him sent shivers down his spine, but he had to stay strong.

Marius looked at his advisor. "Amélie, you'll be with us the whole time, right?"

"Of course, Your Majesty. I will there for any task you need me to do." She smiled warmly, then pulled out some spare paper and a quill and ink from her bag, preparing to take notes.

"Amélie, you'll be in charge of the jewelry exchange on the dais but also of making sure there is an escape route back into the château from the dais we'll have set up for the ceremony," Marius commanded. "If something should happen, Sibella and I will run and hide in the safe room."

"The safe room?" Sibella asked, an eyebrow raised.

"It's a protected room within the château should the royal family ever need to hide from an attack or natural disaster," Marius explained. "The location is top secret."

"Only members of the family know of the room's location and how to access it. Not even I know where it is, so Marius will have to show you how to get there himself," Constantin added.

"That's all well and good, Your Majesty," Amélie said, "but we need a plan should anyone be injured."

Marius nodded. "We will need to have a physician ready to stop any bleeding and prepare antidotes for the potential poisons in the arrows. Perhaps we should wear armor under our clothing as well."

Amélie jotted down a note, her quill moving faster than Marius thought it was possible for someone to write. That woman was truly a force of nature.

She paused, her hand hovering above her paper for a moment. "What about the Osmainian royal guests? I thought you wanted to keep the murders a secret from them?"

Marius sighed. That was an unfortunate side effect to this plan that would make him appear less organized than he would like, but things had been going well during their visit so far.

He replied, "Principe Daniel is an understanding man. We will explain the situation to him and allow him to decide for himself whether or not he and the principessa will attend the ceremony."

"I will inform him immediately after we leave here," Amélie said.

"I suggest we adjourn our meeting for today," Constantin concluded. "I'd like to confer with my men about the plan you've suggested. I will bring any further concerns to you before the wedding."

"Thank you, Constantin," Marius said, standing.

"Don't thank me," the général replied. "If this plan works, it will be because your beautiful bride-to-be suggested it."

Marius glanced across the table at Sibella, who, to no surprise, was still sitting quietly. Constantin's compliment brought a faint blush to her cheeks, but she still looked a bit detached from the meeting, as if the woman Marius had once loved was gone, only a shell of herself left behind. It broke his heart to see her like this, and to know that it was all his fault.

Beyond all reason, he hoped she would come back to him one day.

23

Day 91 of Autumn

Sibella hadn't stopped looking in the mirror all night.

She felt horribly vain, but she couldn't help it. It was New Year's Eve, and there was a massive ball just two floors below her chambers, but she couldn't bear to break away from where she sat at her vanity, staring at herself.

She hardly recognized the face looking back at her, and the experience was unsettling. The woman she saw was regal, wearing a dark blue gown so expensive and complex that even Sibella would have shuddered if she'd been the one commissioned to make it. The neckline was low, leaving very little to the imagination, and her corset had been cleverly tied to make her waist nearly disappear.

Her sleeves were large and poofy, and jewels glittered on the sheer fabric when she moved. The skirt was very large as well—not held out with hoops, but with so many layers of delicate fabric that it billowed around her in waves. She'd never seen a skirt cut like this before, with an overskirt of glittering material draped over the back and sides, cascading down the back in a train but leaving the front open to display the silver petticoat beneath. It was beautiful, to be sure, but she'd never worn anything like it before. Even when she'd been courting Principe Daniel, she'd worn the plainer gowns that she was accustomed to.

Her hair was styled in a complicated updo, and a small silver tiara adorned the top. It was all beautiful, but it left Sibella feeling like she'd somehow stepped into someone else's life. The only thing left that indicated she was still herself was the splint on her wrist, which the royal physician said would only need to stay on for a few more days. After that, the Sibella she'd been for so long would be gone forever.

She knew she would grow into her new role as reine in time, but that didn't make her feel any less like an impostor now. It had been easy to fake confidence when she'd been engaged to Daniel. For one thing, she had known no one in Osmain. It had been much easier to put on a façade when there was no one watching who knew her. And secondly, she wouldn't have been jumping straight onto the throne back then. She would have only been the principessa, a position of renown to be sure, but not one with nearly as much power or responsibility as the reine would have.

When Sibella had dreamed of this moment, of becoming a *somebody*, she never expected to feel like she didn't belong. If her father had made the choice to decline the title of Ambassador of the Sun and raised her as his own, this would have been her life, and Sibella would have felt comfortable in her own skin. But he hadn't. For one more night, she was just a seamstress in a pretty dress. It wasn't nearly enough time to say goodbye to the girl she'd been.

To make matters worse, settling into the château hadn't been easy. From the moment she'd arrived—and Marius had announced his intention to marry her—she'd been flanked by servants and guards, all asking her a million questions to prepare for the task of serving her. It hadn't taken long for Sibella to become over-whelmed.

She thought about reaching out to her mother for support but wasn't quite sure what to say. They still hadn't reconciled from their fight, and at this point Sibella was sure her mother had heard the news of her engagement. Every time she tried to draft a letter, she scrapped it—resigned to face this alone, at least for now.

She found herself hiding away in her strange new chambers more and more frequently. She'd become such a recluse that she hadn't seen her fiancé since their meeting with Constantin several days before. Between Marius's constant workload and her lingering distrust of him, she hadn't sought him out. Yet tomorrow, they would stand before all of Esmar, and he would place a crown on her head that would bind them together forever.

And after that... well... Sibella was no fool. Marius was a roi without an heir, and she knew what would be expected of them as soon as their marriage was finalized. While she'd never sought out any kind of sexual relationships in the past, Sibella knew what to expect. She'd heard detailed accounts from both of her brothers over the years, and she had also touched herself enough to know what pleasure felt like.

Still, she wondered how her wedding night would go. The idea of being intimate with Marius both frightened and excited her. She couldn't deny that it sounded appealing on the surface, especially after their encounter at the observatory, but as long as Sibella kept her heart closed to the love he'd professed for her, it would feel rather awkward to bare herself before him.

She wondered where he was now. Probably at the ball downstairs, dancing the night away. Who was he dancing with? Would he change his mind about marrying Sibella in favor of someone else because of the way she was treating him? Or maybe he was in his office again, making final preparations for the wedding with his head of staff. Was he happy? Did he long to see her?

A sharp knock at the door startled her and she cleared her throat. "Come in!"

The handle turned, the door opening just a crack.

Sibella let herself imagine for a moment that Marius might be on the other side, but alas—Luciana stepped through, then closed the door behind her. She looked like the perfect picture of a principessa in her traditional Osmainian gown. The lavish dress was made of beautiful shining gold and deep purple fabrics, and the empire waist flared out into a train behind her. Unlike Sibella, Luciana had left her curly hair to cascade down her back. Sibella wondered how her cousin never had a single hair out of place, but that was just Luciana's way. She made everything she did look easy.

"What can I help you with, Your Highness?" Sibella said, eyeing her cousin suspiciously, unable to keep the hint of venom out of her voice. She'd never particularly gotten along with Luciana, and a visit from her now most likely meant she wanted something.

"Oh please," Luciana said, crossing her arms. "Drop the formalities. You never called me by my title last summer, so don't start now."

Sibella narrowed her eyes and turned back to her vanity. "I don't appreciate you invading my private space to antagonize me."

"If you were at the ball right now, I wouldn't be invading your space," Luciana countered. "I haven't seen you once since you arrived at the château. Daniel and I will be leaving soon, and I wanted to see you before we departed."

"How kind of you," Sibella muttered, rolling her eyes. She watched in the reflection of her mirror as Luciana stepped closer and put her hand on Sibella's shoulder. The touch sent a shiver through her.

"We can't keep pretending like the other doesn't exist, Sibella. We're going to be wives to two of the most important men in the realm. Men who are good friends. We have to put aside our differences and find peace, for the sake of our kingdoms. Besides," Luciana said, her tone eerily even, "you're the only family I have left."

Sibella turned to face her cousin, her last living relative on her father's side. Luciana's icy blue eyes, the same ones Sibella had seen in her own face a million times, seemed to plead for understanding. Sibella wanted to tell Luciana everything. How she'd struggled for years, wishing for a scrap of attention from her father, the man who had willingly made Luciana Reina of Askaña. She wanted to tell her that they would never be family. But she couldn't do it. Sibella had only ever hated Luciana for possessing things that Sibella never could, and that was no longer the case. They were both wealthy and powerful women. She had no real reason to despise Luciana anymore. In fact, while Sibella didn't particularly care for her cousin, she was surprised to find her hatred had dissipated since their last meeting.

Sibella shrugged. "Rest assured, I hold no ill will toward you."

Luciana smiled. "I'm glad to hear it. I hope one day we can build trust between us and become friends."

Sibella smiled back weakly but said nothing. She didn't care to put on a show for Luciana, acting as if everything was alright, like they were suddenly best friends. It would take time and effort for Sibella to be ready to open up to Luciana. This didn't seem to deter the principessa, however.

"Why haven't you made an appearance downstairs yet?" Luciana asked. "This could be the debut into society you need."

"I don't feel like it," Sibella said honestly. "This dress, this tiara, this château… it's all wonderful, but I'm not used to it being mine. I need time. You'll have to give Roi Marius my regrets."

Luciana looked at Sibella in a way that made her feel much too exposed for her liking. When she finally spoke, she said, "Marius isn't at the ball. He didn't stay for very long. He saw you weren't there and left. He said something about how he had a lot of work to do."

This caught Sibella by surprise. He'd been looking for her, wanted her company, even after she'd been constantly pushing him away. Despite his lies, Marius cared.

"I can tell you're thinking about him," Luciana said. "I'm not going to tell you what to do, but if I've learned anything this year, it's that you have to tell people how you feel before it's too late. It's the only way to make sure you find your happiness."

Before she could think, Sibella blurted, "And are you happy?"

Luciana didn't hesitate before nodding. "Of course. But it hasn't been easy. All the studying in the world couldn't prepare me for the realities of becoming an Osmainian. The culture, the people… everything is different than it was in Askaña. And knowing that I'll have to help lead this new place one day is daunting, to say the least. But I do it anyway, because I love Daniel, just as you love Marius."

Sibella's eyes widened. She hadn't expected Luciana to throw around words like that so casually. But wasn't she right? Could Sibella be a great reine if she allowed Marius back into her heart?

Luciana continued, "You clearly have him wrapped around your little finger. He's spoken of nothing but you since I arrived here. You need to tell him how you feel before he slips away."

Sibella's first instinct was to scoff, to brush Luciana off. But the more she thought about it, the more Sibella found herself blinking back tears. She hadn't expected Luciana's words to hit her so hard, but her cousin was right. She had to find Marius. Her heart belonged to him. It had been his since the night they'd met at the masquerade ball, and it would be for the rest of her life. He was sweet, he was witty, and made her feel like she was the only woman in the realm. Despite his lies, despite the shock of his title, she loved him.

She'd pretended that she'd only accepted his proposal because it was the sensible thing to do, but Sibella knew the truth. She couldn't stand being apart from him. Even in her anger, she'd thought about him constantly.

Sibella stood sharply and asked Luciana, "Do you know where he is?"

"In his study, I'd imagine," she replied.

"Do you know how to get there from here?" Sibella asked, taking Luciana's hand in her own, practically begging. Sibella expected Luciana to give her directions, but she was surprised when Luciana didn't say anything more. She held Sibella's hand, opened the door to the hallway, and gestured for her to follow.

SIBELLA DIDN'T BOTHER KNOCKING. She burst into Marius's study with all of the desperation and fire that had possessed her soul. He looked up from the stack of papers in front of him when she entered, his face at first twisting into a scowl of irritation at the interruption before melting into one of shock. Sibella felt like an idiot standing in front of him, this man who was obviously busy and probably wouldn't want to hear from her anyway.

But there he was, quill in hand, a document in front of him on his desk. Just the mere sight of him sent her heart into a frenzy. He wore reading glasses, and Sibella was both surprised that she hadn't known he wore them, and endeared by the way they made him look even more handsome and intelligent than before.

The space was exactly as she'd imagined it would be. It was simple, with his desk and chair facing the door and only bookshelves behind. The only light in the room came from candles along the walls and a small window behind the desk. The walls were lined with books, neatly arranged on the shelves. It wasn't exactly a cozy room, but it somehow felt right for Marius.

"Sibella?" he mused, rising from his blue velvet chair. "What are you doing here?"

"I came to tell you..." She faltered. What could she even say that wouldn't end with her embarrassing herself? She swallowed, nerves fighting to keep her from saying anything else. "I realize you're probably busy. I'm sorry if I'm interrupting your work—"

Marius laughed. "Don't be. I was only trying to distract myself, anyway. There's nothing here that can't wait." He took her in as she stood in the doorframe and said, "You look stunning."

A blush rose in her cheeks at his words, and despite herself she said, "I don't feel like me."

"No," Marius agreed, stepping closer to her. "You don't look like the poor girl who worked so hard every day to take care of herself. You look like a reine."

He took another step toward her. He was close enough to touch, but he kept his hands firmly set at his sides. Sibella found herself wishing that he would reach out to her. She craved the feel of his skin on hers.

There was an undeniable sadness in his eyes as he continued, "I'm sorry for everything, Sibella. I don't want you to be my wife just because you felt obligated to accept my proposal. I want you to get to know me. The real me. And I hope that one day you can forgive me, and that we can reach a place of mutual respect."

It was painful to see Marius like this, so resigned to a future that would surely leave them both miserable. Sibella couldn't take it anymore. She wanted more from Marius than just his respect. She wanted happiness with him. She had to be brave and tell him the truth, whatever the outcome might be.

"I love you," Sibella blurted. Marius's eyes widened in surprise, but Sibella continued. She'd started talking, and now she couldn't stop. "I'm sorry, too. I'm sorry I've pushed you away instead of just talking to you. My life has never been easy, and it seems like every good thing that's ever come my way has somehow let me down— my father, my sewing career, Raphael. I've been so afraid that you would join them on the list of my failures."

"Sibella," Marius said, taking her hand in his and looking deeply into her eyes, "I will never let you down again. I promise you, as long as you're my wife, I'll take care of you. Not only will I provide you with all the material comforts, but I will ensure you are given the love you should have been receiving all along. The people of Esmar will adore you, I'm sure. You'll win over the château staff soon enough. Amélie and Constantin already seem to like you. And there's me. Believe me when I say I would do anything for you."

Sibella couldn't help it when tears sprang to her eyes. She tried to keep them in, but it proved difficult when Marius continued. "And when you and I have children, it will not be just because I need an heir. It will be because I want a family with you, because you deserve to know what it is like to belong to a family full of love."

A tear slipped out of her eye and Marius gently wiped it away. He was beyond any of her wildest dreams for a husband. He was kind and generous and... he was too perfect for someone like her, too good to be true.

"Can I tell you something?" Sibella asked softly.

"Of course," Marius replied. There was so much concern in his voice, so much genuine affection, that another tear rolled down her cheek.

She sighed. "The ugly truth that I've been too stubborn to admit, even to myself, is that I wasn't angry with you about the deceit for long. I've been afraid to come to you, to tell you how I feel, because there is no reason a man like you should see anything of worth in someone like me. It would be one thing if I was marrying you for political advantage, but that's not so, and that's certainly not the reason you've chosen to marry me."

Marius nodded, confirming her words.

She took a deep breath, then continued. "I've been told all my life by almost everyone around me that I'm worthless. If you hear that kind of thing long enough, well, one day you believe it. When you lied to me about your identity, it scared me. I thought if I didn't push you away, I would only get hurt again because there is no reason for a roi to want someone like me."

"To be honest, I don't know what love looks like. But I'm sure that what I feel for you is as true as it gets. And if you feel the same way, I don't know what to do with that."

"You don't think you're worthy of love," Marius said. He said it plain and simple, as if it were a problem to be fixed and not something to pity. Sibella nodded. It was strange to be so completely open and vulnerable with someone, but at the same time, an immense weight lifted off her shoulders.

Marius stepped closer and cupped her face in his hands. He lightly touched his forehead to hers, and Sibella closed her eyes as he steadied her.

"Let me show you," Marius said, his breath dancing across Sibella's lips as he spoke, reminding her just how close he was.

"Show me what?" Sibella whispered.

Marius wasted no time replying. "How worthy you are of my love."

There was no pleading, no explaining, no words. Marius touched his lips to hers, and Sibella was undone. She hadn't quite realized how badly she'd needed to feel his kiss again until that moment. It wasn't as fiery as their last one had been, but it was no less passionate. He took his time with each kiss, leaving Sibella hot with desire and desperate for more. She ran her hands along his chest and back, needing to touch him, to feel his body against hers.

When Marius broke off their kiss, Sibella nearly cried out to beg for him to continue. She'd only gotten a small taste of him, and he was gone again, just like that. But Marius had more tricks up his sleeve. He went to the door and twisted the lock, ensuring their privacy, then stepped behind her, wrapping his arms around her and holding her tight. Sibella leaned against him, feeling his warmth spreading throughout her body.

He leaned down to whisper in her ear, the words sending shivers through her. "Tomorrow could be dangerous. If you're right and the murderer does attend our wedding, we might not be able to have the wedding night I want to give you."

There it was. The cruel reminder that they would likely have to cope with an assassination attempt at their wedding ceremony. While there was a solid plan in place to catch the culprit, the reminder that one or both of them could get seriously hurt was enough to send fear coursing through her. She didn't know what she would do if anything happened to Marius.

He brought Sibella back into the moment as he lightly kissed her neck. She gasped at the sensation but didn't stop him, instead tilting her head to leave her neck even more exposed. He whispered once more, "What would you think about having our wedding night a little early?"

Sibella fell silent as she considered his proposition. It hadn't been very long ago that she'd been frightened of the idea, but everything had changed since then, hadn't it? She loved Marius, and he loved her, and there was no reason for Sibella to deny herself the pleasure of being with him now. Especially when he was standing so close to her that she couldn't help but be intoxicated by him.

She nodded her assent. She expected the gesture to change something in Marius, to make him more frenzied, but he didn't rush into anything. Instead, he kissed her neck again and again, each time unfastening one of the many clasps on the back of her gown. As her dress loosened, he ran his hand gently across the bare skin of her back, making Sibella tremble with anticipation. She was weak from the way he could make even the smallest touch feel meaningful.

When he'd finished with all of her clasps, Marius slid the dress off her arms and shoulders, letting it fall to the floor. He reached up to her hair, removing the tiara and tugging out all of the pins that held her elaborate hairstyle in place. As her golden waves cascaded down her back, she felt more like herself than she had all evening.

Sibella, now wearing only her undergarments, felt Marius's eyes surveying every inch of her exposed figure. She stepped out of the dress, kicking it to the side, then turned to face him. When she did, she couldn't deny that there was a twinkle in his eye. She smiled slightly, relieved that he was pleased by what he saw. He moved toward her, tracing his hands down the length of her torso.

"Stars above, Sibella," Marius said, his voice low and seductive. "You do things to me."

When his hands reached her hips, Marius tugged her toward him until their bodies were pressed against one another. She could feel the evidence of his desire brush against her, ready to make her his. She couldn't wait another second. He was taking things slowly, teasing her, and it left her more desperate for him than she'd ever thought imaginable.

Not wanting to waste any more time, Sibella reached up and practically ripped Marius's jacket off his shoulders. She tossed it aside then got to work on his vest, unbuttoning it far more quickly than he had undone her dress. Marius finished stripping himself, stepping out of his breeches and then lifting his shirt over his head to expose his bare chest. He was slim, but his muscles were defined and far more appealing to Sibella than she would have thought.

She knew she was staring, but she couldn't help it. He was beautiful, and he'd chosen her. He *loved* her. It was almost too much to bear. When he'd finished undressing and was left in just his underwear, he closed the distance between them once again, kissing Sibella with a sweet tenderness that made her melt.

She hadn't even realized he'd been pushing her backward with each kiss until her back bumped lightly against the edge of the desk. Marius reached behind her, pushing all of his documents to the side, a few of the pages fluttering to the ground. He lifted Sibella off the floor and sat her down at the edge of the desk.

"Is this your first time?" he asked.

"Yes," Sibella admitted. "What about you?"

Marius shook his head. "I've done it before, but it was a long time ago. I'll be gentle, I promise."

Sibella looked into his deep blue eyes and nodded for him to continue. Despite everything, she trusted him. She knew he would take care of her.

"Lie down for me," Marius commanded softly. Sibella obeyed, and Marius's hands found their way to the waistband of her bloomers. She instinctively lifted her hips as he slid them off her, leaving her bottom half bare. One of his hands found her good hand, squeezing it tight. The other trailed along the length of her leg and up into her core.

"Marius!" Sibella gasped as he touched her, softly at first, but then he began to move faster.

"I love it when you say my name," he said, sliding a finger inside of her and leaning over her so she could look him in the eye.

Sibella said nothing in response. She couldn't. She was so overcome with the sensations Marius sent through her that she lost all her words. She held his hand as tight as she possibly could as her breathing came more rapidly and she edged closer to release.

But just when she thought she might explode if he touched her any more, his hand fell away. Sibella sat up, confused.

"I didn't finish," she said. Sibella wasn't sure where the last of his undergarments had gone, but he was standing before her without a scrap of fabric to cover him.

Marius smiled, wearing a more devilish expression than he'd ever worn before. "I know."

Then he kissed her even deeper. He slid his tongue into her mouth and Sibella grasped his shoulders, pulling him closer. She could feel the hardness of his cock pressed against her and knew it wouldn't be long before he entered her.

With a steadying hand on her hip, Marius pushed forward, and Sibella bit her lip to stifle a gasp at the new sensation. She wanted to be good for him, to be the partner he deserved, and she couldn't let on that she felt any discomfort at the overwhelming feeling of him inside of her.

Seemingly picking up on how she was feeling, Marius's hands slid to her back where her stays were tied and tugged on the laces until they fell loose. From there it only took one swift movement for the garment to drop away, leaving Sibella fully bare before him. On its own, that might not have been enough to distract her from his slow movements as he pulled in and out of her, but when he took her breast in his hand and traced his fingers across her sensitive nipple, Sibella forgot all about anything else.

Marius continued to move, slow and steady, and when the first twinges of pleasure spread through Sibella's body, she put her good hand behind her on the desk to steady herself. If she'd thought him touching her with his hands was enjoyable, it was nothing compared to this. He traced his lips down her neck and she sighed a deep sigh of contentment.

He was going slow, and the moment was sensual and intimate, but as Marius continued, Sibella found herself hungry for something more. The fact that she could even think at all didn't seem right to her. She wanted him to do more than make love to her. She wanted him to fuck her until every thought she had was replaced by breathless gratification.

"Faster," Sibella commanded, wrapping her legs around him and pinning him against her body.

"Faster?" Marius asked, clearly surprised.

Sibella nodded. He looked into her eyes, and she saw the exact moment he lost his restraint. He took no time at all to push into her faster, harder. Sibella gasped at his intensity at first, but it was exactly what she'd asked for. Gone was the Marius who thought things through, took every movement slowly, made every touch count. This Marius was lost in her, and it made Sibella feel more desirable than she'd ever thought possible.

As he moved, Sibella ran her hand up his chest and into his hair, needing to feel as much of him as she could. She could feel every beat of their hearts, every breath. The pressure that had been building inside of her since he'd first started touching her was going to reach its climax soon. She couldn't catch her breath, her heart beating out of control in her chest.

"Don't stop," Sibella panted. "I think I might..."

Sibella never finished her sentence. She closed her

eyes as she released all of the pleasure Marius had built inside of her. The sensation was incredible and she felt like she had left the earth, her soul cast up into the heavens. For a moment, everything was perfect.

"Oh, Marius!" she cried.

He wrapped an arm around her, holding her tightly as he followed suit, moaning as he emptied himself inside of her. Sibella figured he'd been restraining himself, trying to make sure she finished before he did. It was sweet, and Sibella grinned widely as he deflated, pulling himself out of her and sagging against the desk.

"That was…" Marius trailed off, at a loss for words. Sibella didn't need him to finish his sentence to know what he meant.

He opened his arms, beckoning her toward him. She pushed herself off the desk and fell into his embrace. He held her tightly and Sibella breathed in his scent—the smell of fresh parchment and clean linens—trying to etch it into her memory forever. Now that she'd let herself fall for Marius, there was no going back. For the first time, Sibella let herself really consider what being his wife would be like.

She would never want for anything ever again. There would be no scraping by, no worries about where their next meal would come from, no abuse like Raphael had inflicted on her for so long. It wouldn't be easy, with Marius's stressful job of ruling an entire kingdom, but they would manage it. Because they had each other.

Sibella's thoughts were interrupted by the sound of

bells pealing in the belltower outside. She pulled away from Marius enough to listen. Twelve chimes, one for each hour.

"Midnight," Sibella said. "Happy New Year, Marius."

"Happy New Year, Sibella," he replied, kissing her deeply.

When he broke their kiss, he said, "Stay with me tonight."

"I'd love to," Sibella said. "But my things—"

"I'll have Amélie fetch them and bring them to my chambers."

"What would people think if word got out that we spent the night together before our wedding?" she asked.

Marius only shrugged in response. "I don't care." He leaned toward her, mere inches from her lips. "Right now, I only care about one thing, and that's you. I want to know every little detail about you, and I want you to get to know the real me."

Sibella thought about Marius. The man who had been so kind to her, so patient, so loving. A man who just wanted to be seen as something more than a political pawn. She knew him, probably better than most, because she'd been able to see him without the pretense of a crown in the way. He wasn't perfect, but Sibella loved him, flaws and all.

She kissed him lightly, then said, "I already know you."

"It is with a heavy heart that I report that my parents, the dear Roi and Reine of Esmar, have been killed. I hope that we can continue the tradition of peace and goodwill between our kingdoms now that I am roi."

Marius Roche to Antonio DiAngelo, day 89 of spring, year 728

24

Year 739
Day 1 of Winter

The crowd was larger than Sibella had expected.

Despite the short notice, it seemed that the people of Esmar were eager to attend the royal wedding. Sibella didn't want to know what the rumor mill was saying about her, given that one day she hadn't officially existed at all, and the next she was engaged to the roi. She was sure it would take her a while to truly break into society, but she didn't care. No one would dare disrespect the reine.

Besides, Marius had made it very clear to her the night before that his was the only approval that mattered. And if telling her hadn't been enough, he'd also practically worshiped her when she'd arrived in his bedroom, making love to her until they were both too exhausted to continue.

Heat rose to Sibella's cheeks as she thought about him, and although no one could see what she'd been thinking about, she turned so no one could see her reddened face. She didn't want anyone to ask her personal questions about her and Marius's relationship. His love for her was Sibella's little secret, the only thing in the world that was hers and hers alone, and she wanted to keep it that way.

"Are you ready, Your Highness?" Amélie said, rushing back to where Sibella stood. It was jarring to be addressed by a royal title, but she knew Amélie was only trying to show respect.

The older woman stopped short when she caught sight of Sibella, eyeing her up and down. Sibella had insisted she choose her own gown for the occasion. If she couldn't sew it herself, she at least wanted to pick out the design. She'd settled on a high-necked ballgown of the palest blue, covered in silver and white crystals that made it shimmer in the light. The long sleeves covered the splint on her wrist, making her injury invisible to the average wedding guest.

Amélie smiled. "You look beautiful."

Such a simple phrase, but it made Sibella beam. It somehow meant a lot to her that she had Amélie's approval. It was clear that she was as close to Marius as family. Probably even closer than family, considering that Marius's only living relative was Prince Charlie, whom Sibella still hadn't seen since that night at the tavern. She wondered if she would see him at the ceremony.

As Sibella prepared to step onto the makeshift dais that had been erected in front of the château, she took one last deep breath. This was it. She was going to marry the love of her life, all strings attached, and all she had to do was try not to get assassinated in the process.

She'd tried forgetting the danger they were in, but with the surplus of guards surrounding her now, it was hard to ignore. It seemed that every doorway in the château had a guard positioned there, eyeing everyone in the room for signs of suspicious behavior. The wedding was to take place outdoors in the courtyard at the front of the château. While the space was quite open, guards had been stationed at the front gates, searching everyone filtering in to watch the proceedings. Sibella knew in her soul that the killer would be attending the ceremony. She shivered at the thought, prompting Amélie to clap her hands, getting the attention of some of the many servants buzzing around.

"Let's get on with this wedding before our new reine freezes to death," Amélie said sternly.

It didn't take long for Sibella to hear a band strike the first chords of a traditional Esmarish wedding song from the other side of the doorway. The voice of the officiant cut through the music, announcing Marius with a flourish. There was a roar of applause as he stepped on stage, and then the officiant began to announce Sibella's name. She took a deep breath. This was it.

Amélie gently pushed her forward. "Go ahead, Your Highness."

Sibella's legs were like lead as she put one foot in front of the other. She climbed the steps and walked through the doorway, and at once all her anxieties came to a head. There were so many people there. So many that Sibella could barely make out where the crowd ended. She couldn't tell if they were applauding her like they had Marius. The only thing she could hear was a roaring in her ears.

She tried not to look at the faces of those up front, but it proved difficult. The most important noblemen and women in Esmar were seated in a separate section from the commoners, and their expressions ranged from contempt to amusement. She caught sight of Prince Charlie in the front row, his arms crossed and a smirk on his face. He must have found his brother's marriage to a nobody hilarious.

Marius had assured Sibella that Charlie had been informed about the parts of their plan that included him. There was, after all, significant risk to his life as well. Marius had explained to her that he suspected Charlie escaped unscathed by the killer the first time around by sheer luck, and he had no desire to test fate with Charlie's safety again. Sibella had agreed, and she'd trusted Marius to tell his brother what he needed to know.

When Sibella reached her destination, right across from Marius, he caught her eye and nodded reassuringly.

"You're doing great," he said softly. "Just look at me."

Sibella took a deep breath and tried to ignore the thousands of eyes trained in her direction as the officiant began the ceremony. Most guests likely couldn't hear him due to the distance, but the small man had a surprisingly loud voice, and Sibella wished she could plug her ears as he practically screamed his opening speech.

"Friends, welcome. We are gathered here today to join our beloved roi and our new reine in marriage. Please bring forward the jewelry offerings," he bellowed.

Amélie rushed on stage, carrying a delicate silk pillow with the traditional silver pieces that would symbolize their union. Sibella still hadn't seen hers, but for Marius, she'd chosen a plain silver ring, the only embellishment being her name etched in the metal. No jewels, nothing that might make Marius feel overly flashy or call too much attention. She knew enough about him to know that he wanted their love to be private, between them alone. Beneath his crown, he was a simple man.

"Do you, Roi Marius, take Sibella Bellerose to be your wife and reine?" the officiant asked. There were no extravagant vows or speeches to prolong the ceremony in Esmar. Some other kingdoms had lengthier wedding ceremonies, but in Esmar the public ceremony was considered a legal formality. The real celebration would take place later with a private crowd. There were sure to be parties and festivals all over the kingdom in the coming days to celebrate such an important marriage.

"I do," Marius said. He smiled broadly as Sibella reached over to the pillow Amélie held. She took the ring and slid it onto his finger. Before she could pull her hand away, Marius squeezed it tight. He didn't say anything, but his pure joy was evident in the way his blue eyes sparkled.

"And do you, Mademoiselle Bellerose, take Roi Marius to be your husband? Do you vow to protect and serve the kingdom of Esmar with wisdom as long as you reign?"

Sibella nodded. It took no strength to utter the words that she knew would keep her beside the man she loved forever. "I do."

Marius took a shining silver necklace off the pillow. It held a simple pendant, shaped like a shining star, with sparkling diamonds mounted in the silver. His name was inscribed at the bottom. Sibella beamed radiantly as he reached around her, clasping the chain around her neck. She was honored beyond words that she was the woman lucky enough to wear Marius's name close to her heart.

He stepped away, a smile on his lips.

And that was when the arrow hit.

It flew in from behind and struck him in the back without any warning. There had been no sounds of the bow string being released, nor of the arrow as it sped through the air. Sibella screamed, but her yell was lost as the crowd before them erupted into chaos. Some guests ran, some looked around for the source of the arrow, some just stared at their roi, stunned. Sibella tried to see where the shot had come from. Maybe she could see their hidden assailant before they took another shot. Based on where the arrow had hit, the assassin couldn't have been in the crowd, but instead on the roof of the château.

Marius took Sibella's hand. His grip was firm, without any room for negotiation. He said nothing and ran off the stage, pulling a stunned Sibella behind him. Knowing it was going to happen and watching the arrow hit Marius were two very different things, and Sibella was deeply shaken. More so, perhaps, than Marius, who ran faster than Sibella could keep up with.

They flew through the entrance to the château, running through hallway after hallway. Sibella was out of breath and panting by the time they finally reached the camouflaged door that led to the royal safe room. There was no guard standing by the hidden entrance, as that would have meant disclosing the secret location.

Marius ran down the stairs two at a time, still not letting go of her hand. When they reached the landing, he pulled a key out of his pocket and used it to unlock the entrance to the protected room. He pushed open the heavy metal door and together they stumbled inside.

"Are you alright?" he asked, running a hand through

his hair to compose himself after their rapid flight from the ceremony.

"Me?" Sibella asked, eyes wide. "You're the one who's been hit with the arrow!"

Sibella walked behind him to investigate the damage. Sure enough, there was a hole in his coat where the arrow had sliced through the fabric. It had fallen out somewhere while they'd been running, and Sibella hadn't stopped to retrieve it to see if it was poisoned.

"Did your armor hold up?" she asked, worry rising in her chest. They had decided on the armor during one of their later meetings with Constantin and his guards. Nothing too bulky, just enough to stop an arrow. Sibella herself wore a similar light breastplate underneath her modest gown.

"Don't worry. I'm fine," Marius said, turning to her and tucking a flyaway strand of hair behind her ear. "All I felt was the impact pressure from the arrow as it hit the armor. It definitely didn't make it past that."

"Good." Sibella breathed, wrapping her arms tightly around him. Held firmly in his strong embrace, she let her heart rate settle.

Their moment of rest didn't last long. The sound of footsteps outside brought Sibella to attention, but it was too late. Marius didn't get to the door they'd carelessly left open fast enough to close it before a hooded figure entered the safe room. The hood was pulled down low enough that Sibella couldn't see the face of the person wearing it, but they held a bow in one hand

and a bloody knife in the other. Marius and Sibella were in the presence of the very assassin they'd been hunting.

Marius stepped in front of his new wife protectively, but she fought against him. It should be Sibella standing between them, protecting Marius. She couldn't let him die, not ever, but especially not now when she'd just begun to allow herself to hope that she might be happy with him. How could she ever continue to live if Marius was gone?

The hooded killer didn't seem to have any more arrows with them, at least none that were visible. Sibella's eyes fixed on the knife in their hand, the way the crimson blood dripped from the blade onto the cold white marble floor. Her knees grew weak at the sight of it. How many loyal guards had just been cut down by that very blade?

She eyed the staircase behind the figure—her and Marius's only chance of escape. It would be nearly impossible to get through the doorway without being stabbed, especially if the killer was trained enough to best some of Marius's own highly capable guards.

"Who are you?" Sibella asked, her voice shaking with terror.

The figure slowly lifted their hood, exposing the face underneath. At first, Sibella wasn't sure who she was looking at. The woman looked about the same age as Sibella's mother, and she looked at Sibella with a soulless expression, as if murdering them at their own wedding was a chore to be taken care of rather than a merciless crime.

Her graying brown hair was tied back in a bun, her cheeks hollow and starved. But her large brown eyes were so familiar to Sibella that she did a double take. And the way her jaw clenched, it reminded her of... no. Those were Simon's eyes. The same doe-eyed expression he always wore. And that was Leo's jaw, the cold, determined look he used when he would torment her.

And the way she looked down at Sibella was the same way the portrait that hung in Raphael's grand staircase seemed to always have an eye on her.

"Madame Juliette?" Sibella practically gasped. "But you're... you *died!*"

As if to confirm Sibella's suspicion, Juliette's lips curled up in a menacing smile. She shrugged. "In a way, yes. I did."

Now it made sense why they'd never found the body of the former duchesse. She'd somehow faked her own death expertly enough that it had fooled everyone.

"I found that old bow in Raphael's cellar. I thought it had been his, but it was yours," Sibella said, hands shaking at her sides.

"Naturally," Juliette said flippantly. "I've always enjoyed hunting."

Sibella's blood ran cold. *Hunting.*

"But Raphael... Leo and Simon..." Sibella began. "They all think you're dead!"

It was so brief that Sibella thought she'd imagined it

at first, but the faintest bit of pain flashed through Juliette's eyes at the mention of her sons. Just as quickly as it appeared, it was gone, and her steely expression returned.

"My sons can never know what I've sacrificed for them," Juliette said, raising her blade. "I'm sorry you've involved yourself in this business, Sibella. I always hate being forced to harm people like me."

Before Sibella could ask what that meant, Juliette lunged toward her, dagger up and ready to kill. Sibella screamed and stumbled backward, tripping over the hem of her wedding gown and falling to the floor with a thud. She knew she didn't have a hope of taking down Juliette with force, especially unarmed. She only hoped she could provide enough of a distraction that Marius would make it out of the room alive.

Sibella held up her arm to shield her face, bracing for the shock of cold steel, but it never came. Instead, she heard a metallic clang as Marius dove in front of her, holding nothing but a small candelabra. His move had successfully blocked Juliette's strike, but Sibella knew that Marius's makeshift weapon was no match for a real one. Sibella had to act now, while Juliette was surprised.

From her position on the ground, Sibella swung her leg out, kicking Juliette off balance. All it took was a shove from Marius, and the duchesse fell to the floor across from Sibella. Marius held her down with his foot while Sibella rose to her feet. She was frightened and out of breath, but she didn't waver. She stood at Marius's side as he plucked the dagger from Juliette's hand and held it toward the crazed woman threateningly.

"You killed them," Marius cried, his hand shaking from anger rather than fear. "You were already a duchesse, but that wasn't enough for you. Why?"

Juliette remained frustratingly silent, betraying no emotion. Fueled by rage, Marius screamed, "Tell me why!"

Sibella wondered for a moment if he would use Juliette's own weapon against her. She couldn't say she'd blame him, after all the trauma the woman had inflicted on him. Juliette deserved to have that knife twisting inside of her, draining her of what little humanity she had left. But Marius didn't strike, and Sibella also understood why. He wanted to hear the reasons from her directly—to know what had possessed this woman to commit such atrocities.

Still, Juliette said nothing. Sibella could sense Marius's control over her fading—she was frustrating him enough that he would let his guard down. The bunker was well hidden, and no one but the royal family could find it. Even if the assassin had left the camouflaged door at the stairs open, it would likely be a while before any guards found them. Sibella couldn't entertain the idea of leaving Marius alone with Juliette to go get help, considering how dangerous she was, but that meant their only option was to detain her until help arrived. If Marius was ever going to get the answers he needed, he would need Sibella's help.

She stepped forward, stomping on Juliette's outstretched hand. The woman cried out in pain and Sibella put even more weight on her foot, feeling the bones strain under the pressure. She found no pleasure in harming anyone, but Sibella would defend herself and Marius at any cost. If that meant returning Juliette's violence and watching the woman fight back tears, then so be it.

"Tell him everything," Sibella commanded. "Or should I start snapping bones?"

"Marius, I'm your aunt!" Juliette cried. Sibella remembered Simon's story about his mother, how she'd been raised adjacently to the royal family. Of course she would know their secrets, and how to find them in the safe room. Sibella didn't release Juliette's hand. Not now that the tables were turning.

"What?" Marius sputtered, struggling to keep his composure.

"I am the oldest child of Roi Charles," Juliette explained. One look at Marius confirmed that he'd had no idea, the shock on his face evident.

Juliette continued. "I was illegitimate, so I was removed from the line of succession, but my father took pity on me and sent me to be the ward of a member of his court. It allowed me to move in proper society, but I had been denied my rightful place. When I married Raphael, who was himself distantly in line for the crown, I knew what I had to do. I had to get my family back on the throne, as we deserved. But eventually I saw my husband for what he was. A monster. I could never make a man like him Roi of Esmar, but I could secure the crown for my boys."

Sibella almost pitied this woman. She knew the pain that came with being an illegitimate heir all too well, and she knew the lengths to which the ensuing desperation could take a person. But as she looked upon the shattered woman on the ground before her, she knew that there was at least one major difference in their situations. Sibella had found love, and that had proved to be enough for her. Juliette might have power, but she had never been loved the way she needed to be.

"Do Leo and Simon know you're alive, then? Or were they just going to be pleasantly surprised when they discovered they were next in line to rule Esmar?" Sibella pressed.

"They don't know anything about what I've done. And they never will," Juliette growled.

"There's just one thing that I don't understand," Marius remarked. "You killed plenty of people before you faked your own death, but your job wasn't done yet. What made you decide to disappear?"

Juliette didn't answer, but Sibella found she already knew. "Raphael found out. He knew what you were planning, didn't he? When he discovered you were going to kill him too, you ran away so he couldn't turn you in."

There was no response, but the steely look in Juliette's eyes told Sibella all she needed to know. It explained why Raphael had always seemed so suspicious of everyone. On top of his anger and abusive tendencies, he'd known all along who the killer was, and he'd allowed the murders to continue. Disgust roiled in Sibella's stomach, and when she looked at Marius, he appeared just as ill.

"You ran to Tatria when you left, didn't you?" Marius asked. "That's how you were able to find the girselia to poison your blades instead of snake venom."

This revelation came as a surprise to Sibella, as she hadn't known what poisons the arrows had been laced with, but it all made sense. They had the information they wanted, but it had thrown both of them off balance.

And Juliette chose that moment to strike.

She twisted out from under Marius, rolling to the side, barreling over Sibella's leg and knocking her over once again. She tried to catch herself, but her weight landed on her weak wrist, sending pain shooting through her arm. Before Marius could react, Juliette bounced back to her feet and kicked out, landing a hit on Marius's stomach. He stumbled backward, caught by surprise, but Juliette wasn't done. She swung her fist toward his face, successfully making contact with his jaw.

Sibella heard a piercing noise, and it took her longer than it should have to realize that it was her own frightened cry. She rushed forward, trying to get herself between Juliette and Marius, but there wasn't enough space for her in their close-up brawl.

In desperation, Sibella took to pounding on Juliette's shoulders and pulling at her tightly pinned hair, but the woman was obviously determined to finish what she'd started all those years ago. The only weakness that Juliette showed was her injured hand, which she kept tucked out of reach. Otherwise, she kept fighting like nothing Sibella did affected her.

"Stop! No!" Sibella pleaded, but her cries fell on deaf ears.

The fight was over as quickly as it began. Juliette twisted her knife out of Marius's grip, then began swinging it at him. Marius managed to dodge all her attempts, but Sibella knew that they had been bested. There wasn't much in the small space that could be used as a weapon—a few small cots, a chamber pot, and a cabinet for food rations.

The candelabra that Marius had tossed aside earlier lay close to the door, well out of reach. Also discarded, and forgotten in the heat of the battle, Sibella knew that it was their only chance for survival. But before she could dive for it, Juliette turned her weapon on Sibella, too.

She jumped back instinctively, realizing seconds too late that Juliette was trying to back them further into the room. She wanted them cornered. And with Juliette's attention on both of them, there was no way Sibella could get to the candelabra in one piece.

Her hope that she and Marius might get out of this alive was slipping away by the second, and a chilling sense of despair washed over her.

Juliette made no clever quips, no final speeches. She silently stalked toward them, everything about her unsettling Sibella to her core. She made no noise at all. In the end, Sibella would die not with a bang, but with a whisper.

As she looked into the hardened eyes of the woman who would take her life, Marius took her hand, squeezing it softly as if to reassure her that everything would be okay. Sibella turned her head to look at him one last time. His perfectly styled hair was in disarray, his fine wedding attire ripped and stained with small amounts of his blood. But there was still a spark in his eye, a gleam of fire that told Sibella he hadn't given up yet.

Then there was a loud crack. Sibella whipped her head around to look for the source of the noise, and that was when Juliette crumpled unceremoniously. Her unconscious body hit the floor. And once Sibella peeled her eyes away from where her assailant lay, her jaw dropped. Standing over Juliette, holding the silver candelabra, was Charlie. He looked down at the hand that he'd used to strike her, then, almost as if he'd been burned, he dropped the candelabra and backed away.

"Charlie!" Marius exclaimed, rushing forward to embrace his brother. "Thank goodness you're safe."

Sibella would have been touched at this tender

moment between brothers, but she didn't have time to think about that, as heavy footsteps thundered down the stairs. Several guards, led by Constantin, rushed through the doorway, looking around. Juliette's unconscious body lying on the floor left a look of confusion on a few of their faces, but they relaxed a little when they saw Marius relatively unharmed.

"How did you find us?" Sibella asked the guards, still in disbelief at her sudden rescue. "I thought only the royal family knew how to find this room?"

"Prince Charlie led us here," Constantin said. "We're sorry we didn't arrive sooner. The aftermath of what this woman did left the château in chaos."

Another guard glanced at Juliette, then back at Marius. "This is the woman who made an attempt on your life, is she not?"

"She is," Marius said. "She has also admitted to many other crimes, including that of the murder of my parents, the previous roi and reine."

The guards moved to bind Juliette's arms and legs. As their ropes were tightened and they tied them off, Juliette moaned and opened her eyes. When she saw what was happening, she thrashed against the guards and her bonds, but it was useless. She was trapped.

Marius looked at Sibella with pride in his eyes and her heart melted under that gaze. She knew that having Juliette arrested for high treason wouldn't be enough to fill the void in Marius's heart that being orphaned had left, but it was the best closure he could hope to have. It also made her happy to realize that all their sleuthing hadn't been for nothing. Sibella knew more about the case than she would have otherwise, enough to present the full story during the inevitable trial.

"May I speak to her?" Charlie asked, eerily calm. Marius shrugged, and Charlie stepped forward to look Juliette in the eye. Reaching forward, he took her chin in his hand and held her face steady. His touch was soft at first, but quickly tightened, his hand shaking with rage.

"Look at me," he commanded. "Look at a man whose life you tried to destroy. When you are executed, and you surely will be, I hope your death is painful and long, and that your suffering will feel as endless as mine has."

Charlie pulled his hand away as softly as he'd first placed it on her, leaving her without a scratch. He turned to go but must have changed his mind at the last moment, turning back and spitting on her grimy boots before stalking away.

"Sibella," Juliette said, and Sibella turned to face her.

"You shall not speak to Her Highness," one of the guards snapped, and began to drag her away.

"Don't tell them!" Juliette pleaded as she was taken away. "Let them think I've been dead all along!"

Sibella didn't need to ask who she meant. She didn't want Simon and Leo to know what she'd done. Sibella didn't reply, even as Juliette screamed and fought the whole way up the stairs, but in her heart, Sibella knew she could never promise that. The trial would have to be public enough to assure the court that there was no further danger, and while it might break Simon's heart to know what his mother had become, Sibella couldn't protect him like she wanted to.

Constantin, the only guard left behind, put a hand on Marius's shoulder. "Are you alright, Your Majesty?"

Marius nodded. He had a strong front, but Sibella could tell he was hurting. Underneath his wise, stately exterior, he was still just a man.

"And you, Your Highness?" Constantin asked, gesturing to Sibella.

She took a deep breath. She thought about her father and the way he'd disowned her. She thought about Raphael and Leo and how they'd taught her to feel worthless for years. And then she thought of her mother and Simon, and the love she had for her real family. She thought about Marius. He was right there, and he was hers, and when she saw herself now, she no longer only saw Rey Nicolas's bastard child, or a struggling seamstress. She saw her future self, and she was radiant. She was happy.

Sibella smiled. "I believe I will be."

25

Day 1 of Winter

*M*arius and Sibella were late to their own wedding reception.

The staff had been spread thin following the events at the ceremony. Chaos had erupted outside, leaving a large mess to be cleaned up. Some staff had been tasked with spreading the news that Roi Marius and Reine Sibella were officially married, and that they were both safe and well. Others had gotten behind on their daily tasks and had to work double time to get everything finished. Marius had hardly been able to put together a list of things that needed to be done before Amélie had informed him she'd already set a plan in motion that would "fix everything."

In the end, Marius and Sibella were finally ready an hour after they were originally expected, but Marius suspected no one would care. Not after the day they'd had. The group at the private party was small, and as Marius glanced around the cozy space, he found he was glad to only be around people he could trust.

The party was held in a cozy private reception room with navy blue walls and intricately carved wooden furniture. A fire crackled in the hearth and a musician plucked out a relaxing melody on the piano. Marius looked around at his guests. Constantin stood watch while Amélie ran around the room, frantic as always, checking items off her infinite to-do list. Daniel and Luciana sat on a sofa nearby, chatting with Simon and Thomas.

Sibella, of course, had positioned herself next to Marius at the dining table. She looked angelic in a simple gown of pure white silk, and her hair fell down past her shoulders in golden waves that the servants hadn't had time to tie back before they'd left for their reception. Maybe he was imagining it, but Marius swore that Sibella looked more like her true self in that moment than he'd seen before. With the silver crown of the reine on her head, she was more beautiful than ever.

Marius smiled and took his wife's hand. His wife. It was still strange to think that she was his, especially after their ceremony had been interrupted, but it was a relief to be safe at last. He hadn't realized how much his parents' killer being at large had hung over him, like a storm cloud that permeated everything he did. Now that he was relieved of that burden, he wasn't quite sure what to do with himself.

"Marius," a voice said softly behind him. He knew the voice before he turned around. Charlie.

"Brother! You made it!" Marius said jovially, gesturing to the seat across from him at the table. "Join us."

Charlie cleared his throat, and his normally expressive face showed that he was nervous about something. "I would love to but first, I need to speak with you. Alone."

Marius wanted to blow him off, to promise to listen to him later, but he and Charlie had only just promised one another that they'd do a better job at being brothers, and Marius had a suspicion that right now, he needed to listen. Marius stood, leaving his glass of champagne at his seat, and took Sibella's hand.

He kissed her knuckles and softly said, "I will return in just a moment."

To her credit, Sibella seemed unfazed by his departure. She only nodded and said, "Of course. I'll go speak with my cousin while you're gone."

Sibella smiled at him, and Marius's heart melted at the sight of her, so happy and trusting. He turned away from the party, following Charlie out of the room and into the hallway. The reception hall was just off the main entrance to the château, in a space that would have usually been reserved for visitors making calls to its residents. The hall was lined with guards, but otherwise distant from prying ears. Still, Charlie kept his voice down.

"I'm sorry to take you away from your party. I know tonight is not about me, but I need to tell you something."

"Go on," Marius prompted, impressed by Charlie's growth over the past season. It seemed like only yesterday he would have interrupted the reception to say what he wanted in front of everyone, or even not come at all.

Charlie took a deep breath, then spit it out. "I'm leaving Esmar."

Marius's eyes widened and he clenched his jaw to keep it from falling open in shock. Charlie wasn't the most responsible of princes, it was true, but to leave his own kingdom behind? The only response Marius could muster was a weak, "What?"

"I've been speaking with Principe Daniel," Charlie explained. "He's traveled to three of the five kingdoms and plans to see them all eventually, and I realized that I haven't seen much of the realm. And now that you're married and will likely have heirs soon, I'm not needed here anymore. I want to go. I want to figure out who I am without Esmar."

There was an unusual light in Charlie's eyes as he spoke about his plans. He wanted this. It was so long since he'd heard Charlie be passionate about anything that Marius didn't know how to refuse him. But how could his brother leave him, just as they'd started to make up for lost time? Not to mention the rumors this would spark in court.

"Charlie," Marius said, "I'm not sure this is a good idea."

"I'm not sure either," Charlie said, shrugging. "But I need to do this. I've already made arrangements with Daniel and Luciana. I'll be returning to Osmain with them when they leave tomorrow."

"*All* the kingdoms, Charlie? How do you plan on visiting Askaña when we have no formal alliance with Rey Hugo? How will you see Tatria when Tsarista Saffron has it out for you personally?" Marius asked, trying to control his voice as it threatened to rise.

"They don't need to know I'm there," Charlie said. "I don't have to stay with the royal family. In fact, I think it would do me some good if I didn't."

Marius could think of a million things that could go wrong with this plan. What if Charlie went missing and there was no way to find him because he'd been traveling alone without the protection of his title? How would Marius find Charlie if he needed him?

"I can't just let you disappear, Charlie. I'm responsible for your well-being," Marius said.

"I won't disappear forever, Marius." Charlie crossed his arms defensively. "I'll write to you."

"How will I know where to send my responses?"

"I'll tell you my current address whenever I send a letter, and I won't move on until I get a reply," Charlie promised.

Marius knew he was fighting a losing battle. Charlie was an adult, and while Marius might not like his choices, he didn't feel entitled to stop him. Still, Charlie had a responsibility to Esmar that he couldn't just abandon.

"You know I'll support you, Charlie, but you're going to have to do this on my terms," Marius said, crossing his arms and trying to appear as authoritative as possible.

"What are they?" Charlie asked. Marius noticed that he wasn't quick to agree.

"I'm lifting your ban from participating in court functions. I need you to stay active in your role as prince, at least for the next few years. Once you're done with your stay in Osmain, I want you to come home—and we can figure out where you can go next that will be of benefit to Esmar. It can be an official duty, because I don't need to spend time quelling rumors that you've abandoned your title. I won't give you any assignment that I don't think you can handle, and in return I'll cover your travel and lodging expenses."

Charlie considered the offer for a moment, his lips pursed in thought. But eventually he nodded and stuck out his hand. "Deal."

As they shook on their agreement, the front door swung open. The night was dark and cold air flooded into the hallway, sending a shiver down Marius's spine. Through the haze of a few outdoor candles, Marius could make out the form of one of his guards, and behind him, the silhouettes of two tall men and one thin woman.

The guard rushed inside, and when he saw Marius and Charlie before him, his eyes widened. Bowing before his roi, he said, "Your Majesty. Someone has called upon you. I tried to inform him that it is your wedding night, but he insisted upon seeing you. Something about being separated from his daughter?"

Marius almost groaned. He knew who the intruder would be even before he stepped confidently over the threshold of the château. It came as no surprise to Marius when Raphael strode into the light, a scowl on his face. Trailing behind him was Leo and a woman who looked so much like Sibella that Marius didn't need to ask her name to know that this had to be her mother.

"My sincerest apologies, Your Highness," the guard continued to ramble. "I never thought you'd be in the hallway. I only meant to find the général."

Marius held up a hand to silence the guard. "Please go fetch Constantin. He is watching over my reception as we speak."

The guard hurried into the reception room, leaving Marius and Charlie alone with their uninvited guests. There were still plenty of guards nearby, but they watched with curiosity, waiting for a cue from Marius or any sign of a threat.

"What do you want?" Marius asked.

"I want to see my daughter," Raphael huffed. "You took her from me, and now I want to see her. It was

insulting enough to have to watch the wedding ceremony with the commoners, but to be excluded from
your private reception is far too insulting. Furthermore,
you never asked my permission to marry my darling
Sibella, and I am outraged! Am I not entitled to some
compensation for this injustice?"

"I never asked your permission because you are not
her father," Marius answered. "You made it very clear to
both her and me that you have no love for the woman,
not to mention you have disowned her. I am not fooled
by your charade. You are only crawling back now
because you want to be closer to the crown. I suggest
you leave now before I expose your numerous crimes
and have you arrested."

"Crimes?" Raphael scoffed. If he was frightened by
the notion of being arrested, he didn't show it, but
Delphine sent him a curious glance. The door down the
hall swung open and Constantin approached the scene,
followed closely by Sibella. She had obviously let her
anger overtake some of her usual grace as she stomped
down the hall, scowling in Raphael's direction. Marius
wasn't surprised to see his wife. In fact, he was proud to
see she'd come to defend herself when she could have
easily hidden from the conflict.

"It looks like the captain of my guard is coming now,"
Marius said. "This is your final warning."

But Raphael held steady. "My daughter is the reine
and I expect to be treated with respect."

Marius shrugged. "Alright, then."

Constantin and Sibella arrived on the scene and Raphael stepped forward, arms out for an embrace. "My sweet daughter."

"Don't touch me," Sibella snapped, taking a step backward. Anger swept over Raphael's face, but it passed as soon as it came. He was trying to appear civil, the ever-concerned father. But no one was falling for it.

"Général, so kind of you to join us," Charlie quipped. "My brother was about to expose this man's crimes, and I, for one, am very curious to find out what they are."

"My father has committed no crimes," Leo argued. "He is a duc. A man of honor."

"Honor?" Marius laughed. "Where should I start?" Marius pretended to consider for a moment before motioning to Sibella, whose injured wrist was still wrapped tight in a splint. "How about the injury he gave to our beloved reine by pushing her down a flight of stairs, breaking her wrist? Or for the countless stories of abuse I've heard? That is enough on its own to justify criminal charges, but that isn't all. The duc knew who killed my parents—and all the other murdered noblemen—and kept her identity a secret for years. That, sir, is treason!"

"What?" Raphael was trying not to lose his composure, but was failing miserably. "I would never!"

"She told me herself, just before we caught her. And now you'll rot in prison together," Marius said. "Arrest him!" Constantin and a few other guards swarmed

Raphael even as he fought them, but they eventually held him fast and began to lead him away.

"Stop! Let go of me this instant! Do you know who I am?" Raphael ranted.

"You are no one," Sibella called after him. "As of this moment, as Reine of Esmar, I am stripping you of your title as the duc des Étoiles."

"You can't—" Raphael started to say, but he was gone around the corner before he could so much as hurl an insult.

One look at his wife's face was all it took for Marius to break out smiling. Sibella looked utterly terrified and angry, but the relief on her features was unmistakable. After her years-long battle with Raphael, Sibella had won. And Marius couldn't have said it better himself—Raphael was no duc. But then again, from the sound of it, neither was Leo—Leo, who right now looked utterly shocked, yet somehow smug. He knew what his father being stripped of his title meant for him. Or at least, what it would usually mean.

"You find this amusing?" Marius asked.

"I am surprised, Your Majesty. I didn't expect to become the duc at such a young age," Leo replied.

"Why would you think you're the duc des Étoiles now?"

Leo said nothing, dumbfounded, but Marius wasn't done. "I have seen enough of your character to know you don't possess the qualities that an Esmarish gentleman should. You have bullied Sibella for years, both to her face and behind her back. It's clear that you enjoy causing pain and discomfort in others, and I don't believe anyone who is so cruel to their own reine should have any power over others."

"Your Majesty, you have to understand," Leo argued, "she wasn't reine at the time, she was a nobody!"

"And that makes it okay to push me around?" Sibella cut in. "I rather think the title should pass over you. Perhaps that would humble you."

"No, please!" Leo begged. "I will be disgraced!"

"Don't worry about it too much," Sibella said coldly. "I'm sure your brother the duc will take good care of you."

Leo was silent, but his seething fury could be felt throughout the hallway. Without waiting for an escort or an official dismissal, Leo stalked away, leaving through the front door.

After he disappeared from view, Charlie glanced around at the four people remaining and shrugged. "Well, that was fun. I'm going back to the party now."

And then there were three. Sibella and Delphine eyed each other like strangers at first, but eventually Delphine said, "Look at you. Reine."

"I'm sorry I didn't tell you," Sibella said, tears forming in her eyes. "This whole thing has been complicated."

"It's okay, Sibella," Delphine said, taking her daughter in her arms. "I've always wanted what's best for you. I know I failed to protect you, and for that I'm truly sorry. But I hope you can forgive me."

"Of course, Maman," Sibella said, holding her mother tight. Marius felt like he was interrupting a private moment, so he stayed quiet as they embraced. When Sibella and Delphine finally separated, he put a hand on Sibella's shoulder, and she turned to smile at him.

Marius cleared his throat and addressed Delphine. "I apologize for having our first meeting under such strange circumstances, but I promise you, I have nothing but love and respect for your daughter. And I assure you that you will be provided for."

"Marius," Sibella said, looking at him pleadingly. "Could she stay somewhere on the château grounds?"

"Of course, if you want her here. I can set her up in the guest house," Marius said. He hadn't intended to offer Delphine a place in his home without Sibella's approval. Otherwise, he would have already asked.

"That's very generous of you, Your Majesty," Delphine said, tears in her eyes and a smile on her face. "I would be honored to accept your offer."

"Maman," Sibella said, gesturing to the door to the reception room where the others sat just beyond. "Why don't you go join the others at the party? We'll be there in just a moment."

"Of course," Delphine said, curtsying politely to Marius and going to join the celebration.

"Come, walk with me," Sibella said to her new husband. Marius held out an arm for her, which she took swiftly, and the guards opened the large double doors that led outside. Marius breathed in the chilly evening air and looked over at Sibella, who shone as brightly as the stars that twinkled above them.

"You'll have to tell Simon that he's now the duc des Étoiles," Marius said, laughing slightly.

"He'll make an excellent duc," Sibella mused.

"I'm confident he will be," Marius agreed. "Just as you will be a wonderful reine."

Sibella blushed and turned her face away, but Marius could still see the unmistakable hint of a smile on her lips. She was humble about it, but Marius knew Sibella was truly happy underneath her nervous exterior.

"How can you be so sure?" she asked.

Marius took her hand and pulled her close, the warmth of her body radiating into every fiber of his being. The rest of the world faded into a hazy blur as he found Sibella's eyes. There was no one but her, and there would never be anyone else.

"Because you," he said, pressing his lips to hers, "were the only one to see me as I am. You see the truth in people, good or bad. And you will use that to help your kingdom prosper."

There would be challenges ahead. Nothing was simple in the life of a roi. But Sibella, this one, perfect woman, would be by his side to keep him grounded, to advise him, and to love him when his work was done. The promise of having her next to him made Marius feel for the first time like he was ready to bear the weight of the crown.

Marius smiled to himself as he gazed at his wife. The truest heaven was not somewhere among the infinite stars. It was in the eyes of the woman he loved.

ACKNOWLEDGMENTS

Thank you to everyone who helped me in my writing and publishing process, especially to the following:

My amazing editors, Hilary and Alexandra. Thank you for your hard work making my book shine!

Amanda. Thank you for listening to my late night rants and always being willing to go the extra mile to help me write.

Everyone who has supported my writing so far. If you bought a copy of Kingdom of the Sea, you helped make this book possible. So thank you!

ALSO BY MADISON HORTON

Kingdom of the Sea

WANT TO SEE MORE OF THE REALM?

Keep an eye out for

Kingdom of the Forest

Book 3 in The Crown Quintet!

ABOUT THE AUTHOR

A lover of storytelling, Madison has been writing since she was in middle school. When she's not typing away at her computer, she can be found sewing fantasy gowns or visiting the Orlando theme parks.

You can find her online at
www.madisonhortonauthor.com